The Man Who Fell Through the Earth

By Carolyn Wells

Originally published in 1919

The Man Who Fell Through the Earth

© 2011 Resurrected Press
www.ResurrectedPress.com

Published by Resurrected Press

This classic book was handcrafted by Resurrected Press. Resurrected Press is dedicated to bringing high quality classic books back to the readers who enjoy them. These are not scanned versions of the originals, but, rather, quality checked and edited books meant to be enjoyed!

Please visit ResurrectedPress.com to view our entire catalogue!

ISBN 13: 978-1-937022-07-5

Printed in the United States of America

FOREWORD

Carolyn Wells is often dismissed by those who judge her by the standards of mysteries that were written several decades after her novels as something of a lightweight in the genre with plots that rely on impossible devices such as secret passages. It is certainly true that Wells, who began her career as a humorist, often writes in a breezy style that would not be out of place in one of the "screwball" comedic films of the thirties. But Wells is also a keen observer and skilled portrayer of the urban middle class of her day, and her mysteries, while perhaps not as elaborate or detailed as those of some later authors, are both entertaining and enlightening, providing the reader with a look into a culture and time that is now gone, New York city in the era from 1910 to 1920.

The Man Who Fell Through the Earth is set during the period just after America entered World War I. It begins traditionally enough with a locked room murder that takes place on the top floor of an office building on Madison Avenue, located as the narrator puts it "between Thirtieth and Fortieth Streets." The twist is that neither victim or assailant are to be found, at least until the end of Chapter Three. The usual string of clews and misdirection follow with suspicion falling first on the beautiful young ward of the murdered man.

The story is enlivened with the subplot of "Case Rivers" an man who is fished from the river with no memories of who or what he is or how he came to be in the river except for a memory of falling for a long time "through the earth." His mystery proves to be at least as interesting as that of the murder, though of course, in the end, they prove to be related.

Entertaining, too, is the detective Penny Wise and his protégé Zizi. This pair provides most of the banter and figure in a number of other mysteries by Wells such as *In the Onyx Lobby*. Almost as entertaining as a comic foil is Mrs. Vail, who, no matter what the situation, seems to have known someone is similar straits.

It is obvious that the goal of Wells' is not to write some profound examination of character. Her goal is to provide a piece of entertainment, a mixture of suspense, romance, and comedy, something for her middle class audience to identify with and pass a few hours of leisure. It is easy to forget that some of the ideas that now appear as clichés, were at the time the book was written still fresh and new. The fact that Wells had a long and successful career proves that she was appreciated by her audience.

Carolyn Wells is not as well known today as she once was, which is a shame. Her works are entertaining without placing too many demands on the reader. Resurrected Press is happy to bring to you *The Man Who Fell Through the Earth*.

About the Author

Carolyn Wells, June 18, 1862 - March 26, 1942 was an American writer and poet. She was best known for her books of poetry and humor until around 1910 she read one of Anna Katherine Green's mysteries and took up the genre. Many of her mysteries featured the detective Fleming Stone. She was married to Hadwin Houghton, heir to the Houghton-Mifflin publishing company. She was a collector of poetry by other authors, and, upon her death, she bequeathed her collection of the works of Walt Witman to the Library of Congress.

Greg Fowlkes
Editor-In-Chief
Resurrected Press
www.ResurrectedPress.com

TABLE OF CONTENTS

Chapter 1: Moving Shadow Shapes...1

Chapter 2: Jenny's Version 13

Chapter 3: The Elevator 25

Chapter 4: The Black Squall..37

Chapter 5: Olive Raynor 49

Chapter 6: Clews...61

Chapter 7: Hudson's Errand...75

Chapter 8: The Man Who Fell Through the Earth 87

Chapter 9: The Man in Boston...99

Chapter 10: Penny Wise and Zizi..111

Chapter 11: Case Rivers..123

Chapter 12: The Link...135

Chapter 13: Olive's Adventure..149

Chapter 14: Where is Manning? 159

Chapter 15: Wise's Pipe Dream 171

Chapter 16: The Snowflake..183

Chapter 17: Zizi's Hunch 195

Chapter 18: Clear as Crystal 207

CHAPTER 1: MOVING SHADOW SHAPES

ONE of the occasions when I experienced "that grand and glorious feeling" was when my law business had achieved proportions that justified my removal from my old office to new and more commodious quarters. I selected a somewhat pretentious building on Madison Avenue between Thirtieth and Fortieth Streets, and it was a red letter day for me when I moved into my pleasant rooms on its top floor.

The Puritan Trust Company occupied all of the ground floor and there were also some of the private offices of that institution on the top floor, as well as a few offices to be let.

My rooms were well located and delightfully light, and I furnished them with care, selecting chairs and desks of a dignified type, and rugs of appropriately quiet coloring. I also selected my stenographer with care, and Norah MacCormack was a red haired piece of perfection. If she had a weakness, it was for reading detective stories, but I condoned that, for in my hammocky moods I, too, dipped into the tangled web school of fiction. And, without undue conceit, I felt that I could give most specimens of the genus Sherlock cards and spades and beat them at their own game of deduction. I practiced it on Norah sometimes. She would bring me a veil or glove of some friend of hers, and I would try to deduce the friend's traits of character. My successes and failures were about fifty fifty, but Norah thought I improved with practice, and, anyway, it exercised my intelligence.

I had failed to pass examination for the army, because of a defect, negligible, it seemed to me, in my eyesight. I was deeply disappointed, but as the law of compensation is usually in force, I unexpectedly proved to be of some use to my Government after all.

Across the hall from me was the private office of Amos Gately, the President of the Puritan Trust Company, and a man of city wide reputation. I didn't know the great financier personally, but everyone knew of him, and his name was a synonym for all that is sound, honorable, and philanthropic in the money mart. He was of that frequently seen type, with the silver gray hair that so becomingly accompanies deep set dark eyes.

And yet, I had never seen Mr. Gately himself. My knowledge of him was gained from his frequent portraiture in the papers or in an occasional magazine. And I had gathered, in a vague way, that he was a connoisseur of the fine arts, and that his offices, as well as his home, were palatial in their appointments.

I may as well admit, therefore, that going in and out of my own rooms I often looked toward his door, in hopes that I might get a glimpse, at least, of the treasures within. But so far I had not done so.

To be sure, I had only occupied my own suite about a week and then again Mr. Gately was not always in his private offices during business hours. Doubtless, much of the time he was down in the banking rooms.

There was a yellow haired stenographer, who wore her hair in ear muffs, and who was, I should say, addicted to the vanity case. This young person, Norah had informed me, was Jenny Boyd.

And that sums up the whole of my intimate knowledge of Amos Gately—until the day of the black snow squall!

I daresay my prehistoric ancestors were sunworshipers. At any rate, I am perfectly happy when the sun shines, and utterly miserable on a gloomy day. Of course, after sunset, I don't care, but days when artificial light must be used, I get fidgety and am positively unable to concentrate on any important line of thought.

And so, when Norah snapped on her green shaded desk light in mid afternoon, I impulsively jumped up to go home. I could stand electrically lighted rooms better in my diggings than in the work compelling atmosphere of my office.

"Finish that bit of work," I told my competent assistant, "and then go home yourself. I'm going now."

"But it's only three o'clock, Mr. Brice," and Norah's gray eyes looked up from the clicking keys.

"I know it, but a snow storm is brewing,—and Lord knows there's snow enough in town now!"

"There is so! I'm thinking they won't get the black mountains out of the side streets before Fourth of July,— and the poor White Wings working themselves to death!"

"Statistics haven't yet proved that cause of death prevalent among snow shovelers," I returned, "but I'm pretty sure there's more chance for it coming to them!"

I hate snow. For the ocular defect that kept me out of the army is corrected by not altogether unbecoming glasses, but when these are moistened or misted by falling snow, I am greatly incommoded. So I determined to reach home, if possible, before the squall which was so indubitably imminent. I snugged into my overcoat, and jammed my hat well down on my head, for the wind was already blowing a gale.

"Get away soon, Norah," I said, as I opened the door into the hall, "and if it proves a blizzard you needn't show up tomorrow."

"Oh, I'll be here, Mr. Brice," she returned, in her cheery way, and resumed her clicking. The offices of Mr. Gately, opposite mine, had three doors to the hall, meaning, I assumed, three rooms in his suite.

My own door was exactly opposite the middle one of the three. On that was the number two. To its left was number one, and to its right, number three.

Each of these three doors had an upper panel of thick, clouded glass, and, as the hall was not yet lighted and

Mr. Gately's rooms were, I could see quite plainly the shadows of two heads on the middle door,—the door numbered two.

Perhaps I am unduly curious, perhaps it was merely a natural interest, but I stood still a moment, outside my own door, and watched the two shadowed heads.

The rippled clouding of the glass made their outlines somewhat vague, but I could distinguish the fine, thick mane of Amos Gately, as I had so often seen it pictured. The other was merely a human shadow with no striking characteristics.

It was evident their interview was not amicable. I heard a loud, explosive "No!" from one or other of them, and then both figures rose and there was a hand to hand struggle. Their voices indicated a desperate quarrel, though no words were distinguishable.

And then, as I looked, the shadows blurred into one another,—swayed,—separated, and then a pistol shot rang out, followed immediately by a woman's shrill scream.

Impulsively I sprang across the hall, and turned the knob of door number two,—the one opposite my own door, and the one through which I had seen the shadowed actions.

But the door would not open.

I hesitated only an instant and then hurried to the door next on the right, number three.

This, too, was fastened on the inside, so I ran back to the only other door, number one,—to the left of the middle door.

This door opened at my touch, and I found myself in the first of Amos Gately's magnificent rooms.

Beyond one quick, admiring glance, I paid no attention to the beautiful appointments, and I opened the communicating door into the next or middle room.

This, like the first, contained no human being, but it was filled with the smoke and the odor of a recently fired pistol.

I looked around, aghast. This was the room where the altercation had taken place, where two men had grappled, where a pistol had been fired, and moreover, where a woman had screamed. Where were these people?

In the next room, of course, I reasoned.

With eager curiosity, I went on into the third room. It was empty.

And that was all the rooms of the suite.

Where were the people I had seen and heard? That is, I had seen their shadows on the glass door, and human shadows cannot appear without people to cast them. Where were the men who had fought? Where was the woman who had screamed? And who were they?

Dazed, I went back through the rooms. Their several uses were clear enough. Number one was the entrance office. There was an attendant's desk, a typewriter, reception chairs, and all the effects of the first stage of an interview with the great man.

The second office, beyond a doubt, was Mr. Gately's sanctum. A stunning mahogany table desk was in the middle of the floor, and a large, unusually fine swivel chair stood behind it. On the desk, things were somewhat disordered. The telephone was upset, the papers pushed into an untidy heap, a pen tray overturned, and a chair opposite the big desk chair lay over on its side, as if Mr. Gately's visitor had risen hurriedly. The last room, number three, was, clearly, the very holy of holies. Surely, only the most important or most beloved guests were received in here. It was furnished as richly as a royal salon, yet all in most perfect taste and quiet harmony. The general coloring of draperies and upholstery was soft blue, and splendid pictures hung on the wall. Also, there was a huge war map of Europe, and indicative pins stuck in it proved Mr. Gately's intense interest in the progress of events over there.

But though tempted to feast my eyes on the art treasures all about, I eagerly pursued my quest for the vanished human beings I sought.

There was no one in any of these three rooms, and I could see no exit, save into the hall from which I had entered. I looked into three or four cupboards, but they were full of books and papers, and no sign of a hidden human being, alive or dead, could I find.

Perhaps the strangeness of it all blunted my efficiency. I had always flattered myself that I was at my best in an emergency, but all previous emergencies in which I had found myself were trivial and unimportant compared with this.

I felt as if I had been at a moving picture show. I had seen, as on the screen, a man shot, perhaps killed, and now all the actors had vanished as completely as they do when the movie is over.

Then, for I am not entirely devoid of conscience, it occurred to me that I had a duty,—that it was incumbent upon me to report to somebody. I thought of the police, but was it right to call them when I had so vague a report to make? What could I tell them? That I had seen shadows fighting? Heard a woman scream? Smelled smoke? Heard the report of a pistol? A whimsical thought came that the report of the pistol was the only definite report I could swear to!

Yet the whole scene was definite enough to me.

I had seen two men fighting,—shadows, to be sure, but shadows of real men. I had heard their voices raised in dissension of some sort, I had seen a scuffle and had heard a shot, of which I had afterward smelled the smoke, and,—most incriminating of all,—I had heard a woman's scream. A scream, too, of terror, as for her life!

And then, I had immediately entered these rooms, and I had found them empty of all human presence, but with the smoke still hanging low, to prove my observations had been real, and no figment of my imagination.

I believed I had latent detective ability. Well, surely here was a chance to exercise it!

What more bewildering mystery could be desired than to witness a shooting, and, breaking in upon the scene, to find no victim, no criminal, and no weapon!

I hunted for the pistol, but found no more trace of that than of the hand that had fired it.

My brain felt queer; I said to myself, over and over, "a fight, a shot, a scream! No victim, no criminal, no weapon!"

I looked out in the hall again. I had already looked out two or three times, but I had seen no one. However, I didn't suppose the villain and his victim had gone down by the elevator or by the stairway.

But where were they? And where was the woman who had screamed?

Perhaps it was she who had been shot. Why did I assume that Mr. Gately was the victim? Could not he have been the criminal?

The thought of Amos Gately in the role of murderer was a little too absurd! Still, the whole situation was absurd.

For me, Tom Brice, to be involved in this baffling mystery was the height of all that was incredible!

And yet, was I involved? I had only to walk out and go home to be out of it all. No one had seen me and no one could know I had been there.

And then something sinister overcame me. A kind of cold dread of the whole affair; an uncanny feeling that I was drawn into a fearful web of circumstances from which I could not honorably escape, if, indeed, I could escape at all. The three Gately rooms, though lighted, felt dark and eerie. I glanced out of a window. The sky was almost black and scattering snowflakes were falling. I realized, too, that though the place was lighted, the fixtures were those great alabaster bowls, and, as they hung from the ceiling, they seemed to give out a ghastly radiance that emphasized the strange silence.

For, in my increasingly nervous state, the silence was intensified and it seemed the silence of death,—not the mere quiet of an empty room.

I pulled myself together, for I had not lost all sense of my duty. I must do something, I told myself, sternly,—but what?

My hand crept toward the telephone that lay, turned over on its side, on Mr. Gately's desk.

But I drew back quickly, not so much because of a disinclination to touch the thing that had perhaps figured in a tragedy but because of a dim instinct of leaving everything untouched as a possible clew.

Clew! The very word helped restore my equilibrium. There had been a crime of some sort,—at least, there had been a shooting, and I had been an eye witness, even if my eyes had seen only shadows.

My role, then, was an important one. My duty was to tell what I had seen and render any assistance I could. But I wouldn't use that telephone. It must be out of order, anyway, or the operator downstairs would be looking after it. I would go back to my own office and call up somebody. As I crossed the hall, I was still debating whether that somebody would better be the police or the bank people downstairs. The latter, I decided, for it was their place to look after their president, not mine.

I found Norah putting on her hat The sight of her shrewd gray eyes and intelligent face caused an outburst of confidence, and I told her the whole story as fast as I could rattle it out.

"Oh, Mr. Brice," she exclaimed, her eyes wide with excitement, "let me go over there! May I?"

"Wait a minute, Norah: I think I ought to speak to the bank people. I think I'll telephone down and ask if Mr. Gately is down there. You know it may not have been Mr. Gately at all, whose shadow I saw "

"Ooh, yes, it was! You couldn't mistake his head, and, too, who else would be in there? Please, Mr. Brice, wait just a minute before you telephone,—let me take one look round,—you don't want to make a—to look foolish, you know."

She had so nearly warned me against making a fool of myself, that I took the hint, and I followed her across the hall.

She went in quickly at the door of room number one. One glance around it and she said, "This is the first office, you see: callers come here, the secretary or stenographer takes their names and all that, and shows them into Mr. Gately's office."

As Norah spoke she went on to the second room. Oblivious to its grandeur and luxury, she gave swift, darting glances here and there and said positively: "Of course, it was Mr. Gately who was shot, and by a woman too!"

"The woman who screamed?"

"No: more likely not. I expect the woman who screamed was his stenographer. I know her,—at least, I've seen her. A little doll faced jig, who belongs about third from the end, in the chorus! Be sure she'd scream at the pistol shot, but the lady who fired the shot wouldn't."

"But I saw the scrimmage and it was a man who shot."

"Are you sure? That thick, clouded glass blurs a shadow beyond recognition."

"What makes you think it was a woman, then?"

"This," and Norah pointed to a hatpin that lay on the big desk.

It was a fine looking pin, with a big head, but when I was about to pick it up Norah dissuaded me.

"Don't touch it," she warned; "you know, Mr. Brice, we've really no right here and we simply must not touch anything."

"But, Norah," I began, my common sense and good judgment having returned to me with the advent of human companionship, "I don't want to do anything wrong. If we've no right here, for Heaven's sake, let's get out!"

"Yes, in a minute, but let me think what you ought to do. And, oh, do let me take a minute to look round!"

"No, girl; this is no time to satisfy your curiosity or. to enjoy a sight of these "

"Oh, I don't mean that! But I want to see if there isn't some clew or some bit of evidence to the whole thing. It is too weird! too impossible that three people should have disappeared into nothingness! Where are they?"

Norah looked in the same closets I had explored; she drew aside window draperies and portieres, she hastily glanced under desks and tables, not so much, I felt sure, in expectation of finding anyone, as with a general idea of searching the place thoroughly.

She scrutinized the desk fittings of the stenographer.

"Everything of the best," she commented, "but very little real work done up here. I fancy these offices of Mr. Gately's are more for private conferences and personal appointments than any real business matters."

"Which would account for the lady's hatpin," I observed.

"Yes; but how did they get out? You looked out in the hall, at once, you say?"

"Yes; I came quickly through these three rooms, and then looked out into the hall at once, and there was no elevator in sight nor could I see anyone on the stairs."

"Well, there's not much to be seen here. I suppose you'd better call up the bank people. Though if they thought there was anything queer they'd be up here by this time."

I left Norah in Mr. Gately's rooms while I went back to my own office and called up the Puritan Trust Company.

A polite voice assured me that they knew nothing of Mr. Gately's whereabouts at that moment, but if I would leave a message he would ultimately receive it.

So, then, I told them, in part, what had happened, or, rather, what I believed had happened, and still a little unconcerned, the polite man agreed to send somebody up.

"Stuffy people!" I said to Norah, as I returned to the room she was in. "They seemed to think me officious."

"I feared they would, Mr. Brice, but you had to do it. There's no doubt Mr. Gately left this room in mad haste. See, here's his personal checkbook on his desk, and he drew a check today."

"Nothing remarkable in his drawing a check," I observed, "but decidedly peculiar to leave his checkbook around so carelessly. As you say, Norah, he left in a hurry."

"But how did he leave?"

"That's the mystery; and I, for one, give it up. I'm quite willing to wait until some greater brain than mine works out the problem."

"But it's incomprehensible, Norah went on; "where's Jenny?"

"For that matter," I countered, "where's Mr. Gately? Where's his angry visitor, male or female? and, finally, where's the pistol that made the sound and smoke of which I had positive evidence?"

"We may find that," suggested Norah, hopefully.

But careful search failed to discover any firearms, as it had failed to reveal the actors of the drama.

Nor did the representative from the bank come up at once. This seemed queer, I thought, and with a sudden impulse to find out something, I declared I was going down to the bank myself.

"Go on," said Norah, "I'll stay here, for I must know what they find out when they do come." I went out into the hall and pushed the "Down" button of the elevator.

"Be careful," Norah warned me, as the car was heard ascending, "say very little, Mr. Brice, except to the proper authorities. This may be a terrible thing, and you mustn't get mixed up in it until you know more about it. You were not only the first to discover the disappearance,—but you and I are apparently the only ones in this corridor who know of it yet, we may be "

"Suspected of the abduction of Amos Gately! Hardly! Don't let your detective instinct run away with you Norah!"

And then the elevator door slid open and I got into the car.

CHAPTER 2: JENNY'S VERSION

THE elevators in the building were run by girls, and the one I entered was in charge of Minny Boyd, a sister of Jenny, who was in Mr. Gately's office.

As soon as I stepped into the car I saw that Minny was in a state of excitement.

"What's the matter?" I asked, sympathetically.

"Oh, Mr. Brice," and the girl burst into tears, "Jenny said—"

"Well," I urged, as she hesitated, "what did Jenny say?"

"Don't you know anything about it?"

"About what?" I asked, trying to be casual.

"Why, about Mr. Gately."

"And what about him?"

"He's gone! Disappeared!"

"Amos Gately? The president of the Puritan Trust Company! Minny, what do you mean?"

"Why, Mr. Brice, only a little while ago, I took Jenny down. She was crying like everything and she said that Mr. Gately had been shot!"

"Shot?"

"Yes, that's what she said—"

"Who shot him?"

"I don't know, but Jenny was nearly crazy! I told her to go to the lunchroom,—that's where the girls go when off duty,—and I said I'd come to her as soon as I could. I can't leave my car, you know."

"Of course not, Minny," I agreed; "but what did Jenny mean? Did she see Mr. Gately shot?"

"No, I don't think so,—but she heard a pistol fired off, and she—she—"

"What did she do?"

"She ran into Mr. Gately's private office,—and, he wasn't there! And then she—oh, I suppose she hadn't any right to do it,—but she ran on to his own personal room,—the one where she is never allowed to go,—and there wasn't anybody there! So Jenny was scared out of her senses, and she ran out here,—to the hall, I mean,—and I took her downstairs,—and oh, Mr. Brice, I've got to stop at this floor,—there's a call,—and please don't say anything about it,—I mean don't tell I said anything—for Jenny told me not to—"

I saw Minny was in great perturbation, and I forebore to question her further, for just then we stopped at the seventh floor and a man entered the elevator.

I knew him,—that is, I knew he was George Rodman,—but I wasn't sufficiently acquainted to speak to him.

So the three of us went on down in silence, past the other floors, and reached the ground floor, where Rodman and I got out.

Waiting to go up, I found Mr. Pitt, a discount clerk of the Puritan Trust Company.

"This is Mr. Brice?" he said, in a superior way.

I resented the superiority, but I admitted his soft impeachment.

"And you say there is something to be investigated in Mr. Gately's offices?" he went on, as if I were a Food Administrator, or something.

"Well," I returned, a little curtly, "I chanced to see and hear and smell a pistol shot,—and further looking into the matter failed to show anybody killed or wounded or—in fact, failed to disclose anybody whatever on the job, and I confess it all looks to me mighty queer!"

"And may I ask why it appeals to you as queer?"

I looked Friend Pitt square in the eye, and I said, "It seems to me queer that a bank president should drop out of existence and even out of his business affiliations in one minute without any recognition of the fact."

"Perhaps you overestimate an outside interest," said Pitt. "You must know it is really none of the business of the Puritan Trust Company what Mr. Gately does in his leisure hours."

"Very well, Mr. Pitt," I returned, "then let us go and interview the young woman who is Mr. Gately's stenographer and who is even now in hysterics in the employees' lunchroom."

Mr. Pitt seemed duly impressed and together we went to find Jenny.

The lunchroom for the employees of the building was a pleasant place, on the ground floor, and therein we found Jenny, the yellow haired stenographer of Amos Gately.

The girl was, without doubt, hysterical, and her account of the shooting was disjointed and incoherent.

Moreover, Mr. Pitt was of the supercilious type, the kind who never believes anything, and his manner, as he listened to Jenny's story, was incredulous and almost scoffing.

So Jenny's story, though to me illuminating, was, I felt sure, to Pitt, of little value.

"Oh," Jenny exclaimed, "I was in my room, the first room, and I didn't mean to listen,—I never do! and then, all of a sudden, I heard somebody threatening Mr. Gately! That made me listen,—I don't care if it was wrong—and then, I heard somebody quarreling with Mr. Gately."

"How do you know they were quarreling?" interposed Pitt's cold voice.

"I couldn't help knowing, sir. I heard Mr. Gately's usually pleasant voice raised as if in anger, and I heard the visitor's voice, high and angry too."

"You didn't know the visitor's voice? you had never heard it before?" asked Pitt.

"No, sir; I've no idea who he could have been!" and the foolish little Jenny bridled and looked like an innocent ingénue.

I broke in.

"But didn't you admit all visitors or callers to Mr. Gately?" I demanded.

Jenny looked at me. "No, sir," she replied; "I received all who came to my door, but there were others!"

"Where did they enter?" asked Pitt.

"Oh, they came in at the other doors. You see, I only looked after my own room. Of course, if Miss Raynor came,—or anybody that Mr. Gately knew personally—" Jenny paused discreetly.

"And did Miss Raynor come this morning?" I asked.

"Yes," Jenny replied, "she did. That is, not this morning, but early this afternoon. I know Miss Raynor very well."

Mr. Pitt seemed a little disturbed from his usual calm, and with evident reluctance said to me, "I think, Mr. Brice, that this matter is more serious than I thought. It seems to me that it would be wise to refer the whole matter to Mr. Talcott, the secretary of the Trust Company."

Now, I was only too glad to refer the matter to anybody who could be considered authoritative, and I agreed at once.

"Moreover," said Mr. Pitt, as he gave an anxious glance at Jenny, "I think it well to take this young woman along, as she is the secretary of Mr. Gately and may know—"

"Oh, no, sir," cried Jenny, "I don't know anything! Please don't ask me questions!"

Jenny's perturbation seemed to make Mr. Pitt's intentions more definite, and he corralled the young woman, as he also swept me along.

In a moment, we were all going into the offices of the Puritan Trust Company.

And here, Mr. Pitt faded from view, and he left us in the august presence of Mr. Talcott, the secretary of the Company.

I found myself in the quiet, pleasant atmosphere of the usual banker's office, and Mr. Talcott, a kindly gentleman of middle aged aristocracy, began to question me.

"It seems to me, Mr. Brice," he began, "that this story of yours about Mr. Gately is not only important but mysterious."

"I think so, Mr. Talcott," I responded, "and yet, the whole crux of the matter is whether Mr. Gately is, at present, in some one of his offices, or, perhaps at his home, or whether his whereabouts are undetermined."

"Of course, Mr. Brice," the secretary went on, "it is none of our business where Mr. Gately is, outside of his banking hours; and yet, in view of Mr. Pitt's report of your account, it is incumbent upon us, the officers of the Trust Company, to look into the matter. Will you tell me, please, all you know of the circumstances pertaining to Mr. Gately's disappearance,—if he has disappeared?"

"If he has disappeared!" I snapped back; "and, pray, sir, if he has not disappeared, where is he?"

Mr. Talcott, still unmoved, responded, "That is aside the question, for the moment. What do you know of the matter, Mr. Brice?"

I replied by telling him all I knew of the whole affair, from the time I first saw the shadows until the moment when I went down in the elevator and met Mr. Pitt.

He listened with deepest attention, and then, seemingly unimpressed by my story, began to question Jenny.

This volatile young lady had regained her mental balance, and was more than ready to dilate upon her experiences.

"Yes, sir," she said, "I was sitting at my desk, and nobody had come in for an hour or so, when, all of a sudden, I heard talking in Mr. Gately's room."

"Do callers usually go through your room?" Mr. Talcott inquired.

"Yes, sir,—that is, unless they're Mr. Gately's personal friends,—like Miss Raynor or somebody."

"Who is Miss Raynor?" I broke in.

"His ward," said Mr. Talcott, briefly. "Go on, Jenny; nobody had gone through your room?"

"No, sir; and so, I was startled to hear somebody scrapping with Mr. Gately."

"Scrapping?"

"Yes, sir; sort of quarreling, you know; I—"

"Did you listen?"

"Not exactly that, sir, but I couldn't help hearing the angry voices, though I didn't make out the words."

"Be careful, Jenny," Talcott's tones were stern, "don't assume more than you can be sure was meant."

"Then I can't assume anything," said Jenny, crisply, "for I didn't hear a single word,—only I did feel sure the two of 'em was scrapping."

"You heard, then, angry voices?"

"Yes, sir, just that. And right straight afterward, a pistol shot."

"In Mr. Gately's room?"

"Yes, sir. And then I ran in there to see what it meant,—"

"Weren't you frightened?"

"No, sir; I didn't stop to think there was anything to be frightened of. But when I got in there, and saw—"

"Well, go on,—what did you see?"

"A man, with a pistol in his hand, running out of the door—"

"Which door?"

"The door of number three,—that's Mr. Gately's own particular private room,—well, he was running out of that door, with a pistol in his hand,—and the pistol was smoking, sir!"

Jenny's foolish little face was red with excitement and her lips trembled as she told her story. It was impossible to disbelieve her,—there could be no doubt of her fidelity to detail.

But Talcott was imperturbable.

"The pistol was smoking," he repeated, "where did the man go with it?"

"I don't know, sir," said Jenny; "I ran out to the hall after him,—I think I saw him run down the staircase, but I,—I was so scared with it all, I jumped into the elevator,—Minny's elevator,—and came downstairs myself."

"And then?" prompted Talcott.

"Then, sir,—oh, I don't know,—I think I lost my head—it was all so queer, you know—"

"Yes, yes," said Talcott, soothingly,—he was a most courteous man, "yes, Miss Jenny,—I don't wonder you were upset. Now, I think, if you will accompany us, we will go upstairs to Mr. Gately's rooms."

It seemed to me that Mr. Talcott did not pay sufficient attention to my presence, but I forgave this, because I felt sure he would be only too glad to avail himself of my services later on. So I followed him and the tow headed Jenny up to the offices of the bank president.

We did not go up in Minny's elevator, but in another one, and our appearance at the door of Mr. Gately's office number one, was met by Norah,—my Norah, who received us with an air of grave importance.

She was unawed by the sight of Mr. Talcott, imposing though he was, and was clearly scornful of Jenny, who had already assumed a jaunty manner.

But Jenny was quite self possessed, and with a toss of her head at Norah she started to explain.

"I was in here, at my desk, Mr. Talcott," she began, volubly; "and in Mr. Gately's office, I heard somebody talking pretty sharp—"

"A man?"

"Yes, sir."

"How did he get in, if not through your room?"

"Oh, people often went through the hall doors of number two or three, and sometimes they came through my room."

"Who went through your room this afternoon?"

"Only three people. An old man named Smith—"

"What was his business?"

"I'm not quite sure, but it had to do with his getting a part salary from Mr. Gately; he was a down and outer, and he hoped Mr. Gately would help him through."

"And did he?"

"Oh, yes, sir! Mr. Gately always was softhearted and never turned down anybody in need."

"And the other callers?"

"There was an old lady, to see about her husband's pension,—and—"

"Well? I suppose not all the callers were beneficiaries?"

"No, sir. One was a—a lady."

"A lady? Describe her."

"Why, she was Miss Olive Raynor,—Mr. Gately's ward."

"Oh, Miss Raynor. Well, there's no use discussing her. Were there any other ladies?"

"No, sir."

"Nor any other men?"

"No, sir; that is, not through my room. You know, people could go in to Mr. Gately's private offices without going through my room."

"Yes, I know. But couldn't you see them?"

"Only dimly,—through the clouded glass window between my room and Mr. Gately's."

"And what did you see of the callers in Mr. Gately's room just before you heard the shot fired?"

Jenny looked dubious. She seemed inclined not to tell all she knew. But Mr. Talcott spoke sharply.

"Come," he said; "speak up. Tell all you know."

"I didn't hear anybody come in," said Jenny, slowly; "and then, all of a sudden, I heard loud voices,—and then, I heard quarrelly words—"

"Quarrelly?"

"Yes, sir, as if somebody was threatening Mr. Gately. I didn't hear clearly, but I heard enough to make me look through the window between the two rooms—"

"This window?"

"Yes, sir," and Jenny nodded at the clouded glass pane between her room and Mr. Gately's office. "And I saw sort of shadows,—and then in a minute I saw the shadows get up—you know, Mr. Gately and another man,—and then,—I heard a pistol fired off, and I yelled!"

"It was your scream I heard, then!" I exclaimed.

"I don't know," Jenny replied, "but I did scream, because I am fearfully scared of pistol shots, and I didn't know who was shooting."

"What did you do next?" asked Mr. Talcott, in his quiet way.

"I ran into Mr. Gately's room—"

"And you weren't frightened?"

"Not for myself. I was frightened of the shot,—I always am afraid of firearms, but I wanted to know what was doing. So, I opened the door and ran in—"

"Yes; and?"

"I saw nobody in Mr. Gately's room,—I mean this room next to mine,—so I ran on, to the third room,—I am not supposed to go in there,—but I did, and there I saw a man just going out to the hall and in his hand was a smoking revolver."

"Out to the hall? Did you follow him?"

"Of course I did! But he ran down the staircase. I didn't go down that way, because I thought I'd get down quicker and head him off by going down in the elevator."

"So you went down in the elevator?"

"Yes, sir. It was Minny's elevator,—Minny's my sister,—and after I got in,—and saw Minny, I got sort of hysterical and nervous, and I couldn't remember what I was about."

"What became of the man?" asked Talcott, uninterested in Jenny's nerves.

"I don't know, sir. I was so rattled,—and I only saw him a moment,—and—"

"Would you know him if you saw him again?"

"I don't know,—I don't think so."

"I wish you could say yes,—it may be of gravest importance."

But Jenny seemed to resent Mr. Talcott's desire.

"I don't see how you could expect it, sir," she said, pettishly; "I saw him only in a glimpse,—I was scared to death at the sound of the pistol shot,—and when I burst into this room and found Mr. Gately gone I was so kerflummixed I didn't know what I was about! That I didn't!"

"And yet," Norah remarked, quietly, "after you went downstairs and these gentlemen found you in the lunchroom, you were perfectly calm and collected—"

"Nothing of the sort!" blazed back Jenny; "I'm all on edge! My nerves are completely unstrung!"

"Quite so," said Mr. Talcott, kindly, "and I suggest that you go back to the lunchroom, Miss Jenny, and rest and calm yourself. But please remain there, until I call for you again."

Jenny looked a little disappointed at being thus thrust out of the limelight, but as Mr. Talcott held the door open for her, she had no choice but to depart, and we presently heard her go down in her sister's elevator.

"Now," Mr. Talcott resumed, "we will look into this matter further.

"You see," he proceeded, speaking, to my surprise, as much to Norah as to myself, "I can't really apprehend that anything serious has happened to Mr. Gately. For, if the shot which Jenny heard, and which you, Mr. Brice, heard,—had killed Mr. Gately, the body, of course, would be here. Again, if the shot had wounded him seriously, he would in some way contrive to make his condition known. Therefore, I feel sure that Mr. Gately is either absolutely all right, or, if slightly wounded, he is in some anteroom or in some friend's room nearby. And, if this is the case,— I mean, if our Mr. Gately is ill or hurt, we must find him. Therefore, careful search must be made."

"But," spoke up Norah, "perhaps Mr. Gately went home. There is no positive assurance that he did not."

Mr. Talcott looked at Norah keenly. He didn't seem to regard her as an impertinent young person, but he took her suggestion seriously.

"That may be," he agreed. "I think I will call up his residence."

He did so, and I gathered from the remarks he made on the telephone that Amos Gately was not at his home, nor was his niece, Miss Olive Raynor, there.

Talcott made another call or two, and I finally learned that he had located Miss Raynor.

For, "Very well," he said; "I shall hope to see you here in ten or fifteen minutes, then."

He hung up the receiver,—he had used the instrument in Jenny's room, and not the upset one on Mr. Gately's desk,—and he vouchsafed:

"I think it is all right. Miss Raynor says she saw her uncle here this afternoon, shortly after luncheon, and he said he was about to leave the office for the day. She thinks he is at his club or on the way home. However, she is coming around here, as she is in the limousine, and fearing a storm, she wants to take Mr. Gately home."

Chapter 3: The Elevator

MR. TALCOTT returned to the middle room and looked more carefully at the disturbed condition of things around and on Mr. Gately's desk.

"It is certain that Mr. Gately left the room in haste," he said, "for here is what is undoubtedly a private and personal checkbook left open. I shall take on myself the responsibility of putting it away, for the moment, at least."

Mr. Talcott closed the checkbook and put it in a small drawer of the desk.

"Why don't you put away that hatpin, too?" suggested Norah, eying the pin curiously. "I don't think it belongs to Miss Raynor."

"Take it up by the edge," I warned; "I may be jumping to conclusions, but there is a possibility that a crime has been committed, and we must preserve what may be evidence."

"Quite right, Mr. Brice," agreed Talcott, and he gingerly picked up the pin by taking the edges of its ornate head between his thumb and forefinger. The head was an Egyptian scarab,—whether a real one or not I couldn't tell,—and was set on a flat backing of gold. This back might easily retain the thumb print of the woman who had drawn that pin from her hat in Mr. Gately's office. And who, Norah surmised, was the person who had fired the pistol that I had heard discharged.

Placing the hatpin in the drawer with the checkbook, Mr. Talcott locked the drawer and slipped the key in his pocket.

I wondered if he had seen some entry in the book that made him wish to hide Mr. Gately's private affairs from curious eyes.

"There is indeed a possibility of something wrong," he went on, "at first I couldn't think it, but seeing this room, that overturned chair and upset telephone, in connection with the shooting, as you heard it, Mr. Brice, it certainly seems ominous. And most mysterious! Two people quarreling, a shot fired by one or other of them, and no sign of the assailant, his victim, or his weapon! Now, there are three propositions, one of which must be the truth. Mr. Gately is alive and well, he is wounded, or he is killed. The last seems impossible, as his body could not have been taken away without discovery; if he were wounded, I think that, too, would have to be known; so, I still feel that things are all right. But until we can prove that, we must continue our search."

"Yes," I agreed, "search for Mr. Gately and also, search for the man who was here and who quarreled with him."

"Or the woman," insisted Norah.

"I can't think it was a woman," I said. "Although the shadow was indistinct, it struck me as that of a man, the motions and attitudes were masculine, as I recall them. The hatpin may have been left here this morning or any time."

"The visitor must be found," declared Mr. Talcott, "but I don't know how to go about it."

"Ask the elevator girls," I suggested; "one of them must have brought the caller up here."

We did this, but the attendants of the three elevators all denied having brought anyone up to Mr. Gately's offices since the old man and the elderly lady who had been mentioned by Jenny.

Miss Raynor had been brought up by one of the girls also, but we couldn't quite ascertain whether she had come before or after the other two.

While waiting for Miss Raynor to come again, I tried to do a little scientific deduction from any evidence I might notice.

But I gained small information. The desk-blotter, inkwell, and pens were in immaculate order, doubtless they were renewed every day by a careful attendant. All the minor accessories, such as paperweights and letter openers were of individual styles and of valuable materials. There was elaborate smoking paraphernalia and a beautiful single rose in a tall silver vase.

"Can you read anything bearing on the mystery, Mr. Brice," asked Talcott, noting my thoughtful scrutiny.

"No; nothing definite. In fact, nothing of any importance. I see that on one occasion, at least, Mr. Gately kept a chauffeur waiting an unconscionably long time, and the man was finally obliged to go away without him."

"Well, now, how do you guess that?" and Mr. Talcott looked decidedly interested.

"Like most of those spectacular deductions," I responded, "the explanation takes all the charm out of it. There is a carriage check on the desk,—one of those queer cards with a lot of circular holes in it. That must have been given to Mr. Gately when he left his car, or perhaps a taxicab, outside of some hotel or shop. As he didn't give it up, the chauffeur must have waited for him until he was tired."

"He may have gone off with some friend, and sent word to the man not to wait," offered Talcott.

"But then he would have sent the call check out to identify him. What a queer looking thing it is," and I picked up the card, with its seven round holes in a cabalistic array.

"Perhaps the caller left it," spoke up Norah; "perhaps he, or she, came here in a cab, or a car, and—"

"No, Norah," I said, "such checks are not given out at a building of this sort. Only at hotels, theaters, or shops."

"It's of no importance," and Mr. Talcott gave a slight shrug of impatience; "the thing is, where is Mr. Gately?"

Restless and unable to sit still, I wandered into the third room. I had heard of this sanctum, but I had never expected to see inside of it. The impulse came to me now to make the most of this chance, for when Mr. Gately returned I might be summarily, if courteously, ejected.

The effect of the room was that of dignified splendor. It had evidently been done but not overdone by a decorator who was a true artist. The predominant color was a soft, deep blue, and the rugs and textile fabrics were rich and luxurious. There were a few fine paintings in gold frames and the large war map occupied the greater part of a paneled wall space. The chairs were spacious and cushioned, and a huge davenport stood in front of a wide fireplace, where some logs were .cheerily burning.

A cozy place to entertain friends, I ruminated, and then, turning back to the middle room, I reconstructed the movements of the two people I had seen shadowed.

"As they rose," I said to Mr. Talcott, "Amos Gately was behind this big table desk, and the other man,—for I still think it was a man,—was opposite. The other man upset his chair, on rising, so he must have risen hastily. Then the shot was fired, and the two disappeared. As Jenny came into the room at once, and saw the strange man going through the third room and on out to the stairs, we are forced to the conclusion that Mr. Gately preceded him."

"Down the stairs?" asked Mr. Talcott.

"Yes, for the flight, at least, or Jenny would have seen him. Also, I should have seen him, had he remained in this hall."

"And the woman?" asked Norah, "what became of her?"

"I don't think there was any woman present at that time," I returned. "The hatpin was, doubtless, left by a woman caller, but we've no reason to suppose she was there at the same time the shooting occurred."

"I can't think of any reason why anyone should shoot Mr. Gately," said Talcott, musingly. "He is a most estimable gentleman, the soul of honor and uprightness."

"Of course," I assented; "but has he no personal enemies?"

"None that I know of, and it is highly improbable, anyway. He is not a politician, or, indeed, a public man of any sort. He is exceedingly charitable, but he rarely makes known his good deeds. He has let it be known that he wishes his benefactions kept quiet."

"What are his tastes?" I asked, casually.

"Simple in the extreme. He rarely takes a vacation, and though his home is on a magnificent scale, he doesn't entertain very much. I have heard that Miss Raynor pleads in vain for him to be more of a society man."

"She is his ward?"

"Yes; no relation, although she calls him uncle. I believe he was a college chum of Miss Raynor's father, and when the girl was left alone in the world, he took her to live with him, and took charge of her fortune."

"A large one?"

"Fairly so, I believe. Enough to tempt the fortune hunters, anyway, and Mr. Gately frowns on any young man who approaches him with a request for Olive Raynor's hand."

"Perhaps the caller today was a suitor."

"Oh, I hardly think a man would come armed on such an errand. No; to me, the most mysterious thing about it all, is why anyone should desire to harm Mr. Gately. It must have been a homicidal maniac,—if there is really such a being."

"The most mysterious part to me," I rejoined, "is how they both got away so quickly. You see, I stood in my doorway opposite, looking at them, and then as soon as I heard the shot I ran to the middle door as fast as I could, then to the third room door, and then back to the first. Of course, had I known which room was which, I should have gone to door number one first. But, as you see, I was in the hall, going from one door to another, and I must have seen the men if they came out into the hall from any door."

"They left room number three, as you entered number one," said Norah, carefully thinking it out.

"That must be so, but where did they go? Why, if Mr. Gately went downstairs, has he not been visible since? I can't help feeling that Amos Gately is unable to move, for some reason or other. May he have been kidnaped? Or is he bound and gagged in some unused room, say on the floor below this?"

"No," said Talcott, briefly. "Without saying anything about it I put one of the bank clerks on the hunt and I told him to look into every room in the building. As he has not reported, he hasn't yet found Mr. Gately."

And then, Olive Raynor arrived.

I shall never forget that first sight of her. Heralded by a fragrant whiff of fresh violets, she came into the first room, and paused at the doorway of the middle room, where we still sat.

Framed in the mahogany door casing, the lovely bit of femininity seemed a laughing bundle of furs, velvets, and laces.

"What's the matter?" said a soft, sweet voice. "Has Uncle Amos run away? I hope he is in a sheltered place for there's a ferocious storm coming up and the wind is blowing a gale."

The nodding plumes on her hat tossed as she raised her head inquiringly and looked about.

"What do I smell?" she exclaimed; "it's like—like pistol smoke!"

"It is," Mr. Talcott said. "But there's no pistol here now—"

"How exciting! What's it all about? Do tell me."

Clearly the girl apprehended no serious matter. Her wide open eyes showed curiosity and interest, but no thought of trouble had as yet come to her.

She stepped further into the room, and throwing back her furs revealed a slender graceful figure, quick of movement and of exquisite poise. Neither dark nor very fair, her wavy brown hair framed a face whose chief characteristic seemed to be its quickly changing expressions. Now smiling, then grave, now wondering, then merry, she looked from one to another of us, her big brown eyes coming to rest at last on Norah.

"Who are you?" she asked, with a lovely smile that robbed the words of all curtness.

"I am Norah MacCormack, Miss Raynor," my stenographer replied. "I am in Mr. Brice's office, across the hall. This is Mr. Brice."

There was no reason why Norah should be the one to introduce me, but we were all a little rattled, and Mr. Talcott, who, of course, was the one to handle the situation, seemed utterly at a loss as to how to begin.

"How do you do, Mr. Brice?" and Miss Raynor flashed me a special smile. "And now, Mr. Talcott, tell me what's the matter? I see something has happened. What is it?"

She was grave enough now. She had suddenly realized that there was something to tell, and she meant to have it told.

"I don't know, Miss Raynor," Talcott began, "whether anything has happened, or not. I mean, anything serious. We—that is,—we don't know where Mr. Gately is."

"Go on. That of itself doesn't explain your anxious faces."

So Talcott told her,—told her just what we knew ourselves, which was so little and yet so mysterious.

Olive listened, her great, dark eyes widening with wonder. She had thrown off her fur coat and was seated in Amos Gately's desk chair, her dainty foot turning the chair on its swivel now and then.

Her muff fell to the floor, and, unconsciously, she drew off her gloves and dropped them upon it. She said no word during the recital, but her vivid face showed all the surprise and fear she felt as the tale was told.

Then, "I don't understand," she said, simply. "Do you think somebody shot Uncle Amos? Then where is he?"

"We don't understand, either," returned Talcott. "We don't know that anybody shot him. We only know a shot was fired and Mr. Gately is missing."

Just then a man entered Jenny's room, from the hall. He, too, paused in the doorway to the middle room.

"Oh, Amory, come in!" cried Miss Raynor. "I'm so glad you're here. This is Mr. Brice,—and Miss MacCormack,— Mr. Manning. Mr. Talcott, of course you know."

I had never met Amory Manning before, but one glance was enough to show how matters stood between him and Olive Raynor. They were more than friends,— that much was certain.

"I saw Mr. Manning downstairs," Miss Raynor said to Talcott, with a lovely flush, "and—as Uncle Amos doesn't—well, he isn't just crazy over him, I asked him not to come up here with me, but to wait for me downstairs."

"And as you were so long about coming down, I came up," said Mr. Manning, with a little smile. "What's this,—what about a shot? Where's Mr. Gately."

Talcott hesitated, but Olive Raynor poured out the whole story at once.

Manning listened gravely, and at the end, said simply: "He must be found. How shall we set about it?"

"That's what I don't know," replied Talcott.

"I'll help," said Olive, briskly. "I refuse to believe any harm has come to him. Let's call up his clubs."

"I've done that," said Talcott. "I can't think he went away anywhere—willingly."

"How, then?" cried Olive. "Oh, wait a minute,—I know something!"

"What?" asked Talcott and I together, for the girl's face glowed with her sudden happy thought.

"Why, Uncle Amos has a private elevator of his own. He went down in that!"

"Where is it?" asked Manning.

"I don't know," and Olive looked about the room. "And Uncle forbade me ever to mention it,—but this is an emergency, isn't it? and I'm justified,—don't you think?"

"Yes," said Manning; "tell all you know."

"But that's all I do know. There is a secret elevator that nobody knows about. Surely you can find it."

"Surely we can!" said I, and jumping up, I began the search.

Nor did it take long. There were not very many places where a private entrance could be concealed, and I found it behind the big war map, in the third room.

The door was flush with the wall, and painted the same as the panel itself. The map simply hung on the door, but overlapped sufficiently to hide it. Thus the door was concealed, though not really difficult of discovery.

"It won't open," I announced after a futile trial.

"Automatic," said Talcott. "You can't open that kind, when the car is down."

"How do you know the car is down?" I asked.

"Because the door won't open. Well, it does seem probable that Mr. Gately went away by this exit, then."

"And the woman, too," remarked Norah.

As before Mr. Talcott didn't object to Norah's participation in our discussion, in fact, he seemed rather to welcome it, and in a way, deferred to her opinions.

"Perhaps so," he assented. "Now, Miss Raynor, where does this elevator descend to? I mean, where does it open on the ground floor?"

"I don't know, I'm sure," and the girl looked perplexed. "I've never been up or down in it. I shouldn't have known of it, but once Uncle let slip a chance reference to it, and when I asked him about it, he told me, but told me not to tell. You see, he uses it to get away from bores or people he doesn't want to see."

"It ought to be easy to trace its shaft down through the floors," said Amory Manning. "Though I suppose there's no opening on any floor until the street floor is reached."

Manning was a thoughtful looking chap. Though we had never met before, I knew of him and I had an impression that he was a civil engineer or something like that. I felt drawn to him at once, for he had a pleasant, responsive manner and a nice, kindly way with him.

In appearance, he was scholarly, rather than business like. This effect was probably due in part to the huge shell rimmed glasses he wore. I can't bear those things myself, but some men seem to take to them naturally. For the rest, Manning had thick, dark hair, and he was a bit inclined to stoutness, but his goodly height saved him from looking stocky.

"Well, I think we ought to investigate this elevator," said Talcott. "Suppose you and I, Mr.

Brice, go downstairs to see about it, leaving Miss Raynor and Mr. Manning here,—in case,—in case Mr. Gately returns."

I knew that Talcott meant, in case we should find anything wrong in the elevator, but he put it the more casual way, and Miss Raynor seemed satisfied.

"Yes, do," she said, "and we'll wait here till you come back. Of course, you can find where it lands, and—oh, wait a minute! Maybe it opens in the next door building. I remember, sometimes when I've been waiting in the car for Uncle, he has come out of the building next door instead of this one, and when I asked him why, he always turned the subject without telling me."

"It may be," and Talcott considered the position of the shaft. "Well, we'll see."

Norah discreetly returned to my offices, but I felt pretty sure she wouldn't go home, until something was found out concerning the mysterious disappearance.

On the street floor we could find no possible outlet for the elevator in question, and had it not been for Olive's hint as to where to look, I don't know how we should have found it at all.

But on leaving the Trust Company Building, we found the place at last. At least, we found a door which was in the position where we supposed the elevator shaft would require it, and we tried to open it.

This we failed to do.

"Looks bad," said Talcott, shaking his head. "If Amos Gately is in there, it's because he's unable to get out— or—unconscious."

He couldn't bring himself to speak the crueler word that was in both our minds, and he turned abruptly aside, as he went in search of the janitor or the superintendent of the building.

Left by myself I stared at the silent door. It was an ordinary looking door, at the end of a small side passage which communicated with the main hall or lobby of the building. It was inconspicuous, and as the passage had an angle in it, Amos Gately could easily have gone in and out of that door without exciting comment.

Of course, the janitor would know all about it; and he did.

He returned with Mr. Talcott, muttering as he came.

"I always said Mr. Gately'd get caught in that thing yet! I don't hold with them automaticky things, so I don't. They may go all right for years and then cut up some trick on you. If that man's caught in there, he must be pretty sick by this time!"

"Does Mr. Gately use the thing much?" I asked.

"Not so very often, sir. Irregular like. Now, quite frequent, and then, again, sort of seldom. Well, we can't open it, Mr. Talcott. These things won't work, only just so. After anybody gets in, and shuts the door, it can't be opened except by pressing a button on the inside. Can't you get in upstairs?"

"No," said Talcott, shortly. "Get help, then, and break the door down."

This was done, the splintered door fell away, and there, in a crumpled heap on the floor of the car, was Amos Gately,—dead.

CHAPTER 4: THE BLACK SQUALL

IF I had thought Mr. Talcott somewhat indifferent before, I changed my opinion suddenly. His face turned a ghastly white and his eyes stared with horror. There was more than his grief for a friend, though that was evident enough, but his thoughts ran ahead to the larger issues involved by this murder of a bank president and otherwise influential financier.

For murder it was, beyond all doubt. The briefest examination showed Mr. Gately had been shot through the heart, and the absence of any weapon precluded the idea of suicide.

The janitor, overcome at the sight, was in a state bordering on collapse, and Mr. Talcott was not much more composed.

"Mr. Brice," he said, his face working convulsively, "this is a fearful calamity! What can it mean? Who could have done it? What shall we do?"

Answering his last question first, I endeavored to take hold of the situation.

"First of all, Mr. Talcott, we must keep this thing quiet for the moment. I mean, we must not let a crowd gather here, before the necessary matters are attended to. This passage must be guarded from intrusion, and the bank people must be notified at once. Suppose you and the janitor stay here, while I go back next door and tell— tell whom?"

"Let me think," groaned Mr. Talcott, passing his hand across his forehead. "Yes, please, Mr. Brice, do that—go to the bank and tell Mr. Mason, the vice president—ask him to come here to me, —then, there is Miss Raynor— oh, how horrible it all is!"

"Also, we must call a doctor," I suggested, "and, eventually, the police."

"Must they be brought in? Yes, I suppose so. Well, Mr. Brice, if you will attend to those errands, I will stay here. But we must shut up that janitor!"

The man, on the verge of collapse, was groaning and mumbling prayers, or something, as he rocked his big body back and forth.

"See here, my man," I said, "this is a great emergency and you must meet it and do your duty. That, at present, is to stay here with Mr. Talcott, and make sure that no one else comes into this small hall until some of Mr. Gately's bank officers arrive. Also, cease that noise you're making, and see what you can do in the way of being a real help to us."

This appeal to his sense of duty was not without effect, and he straightened up and seemed equal to the occasion.

I ran off, then, and out of one big building back into the other. The storm, still brewing, had not yet broken, but the sky was black, and a feeling of more snow was in the atmosphere. I shivered as I felt the bitterly cold outside air, and hurried into the bank building.

I had no trouble in reaching Mr. Mason, for the bank itself was closed and many of the employees had gone home. My manner of grave importance sufficed to let me pass any inquisitive attendants and I found Mr. Mason in his office.

I told him the bare facts in a few words, for this was no time to tarry,—I wanted to get up and tell Miss Raynor before any less considerate messenger might reach her.

Mr. Mason was aghast at the terrible tidings, and closing his desk at once, he quickly reached for his hat and coat and started on his fearsome errand.

"I will call Mr. Gately's physician," he said, his mind working quickly, as he paused a' moment, "and you will break the news to Miss Raynor, you say? I can't seem to comprehend it all! But my place is by Mr. Gately and I will go there at once."

So I hastened up to the twelfth floor again, trying, on the way, to think how I should best tell the awful story.

The elevator ride had never seemed so short,—the floors fairly flew past me, and in a few moments I was in the beautiful third room of Mr. Gately's, and found Miss Raynor and Mr. Manning eagerly awaiting my news.

"Have you found Mr. Gately?" Amory Manning asked, but at the same instant, Olive Raynor cried out, "You have something dreadful to tell us, Mr. Brice! I know you have!"

This seemed to help me, and I answered, "Yes, Miss Raynor,—the worst."

For I felt that this imperious, self possessed girl would rather be told abruptly, like that, than to have me mince matters.

And I was right, for she said, quickly, "Tell it all,— any knowledge is better than suspense."

So I told her, as gently as I could, of our discovery of the body of Amos Gately in his private elevator, at the bottom of the shaft.

"But I don't understand," said Manning.

"Shot through the heart and alone in the elevator?"

"That's the way it is. I've no idea of the details of the matter. We didn't move the body, or examine it thoroughly, but the first glance showed the truth. However, a doctor has been sent for, and the vice president and secretary of the Trust Company have things in charge, so I came right up here to tell you people about it."

"And I thank you, Mr. Brice," Olive's lovely dark eyes gave me a grateful glance. "What shall I do, Amory? Shall we go down there?"

Manning hesitated. "I will," he said, looking at her tenderly, "but—do you want to? It will be hard for you—"

"I know,—but I must go. If Uncle Amos has been killed—surely I ought to be there to—to—oh, I don't know what!"

Olive Raynor turned a piteous face to Manning, and he took her hand in his as he responded: "Come, if you think best, dear. Shall we go together?"

"Yes," she said; "I dread it, but I must go. And if you are with me I can stand it. What are you going to do, Mr. Brice?"

"I was about to go home," I replied, "but I think I will go back to the Matteawan Building, for I may be able to give assistance, in some way."

I went across to my office and found that Norah had gone home. Snapping on some lights, I sat down for a few minutes to straighten out my bewildered, galloping thoughts.

Here was I, Tom Brice, a quiet, inconspicuous lawyer, thrown suddenly into the very thick of a most mysterious murder case. I well knew that my evidence concerning the shadows I had seen would be eagerly listened to by the police, when the time came, and I wondered how soon that would be. I wanted to go home. I wanted to avoid the coming storm and get into my cozy rooms, and think the thing over, for I had always felt that I had detective ability, and now I had been given a wonderful chance to prove it. I did not intend to usurp anybody's prerogative nor did I desire to intrude. If I were not asked to assist, I should not offer; but I had a vague hope that my early acquaintance with the vital facts would make me of value as a witness and my mental acumen would bring forth some original ideas in the way of investigation.

And I wanted some time to myself, to cogitate, and to formulate some theories already budding in my brain. Now if the police were already on the scene next door, they would not let me get away, if I appeared.

And yet, I longed for further news of the proceedings. So, I concluded to look in at the Matteawan, and if that led me into the clutches of the police inquisitors, I must submit. But, if I could get away before their arrival, I should do so. I was quite willing to be called upon by them, and to tell all I knew, but I wanted to postpone that until the next day, if possible.

Not wishing to obtrude my presence further on Miss Raynor, I went down in an elevator without returning to the Gately rooms. Indeed, I didn't know whether she had gone down yet or not.

But she had, and when I reached the scene, both she and Manning were there and were consulting with the men from the bank as to what should be done.

The doctor came, too, and began to examine the body.

The rest of us stood huddled in the narrow hall, now grown hot and close, but we dared not open the door to the main lobby, lest outsiders should make their way in.

I asked the janitor if there were not some room that could be used as a waiting place, but even as he answered me, the doctor made his report.

It was to the effect that Amos Gately had been shot before he entered the elevator or immediately upon his entrance. That he had died instantly, and, therefore it would seem that the body must have been placed in the car and sent down by the assailant. But this was only conjecture; all the doctor could assert was that Mr. Gately had been dead for perhaps an hour, and that the position of the body on the floor indicated an instantaneous death from a shot through the heart.

And then the janitor bestirred himself, and said he could give us the use of a vacant office on the ground floor, and we went in there,—all except the doctor, who remained by the elevator.

Mr. Mason and Mr. Talcott agreed that the police must be notified and they declared their willingness to stay for their arrival. But the vice-president told Miss Raynor she could go home if she preferred to.

"I'll wait a while," she said, with the quick decision that I found was habitual with her, "the car is still here,—oh, ought we not to tell Connor? He's our chauffeur."

"I'll tell him," volunteered Manning. "I have to go now, I've an important matter to attend to before six o'clock. Olive, may I come up to the house this evening?"

"Oh, do," she answered, "I'll be so glad to have you. Come early, won't you?"

"Yes," said Manning, and after pausing for some further talk with the doctor he went away. I tarried, wondering if I might go also, or if I were needed there.

But as Mason and Talcott were deeply engrossed in a low toned conversation and as Miss Raynor was waiting an opportunity to confer with the doctor, who was their family physician, I concluded I might as well go home while I was free to do so.

So without definite adieux, but with a word to Miss Raynor that she might command my services at any time, I started for home.

The long expected storm had begun, and enormous snowflakes were falling thickly.

As I left the Matteawan, I discerned Amory Manning talking to the chauffeur of a big limousine and knew that he was telling Amos Gately's man what had happened to his master.

I slowed up, hoping Manning would get through the interview and walk along, and I would join him.

When he left the chauffeur, however, he darted across the street, and though I followed quickly, I almost lost sight of him in the blinding snowfall.

I called out to him, but he didn't hear, and small wonder, for the wind roared and the traffic noises were deafening.

So I hurried after him, still hoping to overtake him.

And I did, or, at least, when he finally boarded a Southbound car on Third Avenue, I hopped on the same car.

I had intended taking a Madison Avenue car, but there was none in sight, and I felt pretty sure there was a blockade on the line. The streets showed snowpiles, black and crusted, and the street cleaners were few and far apart.

The car Manning and I managed to get onto was crowded to the doors. We both stood, and there were just too many people between us to make conversation possible, but I nodded across and between the bobbing heads and faces, and Manning returned my greeting.

Stopping occasionally to let off some struggling, weary standees and to take on some new snow besprinkled stampeders, we at last reached Twenty second Street, and here Manning nodded a farewell to me, as he prepared to leave by the front end of the car.

This was only three blocks from my own destination, and I determined to get off, too, still anxious to speak to him regarding the scene of tragedy we had just left.

So I swung off the rear end of the car, and it moved on through the storm.

I looked about for Manning, but as I stepped to the ground a gust of wind gave me all I could do to preserve my footing. Moreover, it sent a flurry of snowflakes against my glasses, which rendered them almost opaque.

I dashed them clear with my gloved hand, and looked for my man, but he was nowhere to be seen from where I stood in the center of the four street corners.

Where could Manning have disappeared to? He must have flown like the wind, if he had already darted either up or down Third Avenue or along Twenty second Street in either direction.

However, those were the only directions he could have taken, and I concluded that as I struggled to raise my umbrella and was at the same time partially blinded by my snowed under glasses, he had hurried away out of sight. Of course, he had no reason to think I was trying to catch up with him, indeed, he probably did not know that I also left the car, so he had no need for apology.

And yet, I couldn't see how he had disappeared with such magical celerity. I asked a street cleaner if he had seen him.

"Naw," he said, blowing on his cold fingers, "naw, didn't see nobody. Can't see nothin' in this here black squall!"

And that's just what it was. A sudden fierce whirlwind, a maelstrom of tossing flakes, and a black lowering darkness that seemed to envelop everything.

"Mad Mary," the great clock nearby, boomed out five solemn notes that somehow. added to the weirdness of the moment, and I grasped my umbrella handle, pushed my glasses more firmly into place, and strode toward my home.

With some, home is where the heart is, but, as I was still heart whole and fancy free, I had no romantic interest to build a home around, and my home was merely two cozy, comfy rooms in the vicinity of Gramercy Park.

And at last I reached them, storm tossed, weary, cold, and hungry, all of which unpleasant conditions were changed for the better as rapidly as I could accomplish it.

And when, finally, I found myself seated, with a lighted cigar, at my own cheery reading table, I congratulated myself that I had come home instead of remaining at the Matteawan Building.

For, I ruminated, if the police had corralled me as witness, and held me for one of their protracted queryings, I might have stayed there until late into the night or even all night. And the storm, still howling outside my windows, made me glad of warmth and shelter.

Then, too, I was eager to get my thoughts in order. I am of a methodical mentality, and I wanted to set down in order the events I had experienced and draw logical and pertinent deductions therefrom.

I greatly wished I had had a few moments' chat with Amory Manning. I wanted to ask him some questions concerning Amos Gately that I didn't like to ask of the bank men. Although I knew Gately's name stood for all that was honorable and impeccable in the business world, I had not forgotten the hatpin on his desk, nor the queer smile on Jenny's face as she spoke of his personal callers. I am not one to harbor premature or unfounded suspicions of my fellow creatures, but

"A little nonsense, now and then,
Is relished by the best of men,"

And Amos Gately may not have been above enjoying some relaxations that he felt no reason to parade.

But this was speculation, pure and simple, and until I could ask somebody concerning Mr. Gately's private life, I had no right to surmise anything about it.

Carefully, I went over all I knew about the tragedy from the moment when I had opened my outer office door ready to start for home. Had I left a few moments sooner, I should probably never have known anything much of the matter except what I might learn from the newspapers or from the reports current among the tenants of the Puritan Building.

As it was, and from the facts as I marshaled them in order before my mind, I believed I had seen shadowed forth the actual murder of Amos Gately. A strange thing, to be an eye witness, and yet to witness only the shadows of the actors in the scene!

I strove to remember definitely the type of man who did the shooting. That is, I supposed he did the shooting. As I ruminated, I realized I had no real knowledge of this. I saw the shadowed men rise, clinch, struggle, and disappear. Yes, I was positive they disappeared from my vision before I heard the shot. This argued, then, that they wrestled,—though I couldn't say which was attacker and which attacked,—then they rushed to the next room, where the elevator was concealed by the big map; and then, in that room, the shot was fired that ended Amos Gately's life.

This must be the truth, for I heard only one shot, and it must have been the fatal one.

Then, I could only think that the murderer had deliberately,—no, not deliberately, but with exceeding haste,—had put his victim in the elevator and sent the inert body downstairs alone.

This proved the full knowledge of the secret elevator on the part of the assassin, so he must have been a frequenter of Mr. Gately's rooms, or, at least had been there before, and was sufficiently intimate to know of the private exit.

To learn the man's identity then, one must look among Mr. Gately's personal friends,—or, rather, enemies.

I began to feel I was greatly handicapped by my utter ignorance of the bank president's social or home life. But it might be that in the near future I should again see Miss Raynor, and perhaps in her home, where I could learn something of her late uncle's habits.

But, returning to matters I did know about, I tried hard to think what course of procedure the murderer probably adopted after his crime.

And the conclusion I reached was all too clear. He had, of course, gone down the stairs, as Jenny had said, for at least a few flights.

Then, I visualized him, regaining his composure, assuming a nonchalant, business like air, and stopping an elevator on a lower floor, where he stepped in, without notice from the elevator girl or the other passengers.

Just as Rodman had entered from a middle floor, when I was descending with Minny.

Perhaps Rodman was the murderer! I knew him slightly and liked him not at all. I had no earthly reason to suspect him,—only,—he had got on, I remembered, at the seventh floor, and his office was on the tenth. This didn't seem terribly incriminating, I had to admit, but I made a note of it, and determined to look Mr. Rodman up.

My telephone bell rang, and with a passing wonder at being called up in such a storm, I responded.

To my delight, it proved to be Miss Raynor speaking.

"Forgive me for intruding, Mr. Brice," she said, in that musical voice of hers, "but I—I am so lonesome,—and there isn't anyone I want to talk to."

"Talk to me, then, Miss Raynor," I said, gladly. "Can I be of any service to you—in any way?"

"Oh, I think so. I want to see you tomorrow. Can you come to see me?"

"Yes, indeed. At what time?"

"Come up in the morning,—that is, if it's perfectly convenient for you."

"Certainly; in the morning, then. About ten?"

"Yes, please. They—they brought Uncle home."

"Did they? I'm glad that was allowed. Are you alone?"

"Yes; and I'm frightfully lonely and desolate. It's such a terrible night I wouldn't ask any of my friends to come to stay with me."

"You expected Mr. Manning to call, I thought."

"I did; but he hasn't come. Of course, the reason is that it isn't a fit night for anyone to go out. I telephoned his rooms, but he wasn't in. So I don't know what to think. I'd suppose he'd telephone even if he couldn't get here."

"Traffic must be pretty nearly impossible," I said, "it was awful going when I reached home soon after five, and now, there's a young blizzard raging."

"Yes, I couldn't expect him; and perhaps the telephone wires are affected."

"This one isn't, at any rate, so chat with me as long as you will. You can get some friend to come to stay with you tomorrow, can't you?"

"Oh, yes; I could have got somebody tonight, but I hadn't the heart to ask it. I'm all right, Mr. Brice, I'm not a very nervous person,—only, it is sort of awful. Our housekeeper is a nice old thing, but she's nearly in hysterics and I sent her to bed. I'll say good by now, and I'll be glad to see you tomorrow."

CHAPTER 5: OLIVE RAYNOR

I DID see Miss Olive Raynor the next day, but not in the surroundings of her own home as I had expected.

For I received a rather peremptory summons to present myself at police headquarters at a shockingly early hour, and not long after my arrival there, Miss Raynor appeared also.

The police had spent a busy night, and had unearthed more or less evidence and had collected quite a cloud of witnesses.

Chief of Police Martin conducted the inquiry, and I soon found that my story was considered of utmost importance, and that I was expected to relate it to the minutest details.

This I did, patiently answering repeated questions and asseverating facts.

But I could give no hint as to the identity, or even as to the appearance of the man who quarreled with Mr. Gately. I could, and did say that he seemed to be a burly figure, or, at least, the shadow showed a large frame and broad shoulders.

"Had he a hat on?" asked the Chief.

"No; and I should say he had either a large head or thick, bushy hair, for the shadow showed that much."

"Did you not see his face in profile?"

"If so, it was only momentarily, and the clouded glass of the door, in irregular waves, entirely prevented a clear cut profile view."

"And after the two men rose, they disappeared at once?"

"They wrestled;—it seemed, I should say, that Mr. Gately was grabbed by the other man, and tried to make a getaway, whereupon the other man shot him."

"Are you quite sure, Mr. Brice," and the Chief fixed me with his sharp blue eye, "that you are not reconstructing this affair in the light of the later discovery of Mr. Gately's fate?"

I thought this over carefully before replying, and then said: "It's quite possible I may have unconsciously done so. But I distinctly saw the two figures come together in a desperate struggle, then disappear, doubtless into the third room, and then I heard the shot. That is all I can state positively."

"You, then, went right across the hall and tried to enter?"

"Yes; tried to enter at the middle door, where I had seen the men."

"And next?"

"Finding that door fastened, I tried the third, because the men had seemed to disappear in that direction."

"The third room was also locked?"

"Yes; or at least the door would not open from the outside. Then I went back to the door number one."

"And that opened at once?"

"Yes; had I tried that first, I should probably have seen the men,—or the girl, Jenny."

"Perhaps. Could you recognize the head of the visitor if you should see it again shadowed on the door?"

"I am not sure, but I doubt if I could. I could tell if it were a very different type of head, but if merely similar, I could not swear it was the same man."

"H'm. We must make the experiment. At least it may give us a hint in the right direction."

He questioned me further as to my knowledge of Mr. Gately and his affairs, but when he found I knew almost nothing of those and had been a tenant of the Puritan Building but a very short time he suddenly lost interest in me and turned his attention to Miss Raynor.

Olive Raynor had come alone and unattended. This surprised me, for I had imagined the young ladies of the higher social circles never went anywhere alone. But in many ways Miss Raynor evinced her independence and self reliance, and I had no doubt a trusted chauffeur waited in her car outside.

She was garbed in black, but it was not the heavy crape material that I supposed all women wore as mourning. A long black velvet cape swathed the slender figure in its voluminous folds, and as this was thrown back, I saw her gown was of black satin, with thinner black material used in combination. Women's clothes, though a mystery to me, had a sort of fascination for my ignorant eyes, and I knew enough to appreciate that Miss Raynor's costume was correct and very smart.

Her hat was black, too, smaller than the one I saw her in the day before, and of a quieter type.

Altogether, she looked very lovely, and her sweet, flower like face, with ity big, pathetic brown eyes, was raised frankly to Chief Martin as she answered his questions in a low, clear voice. A slight pallor told of a night of wakefulness and sorrow, but this seemed to accentuate the scarlet of her fine, delicate lips,—a scarlet unacquainted with the assistance of the rouge stick.

"No," she said, positively, "Mr. Gately had no enemies, I am sure he hadn't! Of course, he may have kept parts of his life or his affairs secret from me, but I have lived with him too long and too familiarly not to know him thoroughly. He was of a simple, straightforward nature, and a wise and noble gentleman."

"Yet you were not entirely fond of your uncle," insinuated the Chief.

"He was not my uncle," returned Olive, calmly. "I called him that but he was no relation to me. He used to be a college chum of my father's and when both my parents died, he became not only my guardian but my kind friend and benefactor. He took me to live with him, and I have been his constant companion for twelve years. During that time, I have seen no act, have heard no word that could in the slightest way reflect on his honor or his character as a business man or as a gentleman."

The girl spoke proudly, as though glad to pay this tribute to her guardian, but still, there was no note of affection in her voice,—no quiver of sorrow at her loss.

"Yet you are not bowed with grief at his death," observed Martin.

The dainty chin tilted in indignation. "Mr. Martin," Olive said, "I cannot believe that my personal feelings are of interest to you. I understand I am here to be questioned as to my knowledge of facts bearing on this case."

The Chief nodded his head. "That's all right," he said, "but I must learn all I can of Mr. Gately's life outside his bank as well as in it. If you won't give me information I must get it elsewhere."

The implied threat worked.

"I do indeed sorrow at Mr. Gately's tragic fate," Olive said, gently. "To be sure, he was not my kin, but I admired and deeply respected him. If I did not deeply love him it was his own fault. He was most strict and tyrannical in his household, and his lightest word was law. I was willing enough to obey in many matters, but it annoyed and irritated me when he interfered with my simplest occupations or pleasures. He permitted me very little company or amusement; he forbade many of my friends the house; and he persistently refused to let me accept attentions from men, unless they were certain ones whom he preferred, and—whom I did not always favor."

"Did he favor Amory Manning?" was the next abrupt question.

Olive's cheeks turned a soft pink, but she replied calmly. "Not especially, though he had not forbidden Mr. Manning the house. Why do you ask that?"

"Had you noticed anything unusual lately about Mr. Gately? Any nervousness or apprehension of danger?"

"Not in the least. He was of a most equable temperament, and there has been no change of late."

"When did you last see him—alive?"

"Yesterday afternoon. I went to his office to get some money."

"He has charge of your fortune?"

"Yes."

"He made no objection to your expenditures?"

"Not at all. He was most just and considerate in my financial affairs. He gave me then what I asked for, and after a very short stay I went on."

"Where?"

"To the house of a friend on Park Avenue, where I spent most of the afternoon."

"At what time were you in Mr. Gately's office?"

"I don't know exactly. About two o'clock, I think."

"Can't you tell me more positively? It may be important."

But Olive couldn't be sure whether she was there before or after two. She had lunched late, and had done some errands, and had finally reached her friend's home by mid afternoon.

This seemed to me most plausible, for society young ladies do not always keep strict note of time, but the Chief apparently thought it a matter of moment and made notes concerning it.

Olive looked indifferent, and though she was courteous enough, her whole manner betokened a desire to get the examination over and to be allowed to go home.

After a little further tedious questioning, which, so far as I could see, elicited nothing of real importance, the Chief sighed and terminated the interview.

Mr. Mason and Mr. Talcott had by this time arrived, and their presence was welcomed by Miss Raynor, who was apparently glad of the nearness of a personal friend.

Of course, their evidence was but a repetition of the scenes I had been through the day before, but I was deeply interested in the attitudes of the two men.

Talcott, the secretary of the Trust Company, was honestly affected by the death of his friend and president, and showed real sorrow, while Mr. Mason, the vice president, was of a cold, precise demeanor, seemingly far more interested in discovering the murderer than appalled by the tragedy.

"We must learn who killed him," Mr. Mason reiterated. "Why, Chief Martin, if the police fail to track down the slayer of Amos Gately, it will be a blot on their record forever! Spare no effort,—put your best men on the case, move heaven and earth, if need be, but get your man! The Company will back you to the full extent of its power; we will offer a reward, when the suitable time comes for that. But the crime must be avenged, the man that shot President Gately must pay the penalty!"

Olive's flashing eyes showed her sympathy with this sort of talk and I could quite understand the attitude of the girl, whose sense of justice cried out for revenge, while she was forced to admit the deprivations of her life with her guardian.

Somewhat later, the three went away together, Miss Raynor and the men from the bank, but I remained, hoping to learn more from further witnesses. And I did. I learned so much that my thoughts and theories were started off along totally different lines; my half formed beliefs were knocked down and set up again, with swift continuance.

First, Jenny Boyd, the yellow ear muffed stenographer came in, wearing her Sunday clothes. Her cheaply fashionable hat was tilted over her pert little face, which showed enthusiastic, if ill advised application of certain pigments. Her gown was V necked and short skirted, but it had a slight claim to style and was undeniably becoming. Her air of importance was such that I thought I had never seen such an enormous amount of ego contained in such a small cosmos.

Minny was with her, but the older sister, in quieter attire, was merely a foil for the ebullient Jenny. Also, they were accompanied by a big, good natured faced man, whom I recognized at once as the janitor of the Matteawan Building, and who, it transpired, was the father of the two girls.

"Here we are," he said, in a bluff, hearty way; "here's me and my girls, and we'd be obliged, Mr. Chief, if you'd cut it short as much as you can, for me and Minny wants to get back."

"All right, Boyd," and Chief Martin smiled at him. "I'll tackle you first. Tell us all about that private elevator of Mr. Gately's."

"I will, but savin' for this murder business, not a word of it would ever have crossed my lips. Well, Mr. Gately, he owned the Matteawan, d'you see? and when it suited his purposes to put in a private elevator up to his rooms on the top floor of the next door building,—The Puritan Building, you know,—what more easy than to run the shaft up in the one building with the opening at the top out into the other house. Anyways, that's what he done—"a long time ago. I had to know of it, of course,—"

"Of course, as superintendent of the Matteawan."

"That's what they call it now, but I like better to be called janitor. As janitor I began, and as janitor I'll work to the end. Well, Mr. Gately, he went up and down in the little car whenever he chose, and no one noticed him at all. It wasn't, after all, to say, secret, exactly, but it was a private elevator."

"But a concealed door in his own office makes the thing pretty secret, I should say."

"Secret it is, then. But it's no crime for a man to have a concealed way of gettin' into or out of his own rooms, is it? Many's the time Mr. Gately's come down laughing fit to bust at the way he got away from some old doddering fool who wanted to buzz him to death!"

"You frequently saw him come down, then?"

"Not to say frequently,—but now and again. If I happened to be about at the time."

"Did anyone else use the elevator?"

"Sometimes, yes. I've seen a few people go up or come down,—but mostly it was the boss himself."

"Did he go up in it yesterday?"

"Not that I seen. But, of course, he may have done so."

"When did he last come into his offices before—before he disappeared?"

"When did he, Jenny? Speak up, girl, and tell the Chief all you know about it."

Although Martin had not addressed Jenny, he turned to her now as if inviting her story.

And Jenny bridled, shook out her feather boa, made a futile attempt to pull her brief skirt a trifle farther down toward a silk stockinged ankle, and began:

"Of course, when Mr. Gately went into his office he most gen'ally went in the middle door, right into his pers'nal office. He didn't go through my room. And, so, yest'day, he went in the middle door, but right away, almost, he opened my door and stuck his head in, and says,'Don't let anybody in to see me this afternoon, unless you come and ask me first.' "

"Wasn't this a general rule?"

"'Most always; but sometimes somebody I'd know'd come, like Mr. Talcott or Miss Olive, and they'd just nod or smile at me and walk right in at Mr. Gately's door. So I says, 'Yes, sir,' and I looked sharp that nobody rushed me. Mr. Gately, he trusted me, and I was careful to do just what he said, always."

"Well, go on. Who called?"

"First, Mr. Smith; and then Mrs. Driggs; and after them, Miss Olive."

"Miss Raynor?"

"Yes, of course!" and Jenny spoke flippantly. "I even announced her, 'cause I had strick orders. Miss Olive, she just laughed and waited till I come back and said she might go in."

"What time was this?"

"Couldn't say for sure. 'Long about two or three, I guess."

Jenny was assiduously chewing gum, and her manner was far from deferential, which annoyed the Chief.

"Try to remember more nearly," he said, sharply. "Was Miss Raynor there before or after the other two callers you mentioned?"

"Well, now, it's awful hard to tell that." Jenny cocked her head on one side, and indulged in what she doubtless considered most fetching eye play. "I ain't a two legged time table!"

"Be careful," advised the Chief. "I want straight answers, not foolishness, from you."

Jenny sulked. "I'm givin' it to you as straight's I can, Mr. Chief. Honest to goodness, I don't know if Miss Olive was just before the Driggs hen or after her!"

"Also, be more careful of your choice of words. Did Mrs. Driggs go back through your room when she left?"

"Yes, I guess she did,—but,—lemmesee, no, I guess she didn't either."

"Isn't your memory very short?"

"For such trifles, yes, sir. But I can remember lots of things real easy. I've got a date now, with—"

"Stop! If you don't look out, young woman, you'll be locked up!"

"Behave pretty, now, Jenny girl," urged her father, who was quite evidently the slave of his resplendent offspring; "don't be flip; this here's no place for such like manners."

"You're right, it isn't," agreed the Chief, and he glared at Jenny, who was utterly unmoved by his sternness.

"Well, ain't I behaving pretty?" and the silly thing giggled archly and folded her hands with an air of mock meekness.

Continued harsh words from the Chief, however, made her at last tell a straight and coherent story, but it threw no light on the mysterious caller. In fact, Jenny knew nothing whatever of him, save that she saw or thought she saw him run downstairs, with a pistol in his hand.

"What sort of hat did the man wear?" asked the Chief, to get some sort of description.

"I don't know,—a soft hat, I guess."

"Not a Derby?"

"Oh, yes! I do believe it was a Derby! And he had on an overcoat—"

"A dark one?"

"No,—sort of—oh, I guess it wasn't an overcoat,—but a, you know, Norfolk jacket, like."

"A Norfolk, and no overcoat on a day like yesterday! I don't believe you saw any man at all, Jenny!"

"Do you know, that's what I think sometimes, Mr. Chief! It almost seems 's if I dreamed it."

"What do you mean! Don't you dare guy me, miss!"

"I'm not," and Jenny's saucy face looked serious enough now. "But it was all so fearful sudden, and I was so struck all of a heap, that I just can't say what was so and what wasn't!"

"That does seem to be your difficulty. You sit over there and think the matter over, while I talk to your sister."

Minny, a quiet, pretty girl, was as reticent as Jenny was voluble. But after all, she had little to tell. She had brought no one up in her elevator to see Mr. Gately beside Miss Raynor that she knew of except the man named Smith and Mrs. Driggs.

"Did these people all go down in your car, too?"

"I'm not sure. The cars were fairly crowded, and I know Miss Raynor did not, but I'm not so sure about the others."

Well, Minny's evidence amounted to nothing, either, for though she told of several strangers who got on or off her car at various floors, she knew nothing about them, and they could not be traced.

The three Boyds were quizzed a little more and then old Joe Boyd, the father, and Minny were allowed to go back to their respective posts, but the Chief held Jenny for further grilling. He had a hope, I felt sure, that he could get from her some hint of Mr. Gately's personal affairs. He had heard of the hatpin, and though he hadn't yet mentioned it definitely, I knew he was satisfied it was not Miss Raynor's, and he meant to put Jenny through a mild sort of third degree.

I was about to depart, for I knew I would not be invited to this session, and, too, I could learn the result later.

Then an officer came in, and after a whispered word to Chief Martin they beckoned to me.

"Do you know Amory Manning?" the Chief inquired.

"I met him yesterday for the first time," I replied, "but I have known of him before."

"Where does he live?"

"Up around Gramercy Park somewhere, I think."

"That's right, he does. Well, the man is missing."

"Missing! Why, I saw him last night,—that is, yesterday afternoon, and he was all right then."

"I've had men searching for him all the morning," the Chief went on, "and he's nowhere to be found. He wasn't at his rooms at all last night." I harked back. I had last seen Manning getting off the Third Avenue car at Twenty second Street,—just where he would naturally get off to go to his home.

I told this, and concluded, "he must have changed his mind, then, and gone somewhere else than to his rooms."

"Yes, it looks that way," agreed the Chief.

"But where did he go? That's the question. He can't be found."

CHAPTER 6: CLEWS

I DIDN'T reach my office until afternoon, and there I found Norah, in a brown study.

She looked up with a smile as I came in.

"I'm neglecting my work," she said, with a glance at a pile of papers, "but that affair across the hall has taken hold of me and I can't put it out of my mind."

"Nor can I. I feel as if I were deeply involved in it,—if not indeed, an accessory! But there are new developments. Mr. Manning is missing."

"Mr. Manning? What has he got to do with it?"

"With the crime? Nothing. He didn't come up here until Miss Raynor came, you know. But—"

"Are they engaged?"

"Not that I know of. I think not."

"Well, they will be, then. And don't worry about Mr. Manning's absence. He'll not stay long away from Miss Raynor. Who is he, anyway? I mean what does he do?"

"He's a civil engineer and he lives in Gramercy Park. That's the extent of my knowledge of him. I've seen him down in the bank once or twice since I've been here, and I like his looks. I hope, for Miss Raynor's sake, he'll turn up soon. She expected him to call on her last evening and he didn't go there at all."

"I shouldn't think he would! Why, it was a fearful night. I was going to the movies, but I couldn't think of going out in that wild gale! But never mind Mr. Manning now, let's talk about the Gately affair. I want to go over there and look around the office. Do you suppose they'd let me?"

"Why, I expect so. Is anybody there now?"

"Yes, a police detective,—that man, Hudson. You know they call him Foxy Jim Hudson, and I suppose he's finding out a lot of stuff that isn't so!"

"You haven't a very high opinion of our arms of the law."

"Oh, they're all right,—but most detectives can't see what's right under their noses!"

"Not omniscient Sherlocks, are they? And you think you could do a lot of smarty cat deduction?"

Norah didn't resent my teasing, but her gray eyes were very earnest as she said, "I wish I could try. A woman was in that room yesterday afternoon; someone besides Miss Raynor and the old lady Driggs."

"How do you know?"

"Take me over there and I'll show you. They'll let me in, with you to back me."

We went across and the officer made no objections to our entrance. In fact, he seemed rather glad of someone to talk to.

"We're sorta up against it," he confessed. "Our suspicions are all running in one direction, and we don't like it."

"You have a suspect, then?" I asked.

"Hardly that, but we begin to think we know which way to look."

"Any clews around, to verify your suspicions?"

"Lots of 'em. But take a squint yourself, Mr. Brice. You're shrewd witted, and—my old eyes ain't what they used to was."

I took this mock humility for what it was worth,— nothing at all,—and I humored the foxy one by a properly flattering disclaimer.

But I availed myself of his permission and tacitly assuming that it included Norah, we began a new scrutiny of the odds and ends on Mr. Gately's desk, as well as other details about the rooms.

Norah opened the drawer that Mr. Talcott had locked,—the key was now in it.

"Where's the checkbook?" she asked, casually.

Hudson looked grave. "Mr. Pond's got that," he said; "Mr. Pond's Mr. Gately's lawyer, and he took all his accounts and such. But that checkbook's a clew. You see the last stub in it shows a check drawn to a woman—"

"I said it was a woman!" exclaimed Norah.

"Well, maybe,—maybe. Anyhow the check was drawn after the ones made out to Smith and the Driggs woman. So, the payee of that last check was in here later than the other two."

"Who was she?" was Norah's not unnatural inquiry.

But Hudson merely looked at her, with a slight smile that she should expect an answer to that question.

"Oh, all right," she retorted; "I see her hatpin is still here."

"If that there hatpin is a clew, you're welcome to it. We don't think it is. Mr. Gately had frequent lady callers, as any man's got a right to have, but because they leaves their hatpins here, that' don't make 'em murderers. No, I argue that if a woman shot Mr. Gately she would be cute enough not to leave her hatpin by way of a visitin' card."

This raised Hudson's mentality in my opinion, and I could see it also scored with Norah.

"That's true," she generously agreed. "In books, as soon as I come to the dropped handkerchief or broken cuff link, I know that isn't the property of the criminal. But, all the same, people do leave clews,—why, Sherlock Holmes says a person can't enter and leave a room without his presence there being discoverable."

"Poppycock," said Hudson, briefly, and resumed his cogitation.

He was sitting at ease in Mr. Gately's desk chair, but I could see the man was thinking deeply, and as he had material for thought that he wasn't willing to share with us, I returned to my own searching.

"Here's something the lady left!" I exclaimed, as on a silver ash tray I saw a cigarette stub, whose partly burned gold monogram betokened it had served a woman's use.

"Hey, let that alone!" warned Hudson. "And don't be too previous; sometimes men have gilt-lettered cigs, don't they?"

Without reply, I scrutinized the monogram. But only a bit remained unburnt, and I couldn't make out the letters.

Norah was digging in the waste basket, and, the scamp! when Hudson's head was turned, she surreptitiously fished out something which she hid in her hand, and later transferred to her pocket.

"Nothing doing!" scoffed Hudson, as he turned and saw her occupation, "we been all through that, and anything incriminating has been weeded out. They wasn't much,—some envelopes and letters, but nothing of any account. Oh, well, straws show which way the wind blows, and we've got some several straws!"

"Is this one?" and Norah pointed to the carriage check, which still lay on the desk.

"Nope. Me and the Chief, we decided that didn't mean nothing at all. It's old, you can see, from its grimy look, so it wasn't left here yesterday. Those things are always clean and fresh when they're given out, and that's sorta soiled with age, you see."

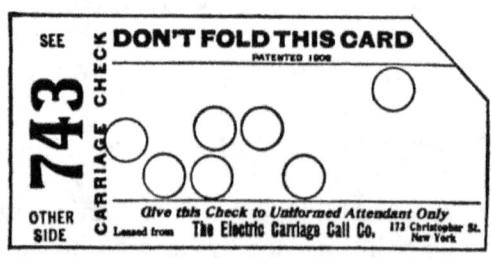

"Well!" I exclaimed, "why would a carriage check be soiled with age? They're used the same day they're given out. Why is it here, anyway?"

Hudson looked interested. "That's so, Mr. Brice," he admitted. "I take it that there check was given to Mr. Gately at some hotel, say. Well, he didn't use it for some reason or other, and brought it home in his pocket. But as

you say, why is it here? Why did he keep it? And, what
did he do with it to give it that thumbed, used look?"

We all examined the check. A bit of white cardboard,
about two by four inches in size, and pierced with seven
circular holes in irregular order. Across the top was
printed "Don't fold this card," and at one end was the
number 743 in large red letters. Also, the right hand
upper corner was sliced off.

"Why," I exclaimed, "here's a narrow strip of paper
pasted across the end, and—look,—it's almost
transparent! I can't read through it—' Hotel St. Charles!'
That's where it came from!"

"Hold your horses!" and Hudson smiled
condescendingly, "that's where it didn't come from! It
came from any hotel except the St. Charles. You may not
know it, but often a hotel will use electric call checks of
other hotels, with a slip of paper pasted over the name.
That's an item for you to remember. No, Mr. Brice, I can't
attach any importance to that check, but I'm free to
confess I don't see why it's there. Unless Mr. Gately found
it in his pocket after it had been there unnoticed for some
time. And yet, it is very much thumbed, isn't it? That's
queer. Maybe he used

it for a bookmark, or something like that."

"Maybe the lady left it here," suggested Norah. "The
same time she left her hatpin."

"Now, maybe she did," and Foxy Jim Hudson smiled
benignly at her. "Any ways, you've made the thing seem
curious, and I guess I'll keep it for a while."

He put the card away in his pocketbook, and Norah
and I grinned at each other in satisfaction that we had
given him a clew to ponder over.

"You know, Mr. Brice," Hudson remarked, after
another period of silent thought, "you missed it, when you
didn't fly in here quicker and catch the murderer
redhanded."

"If I'd known that the first door, Jenny's door, was the only one I could open, of course I should have gone there first. But I'd never been in here at all,—I've only been in the building a week or so, and I did lose valuable time running from one door to another. But I still think it's queer that I didn't see anything of the man Jenny describes."

"One reason is, there wasn't any such man," and Hudson seemed to enjoy my blank look.

"What became of the murderer, then?"

"Went down in the car with Mr. Gately. Private elevator. Shot him on the way down—"

"But man, I heard the shot,—and this room was full of smoke."

"Shot him twice, then. Say the first time, Mr. Gately wasn't killed and could get into the elevator. Then murderer jumps in, too, and finishes the job on the way down. It's a long trip to the ground floor, you know. Then, murderer leaves elevator, slams door shut, and walks off."

I ruminated on this. It seemed absurd on the face of it, and yet

"Why, then, did Jenny say she saw a man?" demanded Norah.

"Maybe she thought she did,—you know people think they see what they think they ought to see. Jenny heard a shot, and running in, she expected to see a man with a pistol,—therefore, she thought she did see him. Or, again, the girl is quite capable of making up a yarn out of the solid. For the dramatic effect, you know, and to put her silly little self in the limelight."

This was not unbelievable. Jenny was most unreliable as a witness. She stumbled and contradicted herself as to the man's hat and had given conflicting testimony about his overcoat.

"Well, as I say, Mr. Brice, the chance was yours to be on the spot but you missed it. Of course, you are not to blame,—but it's a pity. Now, s'pose you tell me again, as near as you can rec'lect, about that other shadow,—the one that wasn't Mr. Gately."

I tried hard to add to my previously related details, but found it impossible to do so.

"Well, could it have been a woman?"

"At first I should have said no, Mr. Hudson. But on thinking it over, I suppose I may say it could have been but I do not think it was."

"You know nowadays the women folks wear their hair plastered so close to their heads that their heads wouldn't shadow up any bigger'n a man's."

"That's so," cried Norah. "A woman's head is smaller than a man's, but her hair makes it appear larger in a shadow. Unless, as Mr. Hudson says, she wore it wrapped round her head,—and didn't have much, anyway."

"You go outside, Mr. Brice," directed Hudson, "and look at the shadows of me and Miss MacCormack, and then come back and tell us what you can notice."

I did this, and the two heads were shadowed forth on the same door that I had watched the day before. But the brighter daylight made the shadows even more vague than yesterday, and I returned without much information.

"I could tell which was which, of course," I reported, "but it's true that if I hadn't known you people at all, I could have mistaken Norah's head for a man, and I might have believed, Hudson, that you were a woman. It's surprising how little individuality was shown in the shadows."

"Well, of course they were clearer yesterday, as the hall was darker," mused Hudson. "After all, Mr. Brice, your testimony can't amount to much unless we can get the actual murderer behind that glass, and some peculiar shape or characteristic makes you recognize the head beyond all doubt."

"I think I could do that," I returned; "for though I can't describe any peculiarity, I'm sure I'd recognize the same head."

"You are?" and Hudson looked at me keenly. "Well, perhaps we'll try you out on that."

They had a definite suspect, then. And they proposed to experiment with my memory. Well, I was ready, whenever they were.

Norah and I went into the third room, Hudson making no objection. At another time we would have been deeply interested in the pictures and the furnishings but now we had eyes and thoughts only for one thing.

We looked behind the war map and saw the elevator door, but could not open it.

"The car's down," spoke up Hudson, who was watching us sharply. "I dunno will it ever be used again. Though I suppose these rooms will be let to somebody else, some time. Mr. Gately's things here will be sent to his house, I expect, but his estate is a big one and will take a deal of settling."

"Who's his executor?"

"Mr. Pond, his lawyer. But his financial affairs are all right. Nothing crooked about Amos Gately—financially. You can bank on that!"

"How, then?" I asked, for the tone implied a mental reservation.

"I'm not saying. But they do say every man has a secret side to his life, and why should Mr. Gately be a lone exception?"

"A woman?" asked Norah, always harking back to her basic suspicion.

Foxy Jim Hudson favored her with that blank stare which not infrequently was his answer to an unwelcome question, and which, perhaps, had a share in earning him his sobriquet.

Then he laughed, and said, "You've been reading detective stories, miss. And you remember how they always say 'Churches lay femmy!' Well, go ahead and church, if you like. But be prepared for a sad and sorrowful result."

The man was obviously deeply moved, and his big, homely face worked with emotion.

But as he would tell us nothing further, and as Norah and I had finished our rather unproductive search of the rooms, we went back to my office.

Here Norah showed me what she had taken from the waste basket.

"I'll give it back to him, if you say so," she offered; "but he could do nothing with it, and maybe I can."

It was only a tiny scrap of pinkish paper, thin and greatly crumpled. I took it.

"Be careful," warned Norah; "I don't suppose it could show finger prints, but anyway, it's a sort of a kind of a clew."

"But what is it?" I asked, blankly, as I held the crumpled paper gingerly in thumb and forefinger..

"It's a powder paper," vouchsafed Norah, briefly.

"A what?"

"A powder paper. Women carry them,—they come in little books. That's one of the leaves. They're to rub on your face, and the powder comes off on your nose or cheeks."

"Is that so? I never saw any before."

"Lots of girls use them." Norah's clear, wholesome complexion refuted any idea of her needing such, and she spoke a bit scornfully.

"Proving once more the presence of what Friend Hudson calls a femmy," I smiled.

"Yes; but these things have great individuality, Mr. Brice. This is of exceedingly fine quality, it has a distinct, definite fragrance, and is undoubtedly an imported article,—from France, likely."

"Can they get such things over now?"

"Oh, pshaw, it may have been imported before the war. This quality would keep its odor forever! Anyway, don't you believe we could trace the woman who used it and left it there? It must have happened yesterday, for the basket is, of course, emptied every day in that office."

"Good girl, Norah!" and I nodded approval. "You are truly a She Sherlock! A bit intimate, isn't it, for a woman to powder her nose in a man's office?"

"Not at all, Mr. Old Fogey! Why, you can see the girls doing that everywhere, nowadays. In the street cars, in the theater,—anywhere."

"All right. How do you propose to proceed?"

"I think I'll go to the smartest Fifth Avenue perfume shops and try to get a line on the maker of this paper."

My door opened then, and the Chief of Police stood in the doorway.

"Will you come over, across the hall, Mr. Brice?" he said.

"May I come?" piped up Norah, and without waiting for the answer, which, by the way, never came, she followed us.

"We have learned a great deal," began the Chief, as I waited, inquiringly. "And, now think carefully, Mr. Brice, I want you to tell me if the head you saw shadowed on the door, could by any possibility have been a woman's head?"

"I think it could have been, Chief; we've been talking that over, and I'm prepared to say that it could have been,—but I don't think it was."

"And the shoulders? Though broad, like a man's, might not a woman's figure, say, wrapped in furs, give a similar effect?"

An icy chill went through me, but I answered, "It might; the outlines were very indistinct."

"We are carefully investigating the movements of Miss Raynor," he went on, steadily, "and we find she told a deliberate untruth about where she spent yesterday afternoon. She said she was at the house of a friend on Park Avenue. We learned the name of the young lady and she says Miss Raynor was not there at all yesterday. Also, we find that Miss Raynor was in this office after the calls of the old people we know about, and not before them, as Miss Raynor herself testified."

"But—" I began.

"Wait a moment, please. This is positively proved by the fact that a check drawn to Miss Raynor by Mr. Gately follows immediately after the two checks drawn to Mr. Smith and Mrs. Driggs."

"Proving?" I gasped.

"That Miss Raynor is the last one known to be in this room before the shooting occurred."

"Oh," cried Norah, "for shame! To suspect that lovely girl! Why, she wouldn't harm a fly!"

"Do you know her?"

"No, sir; but—"

"It is an oft proven fact that the mildest, gentlest woman, if sufficiently provoked to it, or if given a sudden opportunity, will in a moment of passion do what no one would dream she could do! Miss Raynor was very angry with her uncle,—Jenny admitted that, after much delay. Mr. Gately had a revolver, usually in his desk drawer, but not there now. And,"—an impressive pause preceded the next argument, "Mr. Amory Manning is not to be found."

"What do you deduce from that?" I asked, amazedly.

"That he has purposely disappeared, lest he be brought as a witness against Miss Raynor. He could best help her cause, by being out of town and impossible to locate. So, he went off, and she pretended she did not know it. Of course, she did,—they connived at it—"

"Stop!" I cried, "you are romancing. You are assuming conditions that are untrue!"

"I wish it were so," and the Chief exhibited a very human aspect for the moment; "but I have no choice in the matter. I am driven by an inexorable army of facts that cannot be beaten back. What else can you think of that would account for Mr. Manning's sudden disappearance? Attacked? Nonsense! Not in the storm of last evening. Abducted? Why? He is an inoffensive citizen, not a millionaire or man of influence. You said you saw him last night, Mr. Brice. Where, exactly, was that?"

I told of my trip down in the Third Avenue car, and of my getting off at Twenty second Street, meaning to speak to Mr. Manning. Then I told of his sudden, almost mysterious disappearance.

"Not mysterious at all," said the Chief. "He gave you the slip purposely. He went away at once, and has hidden himself carefully. But we will find him. It's not easy for a man to hide from the police in this day and generation!"

"But, Miss Raynor!" I said, still incredulous. "Why? What motive?"

"Because her uncle wouldn't let her marry Amory Manning. When she said she went to her friend, Miss Clark's house, she really went to the home of a Mrs. Russell, the sister of Manning. She was to meet Manning there. I have all this straight from Mrs. Russell."

"And you think it was Miss Raynor's shadow I saw on the door!"

"You said it might have been a woman."

"Very well, then look for another woman! It was never Miss Raynor!"

"Your indignation, Mr. Brice, is both natural and admirable, but it is based on your disinclination to think ill of Miss Raynor. The police are not allowed the luxury of such sentiments."

"But—but—how did she—how did Miss Raynor get out of the room?"

"We do not entirely credit Jenny's story of the man with a revolver running downstairs. And we do think that the person who did the shooting may have gone down in the private elevator with the victim. It would be easy to gain the street unnoticed, and it presupposes someone acquainted with the working of the automatic elevator."

"But Miss Raynor said she had never seen it," I cried, triumphantly. "She said she had only heard her uncle speak of it!"

"I know she said so," returned the Chief.

CHAPTER 7: HUDSON'S ERRAND

FOR a day or two I moped around, decidedly out of sorts. I didn't feel sufficiently acquainted with Miss Raynor to call on her,— though she had once asked me to do so,—but I greatly longed to find out if the police had yet acquainted her with their suspicions. I thought perhaps they were waiting for further proofs, or it might be, waiting until after the funeral of Mr. Gately. There had been, so far, nothing in the papers implicating Olive, and I hoped against hope there would not be. But I felt sure she was being closely watched, and I didn't know what new evidence might be cooking up against her.

The funeral of the great capitalist was on Saturday evening.

I attended, and this being my first visit to the house, I was all unprepared for the wealth of art treasures it held.

I sat in the great salon, lost in admiration of the pictures and bronzes, as well as the beautiful architecture and mural decorations.

A throng of people attended the services and the oppressive fragrance of massed flowers and the continuous click of folding chairs, combined with the whispers and subdued rustling of the audience, produced that unmistakable funeral atmosphere so trying to sensitive nerves.

Then, a single clear, sweet soprano voice, raised in a solemn anthem, broke the tension, and soon the brief obsequies were over, and I found myself moving along with the crush of people slowly surging toward the door.

I walked home, the clear, frosty air feeling grateful after the crowded rooms.

And I wondered. Wondered what would be the next scene in the awful drama. Would they accuse Miss

Raynor,—lovely Olive Raynor, of the crime? How could they? That delicate, high bred girl!

And yet, she was independent of thought and fearless of action. Though I knew her but slightly, I had heard more or less about her, and I had learned she was by no means of a yielding or easily swayed disposition. She deeply resented her guardian's tyrannical treatment of her and had not infrequently told him so. While they were not outwardly at odds, they were uncongenial natures, and of widely divergent tastes.

Olive, as is natural for a young girl, wanted guests and gayety. Mr. Gately, a thoroughly selfish man, preferred quiet and freedom from company. Her insistence met with refusal and the results were often distressing to both of them. In fact, Miss Raynor had threatened to leave her guardian's home and live by herself, but this by no means suited his convenience. The comfort of his home and the proper administration of his household depended largely on Olive's capable and efficient management, and without her presence and care he would miss many pleasant details of his daily existence. He rarely allowed her to go away on a visit, and almost never permitted her to have a friend to stay with her.

I learned of these intimate matters from Norah,— who, in turn, had them from Jenny.

Jenny had not been with Mr. Gately long, but she had managed to pick up bits of information regarding his home life with surprising quickness, and when quizzed by the police had told all she knew,–and, I suspected,—more than she knew,—about Miss Raynor.

Now, I don't suppose the police went so far as to assume that Olive Raynor had killed Mr. Gately because he would not indulge her wishes, but they seemed to think they really had grounds for suspecting.

I was in despair. On Sunday, I could think of nothing but the matter and I wondered if it would be too presumptuous of me to offer Miss Raynor my help or advice. Doubtless she had hordes of advisers, but she might need such a legal friend as I could be to her.

On the impulse, I telephoned and asked if she cared to see me. To my delighted surprise she welcomed the suggestion and begged me to call that afternoon, as she had real need of legal advice.

And so four o'clock found me again at the house of the late president of the Trust Company.

This time I was shown to a small reception room, where Olive soon appeared.

"It's this way, Mr. Brice," she said after a few moments' conversation. "I don't like Mr. Pond,—he's Uncle's lawyer,—I just can't bear the man!"

"For any definite reason, Miss Raynor?" I asked.

"N—no,—well, that is—oh, he's a horrid old thing, and he wants to marry me!"

"Are you quite sure you want to confide these personal matters to me?" I felt I ought to say this, for the girl was nervously excited, and I was by no means sure she would not later regret her outspokenness.

"Yes, I do. I want a lawyer, Mr. Brice, and I will not have Mr. Pond. So I ask you here and now to take my affairs in charge, look after my financial matters, and advise me in many ways when I need your help. You may suppose I have many friends,"—the big brown eyes were pathetically imploring, "but I haven't. Uncle Amos,—of course, you know he was not my uncle, but I called him that,—would not allow me to make many friends and his own acquaintances are all elderly people and he hadn't very many of those. My money is in my own right, Mr. Gately was punctilious in his care of my accounts,—and I want it all taken out of the hands of Mr. Pond and trans ferred to your care. This can be done, of course."

Olive looked imperious and seemed to think the matter all settled.

"Doubtless it can be arranged, Miss Raynor; I will consider it."

"Don't consider,—just say yes! If you don't I must hunt up another lawyer, and—I'd rather have you."

I wasn't proof against her pretty, dictatorial ways, and I agreed to take the steps she desired.

She went on to tell me how she was placed:

Not only in possession of a considerable fortune of her own, Amos Gately's will left her a goodly additional sum, and also the house in which they had lived.

"So you see," Olive said, "I shall continue to live here,—for the present. I have Mrs. Vail now with me,—as a duenna, for propriety's sake. She is a dear old lady, and is of a pliable, manageable sort. I chose her for that reason, largely. Also, she is pleasant and cheerful, and I like to have her about. I was fond of Uncle Amos, Mr. Brice, but we had many dissensions. If he had allowed me a little more freedom, I could have got along with him beautifully,—but he treated me as a child. You see, he took me to live with him when I was a child, and he never realized that I had grown up and had an individuality and a will of my own. I am twenty two years old, and he acted as if I were twelve!"

"And now, absolutely your own mistress?"

"Yes; doesn't it seem strange? And it is all so strange! This house, without him, is like a different house. And the dreadfulness of his death! Sometimes I think I can't stay here,—I must get into other surroundings. But the thought of moving out of here is too much for me, at present, anyway. Oh, I don't know what to do! I can't realize that he is gone!"

Olive did not cry. She sat, dry eyed and tearless, looking so pathetically lonely and so unable to cope with her new responsibilities, that I gladly promised her all possible assistance that I could give, both in legal matters and in any personal or friendly ways.

"Don't think me helpless," she said, reading my thoughts; "I shall rise to the situation, I shall adapt myself to my changed circumstances, but it will take a little time, of course."

"Yes, indeed," I agreed, "and don't attempt to do too much at first. Take plenty of time to rest and to let yourself react from the shock and the awful scenes you have been through."

It was clear to me that the girl had no thought that she was suspected, or that the police were watching her. I wondered whether it would be kinder to give her a hint of this or to leave her in ignorance, when just then a servant entered, saying Mr. Hudson wished an interview with Miss Raynor.

Hudson! Foxy Jim Hudson! Of course, this could mean but one thing.

"Let me stay!" I said, impulsively, and, "Oh, do!" she returned, and in another minute Hudson came in.

There was something about the man's manner that I couldn't help liking and if Olive had to be questioned I felt sure he would do it as gently as anybody could.

Though uncultured, his voice was kindly, and as he put some preliminary questions Olive answered straightforwardly and without objection.

But when he asked her where she had been on the afternoon of Mr. Gately's death, she looked at him haughtily, and said:

"I told all that to the man who questioned me downtown,—that Mr. Martin."

"Did you tell him the truth, Miss Raynor?"

"Sir?"

Into the one word, Olive put a world of scornful pride, but I could note also a look of fear in her eyes.

"Now, let me give you a bit of friendly advice," Hudson said, "you're a very young lady, and you prob'ly think you can tell a little white falsehood and get away with it, but you can't do it to the police. You see, miss, we know where you were on Wednesday afternoon, and you may as well be frank about it."

"Very well, then, where was I?"

"At the house of Mrs. Russell,—the sister of Mr. Manning."

Olive looked at him in amazement. Then her manner changed.

"Since you know," she said, "I may as well own up. I was at Mrs. Russell's. What of it?"

"Only that if you prevaricated in one instance, Miss Raynor, you may have done so in others. Will you tell me why you said you were at the house of your friend, Miss Clark?"

"Of course I will. My guardian was unwilling to have me go to Mrs. Russell's house, because of a personal matter. Therefore, when I wished to go there I sometimes told him that I was going to Miss Clark's. This small falsehood I considered justifiable, because Mr. Gately had no right to say where I should go and where not! If I was untruthful it was because his unjust rules and regulations made me so! I am not a story teller, ordinarily. If I was forced to be one, in order to enjoy some simple pleasures or diversions, it is no one's business but my own."

"That's true, Hudson," I interposed, "why constitute yourself Miss Raynor's Sunday School teacher?"

"Sorry I am to do so," and the good natured face showed real regret; "but I've orders. Now, Miss Raynor, I must put you a few straight questions. Where's Mr. Amory Manning?"

"I don't know! I only wish I did!"

"Now, now, that won't do! I guess you can think up some hint of his whereabouts for me. You can't deceive us, you know."

"Nor do I want to!" Olive's eyes blazed. "Because I found it necessary to evade my guardian's espionage now and then you needn't think I am unable to tell the truth! I have no idea where Mr. Manning is, and I am exceedingly anxious lest some harm has befallen him. If you can find him you will be doing me a great favor."

"Are you engaged to him. Miss Raynor?"

"No, I am not, though I do not concede your right to ask that question. Mr. Manning and I are good friends, that is all."

"Mr. Gately did not approve of his attentions to you?"

"He did not, and that was why I refrained from telling of occasions when I saw or might see Mr. Manning at his sister's house. If that is of interest to you, I've no objections to your knowing it."

"Can you fire a pistol, Miss Raynor?"

I perceived it was Hudson's method to take her by surprise, and so, perhaps, learn something from an answer given off her guard.

"Yes," she replied, promptly, "I am a good shot; why?"

Her wondering eyes were fearless, now, and to me it seemed a proof of her entire innocence that she showed no embarrassment at this inquiry.

But Hudson evidently thought differently. He looked accusingly at her, and continued, "Do you own a pistol?"

"Yes; Mr. Gately gave me one a few years ago."

"Where is it?"

"Down at our country place, on Long Island. I am afraid of burglars there, but not nearly so much so in the city."

"H'm. Now, Miss Raynor, you are the last one known to have seen Amos Gately alive."

"Why, Mr. Brice saw the shooting!"

"Only in shadow. I mean you are the last one known to have talked with him in his office. Was your interview—er,—amicable?"

"Entirely so. I went there for some money, as I occasionally did. My guardian gave me a check and I cashed it at the Trust Company Bank."

"Yes, we know that; and that the check was given to you, and was later cashed, all at about the time Mr. Gately was killed."

"Earlier Mr. Hudson. I was in the bank about half past two."

"No, Miss Raynor. We have the teller's statement that you were there about three o'clock."

"He is mistaken," Olive's voice was confident, and had in it a ring of indignation, "by three o'clock, or very little after, I was at Mrs. Russell's."

"Was Mr. Manning there?"

"No; he expected to come later, after he had attended to some business."

"What was the business?"

"I do not know, but it must have been somewhere in the vicinity of the Puritan Building, for he was near there when I arrived."

"At what time was that?"

"I don't know exactly, perhaps half past three or a little later. I had been at Mrs. Russell's but a few moments when Mr. Talcott telephoned me there."

"How did he know you were there?"

"He called up Miss Clark first, and she told him."

"Your friends, then, aided and abetted you in deceiving your guardian?"

"I resent the way you put that, Mr. Hudson," Olive looked at him haughtily, "but I answer, yes. My friends agreed with me that Mr. Gately was unreasonable in his commands and that I was not bound to obey them."

"But you are now freed from his injustice."

"That is a brutal speech and unworthy of any man! My freedom is too dearly purchased at such a fearful price!"

"Are you sure you think so?"

"What are you implying, Mr. Hudson? Speak out! Do you think I killed my guardian?"

"There are people that do think that, Miss Raynor."

"Leave this house!" cried Olive, rising. "Such words can not be spoken here!"

"Now, now, miss, dramatics won't get you anywheres! There is evidence against you, or so the police think, and it's up to me to tell you that we must ask you not to go out of town without acquainting us of the fact. We do not accuse you, but we do want you where we can communicate with you at will. I am going now Miss Raynor. I came only to make sure on a few points,—which I have done,—and to tell you to remain within call. Indeed, I may as well tell you that any attempt to get away will be frustrated."

"You mean I am under surveillance!"

"That's about it, miss."

Olive looked at him as one might regard a worm of the dust. "Go!" she said, quietly but forcefully. "I shall not leave town, I shall probably not leave this house. Your suspicion is beneath contempt. However, it has taught me one thing,—I shall engage someone else—someone quite outside the stupid police, to discover the murderer of my uncle! And also to trace my friend, Mr. Manning."

Hudson smiled. He looked at Olive almost tolerantly, as if she were a wilful child.

"All right. Miss Raynor. I'll take your word as to your staying here, and I rather guess the police force will yet round up the murderer and will also discover the hiding place of Amory Manning. Good day."

Hudson went away, and Olive turned to me in a passion of rage.

"What insolence!" she exclaimed. "Are such things permitted? To come here and practically accuse me of my uncle's murder!"

"He wasn't your uncle, you know."

"That doesn't matter. I loved him as I would a relative. His sternness and his unreasonable commands were distasteful to me, but that didn't alter my real love and affection for the man. He has been everything to me for the greater part of my life. He has been kindness itself in most matters. He indulged me in all possible ways as to creature comforts and luxuries. He never criticized the ways in which I spent my money, or in which I entertained myself, save in the matter of having guests or making visits."

"And allowing admirers?"

"There were some men he approved of,—you may as well know, Mr. Brice, my guardian wished me to marry his friend and lawyer, Mr. Pond."

"Why, when that gentleman is so greatly your senior?"

"Merely because Uncle was so fond of him. And, too, Uncle never seemed to realize that I was of a different generation from himself. He couldn't understand,—he really couldn't—why I wanted young company and gay parties. He didn't, and he really assumed that I didn't. I think he never realized how greatly he was depriving me when he forbade me society."

"Did it really amount to that?"

"Practically. Or, if I succeeded in persuading him to let me have a house guest or a small party, he made things so unpleasant that I was glad when they were gone."

"Unpleasant, how?"

"Oh, fussing around, as if his comfort were in terfered with,—as if he were terribly incommoded by their presence, and by demanding my time and attention for himself, instead of allowing me to entertain my guests properly."

"Doubtless so you wouldn't do it again."

"Yes, of course. But all that was uncomfortable for me,—almost unbearable,—yet one doesn't kill one's people for such things."

To me this simple statement of Olive Raynor's was more convincing than a storm of denial. She had stormed, with indignation, at the hint of suspicion, but her quiet, dignified refutation went far to assure me of her entire innocence.

"Of course, one doesn't," I agreed, "and now to find out who did do it. Have you any suspicion,—Miss Raynor, even the slightest?"

"No; except that it seems to me it must have been some man who knew Uncle in a business way. Though a generous and charitable man, Amos Gately was scrupulously just, and if he had enemies, they were men whom he had discovered in some wrong doing and he had exposed or punished them. No man had a cause for righteous enmity against him,—of that I'm sure!"

CHAPTER 8: THE MAN WHO FELL THROUGH THE EARTH

"AND it is for me," Olive went on, with a solemn look in her brown eyes, "to avenge the death of my guardian. I am not worried about this surveillance, or whatever they call it, of myself,—it is too absurd to take very seriously. Of course, I shall not leave the city, and I will answer any questions the police may put to me. For, you see, Mr. Brice, the only reason I had for telling falsehoods is a reason no longer. I did resort to 'white lies' because Uncle Amos was so unreasonably strict with me, but I've no further need for that sort of thing, and I assure you you will find me absolutely truthful from now on."

A sad little smile accompanied the words, and an earnest expression on the delicate, high bred face gave me implicit confidence in her sincerity.

"Then," I hastened to advise her, "do not antagonize the police. If they have you under their eye, rest assured they think there is some reason to watch you. Be friendly, or, at least patient with them, and they will all the sooner be aware of their mistake. Moreover, you want their help in running down the real murderer of your guardian. It is a mysterious affair, Miss Raynor."

"Oh, it is, Mr. Brice, and it may be that in penetrating the mystery we may unearth something —you know,— something detrimental to Mr. Gately's character."

"Have you any such fear—definitely, I mean?"

"Not definitely, no. If I had I should tell you. But in a vague, apprehensive way, I feel there must be something in his life that brought this about, and that I as yet know nothing of. But you think, don't you, that we must go ahead and learn all we can?"

"You are not afraid, then, of investigation, for yourself—or, for anyone else?"

I put this query after a moment's hesitation, yet I had to know.

"No, sir," her voice rang out clearly. "I know what you mean, you are thinking of Mr. Manning. And there is another task for you. We must find Amory Manning. That man never went away, voluntarily, without sending me some word. He said he would come up here that night,— the night of Uncle's death. He didn't come, nor did he communicate with me in any way. That means he was unable to do so."

"But what could have happened that would make it impossible for him to send you some word?"

"I don't know—I can't think, I'm sure. But he was attacked or overcome by someone who wanted him put out of the way. Mr. Manning had enemies,—that much I may tell you—"

"Do you know more? That you can not tell me?"

"No; that is, I don't know anything,—but I have some foreboding,—oh, nothing definite, Mr. Brice, but I can't help fearing we shall never see Amory Manning alive again!"

"I don't want to force your confidence, but can't you tell me a few more facts? Why has he enemies? Are they political?"

"Yes; in a way. Don't ask me now anyway. Let us try to find Amory and if we fail, I may decide it my duty to tell you what I now withhold."

And with this I was forced to be content. For Olive Raynor did not talk like a young, inexperienced girl, as I had thought her; she gave me now the impression of a young woman involved in weighty matters, and the trusted holder of important secrets.

"To begin with, then," I said, "suppose we try first to find Mr. Manning,—or to learn what became of him."

"Yes," she agreed; "but how shall we set about it? I've already telephoned to several of his friends, whom I

know, and none of them has seen him since that day,—
the day of Uncle's death. Thank Heaven nobody is foolish
enough to blame that on him!"

"They couldn't very well, as he was with you when the
discovery was made."

"I know it. And for the police to say he ran away to
hide to protect me from suspicion is just about the most
absurd theory possible!"

"I think so, too. Now, to get down to dates. Have you
heard anything of Mr. Manning later than the time when
I saw him get off the Third Avenue car on his way home
that night?"

"No, I haven't. And we know he never reached his
home. His rooms are in a house on Gramercy Park—"

"That's why he got off at Twenty second Street—"

"Yes, of course. He left you there, didn't he?"

"We both got off the car there. My own rooms are in
the same locality. But the snow squall was a whirlwind
at the corner, and my glasses were so covered with flakes
that I couldn't see a thing for a moment, and when I
could, Manning had got out of sight. I didn't know then in
just what direction he lived, so I looked all four ways but
I didn't see him. However, in the black squall, one
couldn't see half a dozen steps anyway."

"Of course, he started toward his home,—perhaps, he
almost reached it,—when whoever was lying in wait for
him attacked him."

"Why are you so sure he was attacked? He may have
had an errand in some other direction."

"I sort of see the thing as a picture. And as he got out
at that corner I naturally see him going straight home. It
is not likely that he would be going on some other errand,
and yet get off at that corner."

"No; I suppose not."

"Well, then, as he never did go home,—hasn't been
there yet,—what theory is there except that he was
prevented from going there? He may have been

kidnaped,—don't smile, it is among the possibilities,—or, he may have met with a serious accident,—slipped and broken his leg or something of that sort. But in such a case, he would have been taken to a hospital, and I should have heard of it. No, Mr. Brice, he was carried off by some powerful enemy. I say powerful, meaning rather, clever or diplomatic, for as I see it, trickery would have been used, not force, to abduct Amory Manning."

"But why abduct him?" I cried in amazement. "What is he? Why is he a menace?"

"I can't tell you, Mr. Brice, unless it becomes gravely necessary. But it has to do with—with men higher up,— and it has nothing to do with my guardian's death,—of that I'm certain."

"Very well, Miss Raynor; I trust you, of course, that goes without saying, but I also trust your judgment in reserving your full confidence in this matter."

"You may. I assure you I will tell you all, if it becomes imperative that I do so. Meantime, let us try to find some trace of him."

"You have tried the hospitals?"

"Yes; I have telephoned to some of them, and I asked our family doctor to inquire of others. He did so, but with only negative results. Now—"

"Now, it's time to call in a detective," I said, positively. "And I don't mean a mere police detective, but a special investigator. Have you any objection to such a course?"

"No; not if we get a good one. I don't know much about such things, but don't some of those all wise detectives have more theories and deductions than results?"

"You have put your finger on a vital flaw in the usual Smarty Cat detective," I laughed. "But I know of a splendid man. He is eccentric, I admit, but beyond that he has none of the earmarks of the Transcendental Detective of the story books. He is intelligent rather than cocksure and efficient rather than spectacular. He is expensive, but no more so than his success warrants."

"That sounds well. But first, Mr. Brice, can't we do a little investigating by ourselves? I had hoped so. To engage a detective is to make the whole affair so public, and I shrink from that."

"Not necessarily, Miss Raynor. If the man I speak of should take the case, he would make no fuss or stir about it. And if you say so, he can also try to find the man who killed Amos Gately."

"Oh, that is what I want! Yes, let us retain—or whatever the procedure is, your detective. What is his name?"

"Don't laugh, but it is Penny Wise!"

"What? How ridiculous!"

"Yes, but true. Pennington Wise is on his visiting cards, but no human nature could refrain from the inevitable nickname."

"He ought to change that name! It's enough to belittle any good work he might do!"

"Well, he doesn't think so. In fact, he has become so used to having people joke about it that he only smiles perfunctorily and goes on about his business."

"Will you ask him to help us?"

"Of course I will, and if not too busy on some other matter he will doubtless begin at once."

"I feel so young and inexperienced," Olive shuddered, "to be deciding these big things. It seems as if someone older and wiser ought to direct me. Oh, I know I have your help and counsel, but I wish I had some relative or near friend on whose judgment I could rely. I am singularly alone in the world, Mr. Brice."

"You have Mrs. Vail?"

"My companion? She is delightful as a chaperon and promises to be most pleasant and congenial in my home life, but she is not capable of giving me any advice of value in these important affairs."

"You are indeed alone, Miss Raynor, but you are amazingly capable for a young woman and you continually surprise me by your grasp of the situation and your ability to rise to its demands."

"If I only had Amory Manning to help me."

Poor child, I knew that was at the bottom of her loneliness, and though I didn't presume to sympathize, I felt privileged to assure her of my personal help as well as my interested performance of my legal duties.

"Well, then, Mr. Brice," she responded, "there is one thing I want you to do for me. I want you to go to the morgue. I can't bring myself to do that, nor do I want to ask anyone else I know to do so."

"Certainly," I replied, instinctively treating the matter casually, for I saw she was deeply moved. "It will be merely a form, but it is better to feel we have made every possible inquiry and left no stone unturned. I will go there at once,—now, if you say so."

She seemed gratified at my prompt compliance, and urged my going immediately.

"Come back this evening and report," she said, and then, with one of those sudden changes of demeanor which I was beginning to learn were characteristic of her, she bade me good afternoon with a quick, curt manner, and practically dismissed me.

I started on my grewsome errand with enough food for thought to set my brain in a whirl. I was deeply in the matter now, and quite satisfied that it should be so. I was the lawyer and adviser of Miss Raynor, and I determined to do my best to deserve and justify her choice. Hitherto obscure, I should now be looked up to by members of my profession with envy—and, doubtless, with criticism. The latter, I meant to take good care, should be favorable.

As I looked at it I had three distinct missions. First, to arrange and attend to all of Miss Raynor's financial matters. Second, to assist her to track down the murderer of Amos Gately. Third, to help her to find, or to learn the fate of Amory Manning.

The first was my only personal charge. The other two must be accomplished by Wise, and for my part I felt sure he would succeed.

My visit to the morgue, as I had surmised, brought no result. The poor unfortunates whose mortal remains had been brought there during or since Wednesday, the day of Manning's disappearance, could by no stretch of the imagination be thought to look like Amory Manning.

Though I had never seen him until that day, I had a vivid picture of the man, large framed, well set up, and with a general air of forcefulness and power. I had watched his face, as we stood in the crowded street car, too far apart for conversation, yet in full view of each other.

His face was strong and scholarly, the latter effect enhanced by his huge, shell rimmed glasses, and he had thick, rather coarse dark hair. Also a dark Vandyke beard and small mustache, both carefully trimmed.

"No," I said to the morgue keeper, "the man I'm looking for isn't here."

I went on to tell him of Manning, in case he knew anything to tell me. But he only said, briefly:

"You're not the first, sir. The police have looked here for Mr. Manning and some others have done so beside."

So the police were ahead of me! Well, that only made it the more certain that what we nought was not here.

"There was another chap, but he wasn't Mr. Manning either," vouchsafed my informant. "Howsomever, the police went to see him. Wanta go?"

"What do you mean?"

"Why, that same afternoon, there was a corpse picked outa the East River, froze stiff. Leastways, we thought he was a corpse, but blamed if the chap didn't come to life!"

I wasn't greatly interested, for if the corpse was taken from the river that afternoon, it couldn't have been Manning. But the morgue keeper went on: "You might take a look, sir, to see if you know him. For the poor

fellow's lost his mind,—no, not that,—but he's lost his
memory, and he dunno who he is!"

"Amnesia?" I asked.

"That's what they call it, and the other thing, too.
Aspasia,—or whatever it is."

"Aphasia," I corrected him, without smiling, for how
should he know anything about what was a mystery to
most skilled physicians.

"Where is he?"

"They carted him over to Bellevue soon's they seen he
was alive. It was a tough job to keep him alive, I heard,
and his memory is completely busted. It would be a
godsend to him if you could identify him. I ask everybody
to take a look on the chance. Somehow, I'm sorry for him."

I wasn't especially interested, but being thus appealed
to in the interests of humanity, I went over to the
hospital, and had no difficulty in gaining a sight of the
patient in question. Indeed, the doctors were most
anxious for visitors to see him, hoping that someone
might identify the man.

My first glance convinced me it was not Amory
Manning, though I had not thought that it was.

This man had thin, light hair and vacant looking,
weak eyes. He was smooth shaven and his voice was
peculiar,—a voice sufficient to identify anyone, I felt sure,
but it was not a voice I had heard before.

No; I didn't know him, and a careful scrutiny made
me positive I did not.

But it was a sorry case. Apparently the man was of
good education and accustomed to cultured surroundings.
Moreover, he had a sense of humor which had not
deserted him, along with his memory.

I sat by his bedside, and I remained rather longer
than I had intended, for I became interested in his story,
and the time slipped by.

"You see," he said, fixing me with his queer looking
eyes, "I fell through the earth."

"You what?"

"I did. I fell through the earth, and it was a long, long fall."

"Well, yes, eight thousand miles, I'm told."

"Oh, no," and he was almost pettish, "I didn't fall through the middle of it."

"Oh," and I paused for further enlightenment.

"It was this way. I remember it perfectly, you know. I was somewhere,—somewhere up North—"

"Canada?"

"I don't know—I don't know." He shook his head uncertainly. "But I know it was up North where it's always cold."

Perhaps the man had been an Arctic explorer.

"Iceland?" I said, "Greenland?"

"Maybe," and he looked uninterested. "But," here he brightened a little, "anyway, I fell through the earth. I fell in there, wherever it was, and came on down, down through the earth till I came out at the other end."

"You mean, you fell through a section or segment of the globe? As if, say, you fell in at London and came out at the Cape of Good Hope!"

"That's the idea! Only I fell out here in New York."

"And you fell in?"

"That's what I can't remember, only it was 'way up North,—somewhere."

"If you had a map, now, and looked at all the Northern countries, it might recall itself to you,—the place where you entered,—where you began your journey."

"I thought so, but the nurse brought me an atlas and I couldn't find the place. I wish I had a globe."

Poor chap. I wondered what had given him this strange hallucination. But as he talked on, I became interested in his own personality.

He was as sane as I was in all respects, save his insistence that he had fallen through the earth. As a child, an ambition of mine had been to dig down to China, and many times I had started the task. Perhaps his childhood had known a similar ambition, and now, his memory gone, his distorted mind harked back to that idea. I changed the subject, and found him remarkably well informed, fairly well educated, and of a curiously analytical temperament, but of his identity or his personality he had no knowledge.

He appreciated this, and it made the thing more pathetic.

"It will come back to me," he said, cheerfully. "The doctors have explained all about this aphasic amnesia, and though mine is the worst case they have ever seen, it will go away some time, and I'll recover my memory and know who I am."

"You can reason and understand everything said to you?"

"Oh, yes; I'm my own man in every respect except in a knowledge of who or what I was before that journey through the earth."

"Then," I tried plain common sense, "then, if you can reason, you must know that you didn't fall through the earth. It would be impossible."

"I know that. My reason tells me it's impossible. But all I know about it is, that I did do it."

"Through a long hole,—miles long?"

"Yes."

"Who bored the hole?"

"It was there all the time. I suppose Nature made it."

"Oh, a sort of rock fissure—"

"No; more like a mine,—a—"

"That's it, old chap! You were a miner, and there was a cave in, and it spoiled your thinker—temporarily."

"But a mine doesn't have an exit at the bottom of it. I tell you I was far away from where I fell in, and I came miles straight down through the solid earth—"

"Could you see plainly?"

"Oh, no, it was dark,—how could it be other wise, inside the earth?"

It was hopeless to dissuade him. We talked for some time, and outside his hallucination he was keen and quick witted. But whatever gave him his idea of his strange adventure he thoroughly believed in it and nothing would shake that belief.

"What are you going to do when you get out of here?" I asked him.

"I don't know, I'm sure. But I can't help feeling that the world owes me a living—especially after I've fallen through it!"

I laughed, for his humor was infectious, and I felt pretty sure he would make good somehow. He was about thirty, I judged, and though not a brawny man, he seemed possessed of a wiry strength.

The doctors, he told me, assured him of speedily returning health but would give no definite promise regarding the return of his memory.

"So," he said, cheerfully, "I'll get along without it, and start out fresh. Why, I haven't even a name!"

"You can acquire one at small expense," I advised him.

"Yes; I've part of it now. I shall take Rivers as a surname, because they pulled me out of the East River, they say."

"How were you dressed?"

"In Adam's costume, I'm told. I regret the loss of a full suit of apparel, more especially as it might have proved my identity."

"You mean you were entirely divested of clothing?"

"Except for a few rags of underwear, entirely worthless as clews to what was doubtless an illustrious personality! However, I'm lucky to have breath left in my body, and when I get back my memory, I'll prove that I really did fall through the earth, and I'll find out where I fell in."

"I sincerely hope you will, old chap," and I shook hands as I rose to go. "As the play says, 'You interest me strangely!' May I come to see you again?"

"I wish you would, Mr. Brice, and by that time I shall have chosen me a first name."

CHAPTER 9: THE MAN IN BOSTON

I COULD not suppress a feeling of elation as I once again rang at the door of Olive Raynor's home that evening. I almost began to feel a proprietary interest in the mansion, as I now was practically the legal adviser of its new mistress. And to be received as a privileged caller, even a welcome one, was a source of gratification to my pride and self respect.

Mrs. Vail was present at our interview this time, and my first sight of her gave me a very favorable impression. A distinguished looking lady, slightly past middle age, she was aristocratic of bearing and kindly pleasant of manner. Perhaps a trifle of condescension mingled with her courteous reception of me, but I put that down to her recent acquirement of a position of importance. No such trait was visible in Miss Raynor's simple and sincere greeting, and as Olive eagerly inquired as to the result of my afternoon's quest, I told her my story at once.

She was greatly relieved that no trace of Amory Manning had been found on the morgue records and though she was duly sympathetic when I told her of the strange case of the man who fell through the earth, it only momentarily claimed her preoccupied attention.

She first satisfied herself that by no chance could this man be Manning, and then turned her thoughts back to her all engrossing theme.

"I am sorry for him," she said, as I described his cheerful disposition and rather winning personality, "and if I can do anything to help him, I will do it. Does he want a position of some sort when he gets well enough to take one?"

"I suppose he will," I returned; "he's an alive sort of chap, and of course he'll earn his living one way or another."

"And he may soon recover his memory," began Mrs. Vail. "I knew a man once who had amnesia and aphasia both, and it was six months before he got over it. But when his memory came back, it came all at once, like a flash, and then he was all right."

"In this case," I said, "the doctors want to find someone who knows the man. It ought not to be difficult to find his friends, or someone who can identify him. Why, that peculiar voice ought to do it."

"Imitate it," directed Mrs. Vail, and to the best of my ability I talked in the monotonous tones of the amnesic victim.

Olive laughed. "I never heard anybody talk like that," she said. "It's absolutely uninflected."

"Yes, that's just what it was. He had no inflections or shadings in his tones."

"A voice is so individual," pursued Olive. "Amory Manning's voice is full and musical; I've often told him he conveys as much meaning by his tones as by his words."

"I knew a man once," put in Mrs. Vail, "who could recite the alphabet so dramatically that he made his audience laugh or cry or shudder, just by his tones."

"Yes, I've heard that done on the vaudeville stage," said Olive. "Now Mr. Brice, what shall be our next step? I don't mind confessing I'm relieved that your errand of today is over with. Our doctor told me there was no chance of Mr. Manning having been killed or injured, without our receiving notification of the fact, somehow. But I've been nervously troubled about it, and nights I've dreamed of seeing him somewhere,—alone and helpless,—and unable to let me know—"

"Maybe he is," said Mrs. Vail; "I knew a man once—"

But Olive cut short the tale of this acquaintance of her friend and kept to the business in hand.

"I can't think of anything better to do," I said, "than to advertise. But why are not other people doing this? Who are Mr. Manning's friends? Who are his business people? Why are they silent?"

"I don't know that they are," Olive returned; "but to tell the truth, I don't know much about Mr. Manning's affairs, in a business way. I know he is a civil engineer, but that's about all. A consulting engineer he is, too. As to his people, I know only his sister, and she doesn't know what to do either. I've seen Mrs. Russell twice since, and we can only sympathize with each other."

"Who is Mr. Russell?"

"Her husband? He's in France, and she's alone with her two little girls. She and Amory are devoted to each other, and he was of such help and comfort to her in her husband's absence. Now, she doesn't know which way to turn."

"I must look these things up," I said; "I must talk with Mr. Manning's business associates,—doubtless Mrs. Russell can tell me of them."

"Oh, yes, of course. You go to see her, and she'll be only too glad to see you."

"And as to a detective? Shall I get in touch with Wise?"

"Yes, I think so. It does seem so queer for me to decide these things! I can't get used to the fact that I'm my own guardian!"

"You're of age, Olive," and Mrs. Vail smiled.

"Oh, yes, and I've had entire control of my money for some time. But Uncle always decided all matters of importance,—though, goodness knows, there never were any such to decide as those that beset us now! Think of my engaging a detective!"

"But Wise is so interesting and so adaptable, you'll really like him. I'll ask him to call here with me some afternoon or evening and you can get acquainted."

"I'd like to meet him," put in Mrs. Vail; "I knew a man once who wanted to be a detective, but he died. I've never seen a real detective."

"Pennington Wise is a real one, all right," I declared. "Of course, Miss Raynor, I shall tell the police that you are employing a private detective, for I don't think it a good plan to do it secretly. It is never wise to antagonize the police; they do all they can, popular prejudice to the contrary notwithstanding."

"Very well, Mr. Brice," and Olive gave me a look of confidence. "I don't care what you do, so long as you attend to it. I don't want to see those horrid police people again."

I thought to myself that she might be obliged to do so, unless Penny Wise could find another way to make them look. But I did not tell her so, for nothing raised her ire like the hint of suspicion directed toward herself in the matter of Amos Gately's murder.

"How dare they!" she exclaimed, her eyes fairly snapping with anger; "to dream that I—Olive Raynor—could—why, it's impossible to put it into words!"

It did seem so. To look at that dainty, lovely girl,—the very ideal of all that is best and gentlest in human nature,—it was impossible to breathe the word murder in the same breath!

I went away from the house, when my visit was over, determined to track down the assassin,—with the help of Penny Wise,—and thereby clear Olive's name from the least taint of the ugly suspicion now held by the police.

The next morning, in my office, I told Norah of all the developments of Sunday.

The warm hearted girl was deeply interested, and eager for me to communicate with Wise at once, for which purpose she slipped a fresh sheet of paper in her typewriter, and waited for my dictation of a letter to the detective.

"Wait a minute, Norah," I laughed; "give me time to open my desk!"

But I did dispatch the letter that morning, and awaited the answer as impatiently as Norah herself.

And then I went down to Police Headquarters.

There a surprise was given me. The Chief had received a letter that seemed to have a decided bearing on the mystery of the murder. He handed it to me without comment, and I read this:

To Police Headquarters;
New York City;
Sirs:

Last Wednesday afternoon, I was in New York, and was in the Building of the Puritan Trust Company. I had occasion to transact some business on the tenth floor, and afterward, when waiting for the elevator to take me down, I saw a pistol lying on the floor of the hallway near the elevator. I picked it up and put it in my pocket,— undecided, at the moment, whether to consider it "findings keepings" (as it was a first class one!) or whether to turn it in at the superintendent's office. As a matter of fact, when I reached the street floor I forgot all about the thing, nor did I remember it until I was back in Boston. And then, I read in the papers the accounts of the murder in that same building, that same afternoon, and I saw it was my duty to return the pistol and acquaint you with these facts. But alas, for dilatory human nature! I procrastinated (without meaning to) until today, and now I send this belated word, with an apology for my tardiness. The pistol is safe in my possession, and I will hold it pending your advices. Shall I send it to you,—and how? Or shall I turn it over to the Boston police? My knowledge of the whole matter begins and ends with the finding of the pistol, which after all, may have nothing to do with the crime. But I found it at three o'clock, or a very few minutes after, if that interests you. I shall be here, at The Touraine, for another week, and will cheerfully allow myself to be interviewed at

your convenience, but, as I said, I have no further information to give than that I have here set forth.
Very truly yours,
NICHOLAS LUSK.

The letter was dated from Boston, on Saturday evening, two days before. Truly, Friend Lusk had delayed his statement, but as he said, that was human nature, in matters not important to oneself.

The Chief was furiously angry at the lateness of the information, and had already dispatched a messenger to get the weapon and to interview the Boston man.

"It's all straight on the face of it," declared Chief Martin; "only an honest, cheerful booby would write like that! He picks up a pistol, forgets all about it, and then, when he learns it's evidence,—or may be,—he calmly waits forty eight hours before he pipes up!"

"Is it the pistol?" I asked, quietly.

"How do I know?" blustered Martin. "Likely it is. I don't suppose half a dozen people sowed pistols around that building at just three o'clock last Wednesday afternoon!"

"How do you fit it in?"

"Well, this way,—if you want to know. Miss—well, that is,—whoever did do the shooting, ran out of the third room, just as Jenny described, and ran downstairs,—it doesn't matter whether all the way down or not, but at least to the tenth—two floors below, and there dropped the pistol, either by accident or by design, and proceeded to descend, as I said, either by the stairs or by taking an elevator at some intervening floor. Now, we want that pistol. To be sure, it may not incriminate anybody,—and yet, there's lots of individuality in firearms!"

"In detective stories the owner's initials are on all well conducted pistols," I remarked, casually.

"Not in real life, though. There's a number on them, of course, but that seldom helps. And yet, I've got a hunch that that pistol will tell its own story, and my fingers itch to get a hold of it!"

"When do you expect it?"

"I've sent young Scanlon after it. He's a live wire, and he'll get back soon's anybody could. See here, this is the way I dope it out. If a woman did the shooting, she'd be more'n likely to throw away a pistol,—or to drop it unintentional like, in her nervousness, but a man—nixy!"

I had foreseen this. And the statement was, in a way, true. A man, having committed murder, does not drop his pistol,—unless, and I divulged this thought to Martin, unless he wants to throw suspicion on someone else.

"Nothin' doin'," was his curt response. "Nobody on that floor possible to suspect, 'ceptin' it's Rodman,—and small chance of him."

"Rodman!" I cried; "why, he got on the elevator at the seventh floor, just after .the shooting."

"He did!" the Chief straightened up; "how do you know?"

"Saw him. I was going down,—in Minny's elevator, you know,—to look for Jenny—"

"When was this?"

"About ten minutes after the shooting—and of course I got on at the twelfth floor, and there were no other passengers at first, so I talked to Minny. But at the seventh Rodman got on, and so we stopped talking."

"His office is on the tenth," mused Martin; "s'posin'— just s'posin' he'd—er—he was implicated, and that he ran downstairs afterward, to his own floor, you know,—and then, later, walked to seven, and took a car there—"

"Purposely leaving his pistol on his own floor!"

"Shucks, no! Dropped it accidentally."

"But you said male criminals don't do that!"

"Oh, pshaw! I say lots of things,—and you would, too, if you were as bothered as I am!"

"That's so, Chief," I agreed, "and there is certainly something to be looked into,–I should say, without waiting for a report from Boston."

"You bet there is! I'm going to send Hudson right up there. He's as good a sleuth as we've got, and he'll deal with the Rodman matter in a right and proper way. If there's nothing to find out, Rodman will never know he looked."

Hudson was duly dispatched, and I returned to the Puritan Building. It was queer, but Rodman had been in the back of my head all along,—and yet, I had no real reason to think him implicated. I did not know whether he knew Mr. Gately or not, but I, too, had confidence in Foxy Jim Hudson's discretion, and I was pretty positive he'd find out something,—if there were anything worth finding out.

And there was!

Rodman, by good luck, was out and his offices locked. Hudson gently persuaded the locks to let go their grip, and, for he let me go with him, we went in.

The first thing that hit me in the eyes, was a big war map on the wall. Moreover, though not a duplicate of Mr. Gately's map, it was similar, and it hung in a similar position. That is, as Rodman's offices were directly under those of the bank president, two floors below, the rooms matched, and in the "third room" as we called it in Mr. Gately's case, Rodman also had his map hung.

There was but one conclusion, and Hudson and I sprang to it at once.

Together, we pulled aside the map, and sure enough, there was a door exactly like the door in Mr. Gately's room, a small, flush door, usually hidden by the map.

"To the secret elevator, of course," I whispered to Hudson, for walls have ears, and these walls were in many ways peculiar.

"By golly, it is!" he returned; "let's open her up!"

He forced the door open, and assured himself that it did indeed lead into the private elevator shaft, and there were the necessary buttons to cause it to stop, if properly used. But now, the car being down on the ground floor, where it had stayed ever since the day of the murder, of course, the buttons could not be manipulated.

"Now," said Hudson, his brow furrowed," to see where else this bloomin' rogue trap lets 'em off! There's somethin' mighty queer goin' on that we ain't caught on to yet!"

He carefully closed the door, readjusted the map, and making sure we had left no traces of our visit, he motioned me out and we went away.

He asked me to return to my office, and promised to see me there later.

When he returned, he told me that he had visited every other office in the building through whose rooms the elevator shaft descended and in no other instance was there an opening into the shaft.

"Which proves," he summed up, "that Mr. Gately and Mr. Rodman was somehow in cahoots, else why would Rodman have access to that secret elevator? Answer me that!"

There were several possible answers. Rodman might have taken his offices after the elevator was built, and might never have used it at all. His map might have hung over it merely to cover the useless door.

Or, Rodman, might have been a personal friend of Mr. Gately's and used the little car for informal visits.

Again,—though I hated myself for the thought,—Mr. Gately might have had guests whom he didn't wish to be seen entering his rooms, and he might have had an arrangement with Rodman whereby the visitors could go in and out through his rooms, and take the private elevator between the tenth and twelfth floors.

I distrusted Rodman; without any definite reason, but all the same I did distrust him, and I have frequently found my intuitions regarding strangers hit pretty nearly right.

It was unnecessary, however, to answer Foxy Jim's question, for he answered it himself.

"There's something about Mr. Gately," he said, and he spoke seriously, almost solemnly, "that hasn't come to light yet, but it's bound to. Yes, sir, it's bound to! And it's on the way. Now, if we can hook up that Boston pistol with Mr. George Rodman, well and good; if we can't, Rodman's got to be put through the grill anyhow. He's in it for keeps—that elevator door isn't easily explained away."

"Does Mr. Rodman," it was Norah who spoke, and as before, Hudson turned to her almost expectantly—he seemed to depend on her for suggestions, or at least, he always listened to them—"I wonder, Mr. Brice," she went on slowly, "does Mr. Rodman look at all like the figure you saw in the shadow?"

I thought back.

"Yes," I said, decidedly, "he does! Now, hold on, Hudson, it's only a memory, you know, and I may easily be mistaken. But it seems to me I can remember a real resemblance between that shadowed head and the head of George Rodman."

"It's worth an experiment," returned the foxy detective, and on the strength of his decision he waited in my office until George Rodman returned to his.

I didn't know, at the time, what argument Hudson used to get Rodman to do it, but his foxiness prevailed and, obeying orders, I found myself watching the shadow of George Rodman's head on Amos Gately's glass door, as Hudson engaged his suspect in animated conversation.

Of course, the scene of the crime was not reenacted, there was merely the shadowed picture of the two men, but Hudson managed to have Rodman conspicuously shadowed in various positions and postures.

And after it was over, and Hudson, back in my office, asked me for my verdict, I was obliged to say:

"Mr. Hudson, if that is not the man I saw quarreling with Mr. Gately, it is his exact counterpart! Were it a less grave occasion, I should not hesitate to swear that it is the same man."

"That's enough, Mr. Brice," and Foxy Jim Hudson went back to Headquarters with his report.

CHAPTER 10: PENNY WISE AND ZIZI

AND so it was at this stage of affairs that Pennington Wise got into the game. He willingly agreed to take up the case, for the mystery of it appealed to him strongly, and by a stroke of good luck he was not otherwise engaged.

He had promised to call at Miss Raynor's, and as she had asked me to be present also, I went up there, reaching the house before Wise did.

"What's he like?" Olive inquired of me.

"Good looking sort of chap, without being handsome," I told her. "You'll like his personality, I'm sure, whether he helps us out of our troubles or not."

"I don't care a fig for his personality," she returned, "but I do want him to solve our two mysteries. I suppose you'll think I'm dreadful,—but I'd rather Mr. Wise would find Amory Manning for me, than to discover Uncle Amos' murderer."

"I don't blame you at all for that. Of course, we want to find the criminal, but even more, I too, want to find Mr. Manning for you."

"And, anyway, I suppose the police think now that Mr. Rodman did it."

"They don't go so far as to say that, but they're hunting up evidence, and they've got hold of some pretty damaging information. It seems Rodman was mixed up in some wrongdoing, and it begins to look as if Mr. Gately was in some way connected with it,—at least, to a degree."

"If he was, then he didn't know it was wrong." Olive spoke with deep conviction, and I didn't try to disabuse her mind.

And then Pennington Wise was announced.

As he entered the room his manner showed no trace of self consciousness, and as I had anticipated. Olive was greatly pleased with her first glimpse of him. But to her surprise, and mine also, he was accompanied, or rather followed, by a young woman, a mere slip of a girl, who paused and stood quietly by.

As Olive smiled at her inquiringly, Wise said:

"That's Zizi. She's part of my working paraphernalia, and will just sit and listen while we talk."

The girl was fascinating to look at. Slight of build, she had a lithe suppleness that made her every motion a gesture of grace, and her pretty smile was appreciative and responsive. She had black hair and very black eyes, which sparkled and danced as she took in her surroundings. But she said no word, acknowledging her brief introduction only by a slight bow, and accepting the chair that Olive offered, she sat quietly, her small gloved hands resting in her lap.

She wore a black suit with a fine set of black fox furs. Unfastening the fur collar, she disclosed a black blouse of soft, thin material which fell away from her slender white throat in becoming fashion.

Her manner was correct in every particular, and she sat in an unembarrassed silence as Wise proceeded to talk.

"I know all that has been in the papers," he said, somewhat abruptly, "now, I'd like you to tell me the rest. I can't help feeling there must be more in the way of evidence or clews than has been made public. First of all, do you think Mr. Rodman the guilty man?"

He addressed himself mainly to Olive, though including me in his inquiring glance.

"I'm sure I don't know," Olive returned; "I won't believe, however, that Amos Gately was involved in any sort of wrong. His honor and integrity were of the highest type,—I knew him intimately enough to certify to that."

"What sort of wrongdoing is this Rodman accused of?" asked Wise.

"Nobody seems willing to tell that," I answered, as Olive shook her head. "I've inquired of the police, and they decline to reveal just what they do suspect him of. But I think it's something pretty serious, and they're tracking it down as fast as they can."

"You see," Olive put in, "if Mr. Rodman is such a bad man, he may have hoodwinked Mr. Gately and made him believe something was all right when it was all wrong."

"Of course he might," said Wise, sympathetically. "Did people come here to the house to see Mr. Gately on business?"

"No; never. Uncle had few visitors, but they were always just his friends, not business callers."

"Then most of our search must be in his offices. You noticed nothing there, Mr. Brice, that seemed indicative?"

Then I told him about the hatpin and the carriage check; and I also related how Norah had found and kept the "powder paper" that she picked out of the waste basket.

Zizi's eyes flashed at this, and she said, "Has she traced it?"

It was the first time the girl had spoken, and I was charmed with her voice. Low and soft, it had also a bell like quality, and seemed to leave a ringing echo in the air after she ceased speaking.

"Yes; to the shop where it was bought," I replied. "As Norah guessed, it came from a very high class perfumer's on Fifth Avenue. But of course he could not tell us to whom he had sold that particular paper."

"I'd like to see it," said Zizi, simply, and again relapsed into silence.

"Norah must be a bright girl," observed Wise, "and she has made a good start by finding the shop. Perhaps we can carry the trail further. It wasn't yours, Miss Raynor?"

"No; I use a paler tint. This one, I have seen it, is quite a deep pink."

"Indicating a brunette possibly. Now, it's not likely it belonged to that old Mrs. Driggs, so we must assume another woman in the office that day. And we must discover who she is."

"There is the hatpin, you know," said Olive. "I have it here, if you care to see it. But the police decided it meant nothing."

"Nothing means nothing," said Zizi, with a funny little smile. "Please let us see the hatpin."

Olive took it from a desk drawer and handed it to the girl, who immediately passed it over to Penny Wise.

He looked at it with interest, for a silent minute.

"There couldn't be a better portrait parle!" he exclaimed. "This pin belongs to a lady with dark, straight hair,—coarse, and lots of it. She has good teeth, and she is proud of them. Her tastes incline to the flashy, and she is fond of strong perfumes. She is of somewhat untidy habits and given to sentiment. She is intellectual and efficient and, if not wealthy, she has at least a competence."

"For gracious goodness sake!" gasped Olive; "and I've studied that hatpin for hours and never could deduce a thing!"

"What I have read from it may be of no use to us," said Wise, indifferently; "I think it will be a sufficient indication of which way to look to find the lady in question, but that doesn't necessarily mean the finding of her will do any good."

"But she may know something to tell us that will do good," Olive suggested; "at any rate, let's find her. How will you go about it?"

"Why, I think it will be a good plan to ask the stenographer, Jenny Boyd, if she ever saw anyone there who fits our description."

"She's the lady of the powder paper, maybe," murmured Zizi, and Penny Wise said, "Of course," in a preoccupied way, and went on:

"That Jenny person must be further grilled. She hasn't told all she knows. She was in Mr. Gately's employ but a short time and yet she picked up a lot of information. But she hasn't divulged it all, not by a long shot!"

"How do you know all this?" asked Olive, wonderingly.

"I've read the papers. I have an unbreakable habit of reading between the lines, and I think Miss Jenny has been persuaded by somebody to suppress certain interesting bits of evidence that would fit right into our picture puzzle."

"May I come in?" said a gentle voice, and Mrs. Vail appeared in the doorway.

As we rose to greet her, Olive presented Mr. Wise, and then Mrs. Vail permitted herself the luxury of a stare of genuine curiosity.

His whimsical smile charmed her, and she was most cordial of speech and manner. Indeed, so absorbed was she in this new acquaintance that she didn't even see Zizi, who sat, as always, back and in the shadow.

"Don't let me interrupt," said Mrs. Vail, fluttering into a chair. "Just go on as if I were not here. I'm so interested, just let me listen! I won't say a word. Oh, Olive dear, did you show Mr. Wise the letter?"

"No; it's unimportant," replied the girl.

"But I don't think it is, my dear," Mrs. Vail persisted. "You know it might be a—what do they call it?—a clew. Why, I knew a lady once—"

"A letter is always important," said Zizi from her corner, and Mrs. Vail jumped and gave a startled exclamation.

"Who's that?" she cried, peering through her lorgnon in the direction of the voice.

"Show yourself, Zizi," directed Wise. "This is my assistant, Mrs. Vail. She is in our council but not of it. I can't explain her exactly, but you'll come to understand her."

Zizi leaned forward and gave Mrs. Vail a pleasant if indifferent smile, then sank back to her usual obscurity.

The girl was, Wise had said, a negligible personality, and yet whenever she spoke she said something!

Mrs. Vail looked bewildered, but apparently she was prepared to accept anything, however strange, in connection with detective work.

"Well," she observed, "as that pretty little thing says, a letter is always important, and I think you ought to show it, Olive. I had a letter once that changed the whole current of my life!"

"What is this letter, Miss Raynor?" asked Wise, in a matter of fact way.

"One I received in this morning's mail," Olive replied; "I paid no attention to it, because it was anonymous. Uncle Amos told me once never to notice an anonymous letter,—always to burn and forget it."

"Good enough advice, in general," said Wise; "but in such serious matters as we have before us any letter is of interest."

"Is the letter written by a woman, and signed 'A Friend'?" asked Zizi in her soft voice.

"Did you write it?" cried Olive, turning to the wraith like girl who sat so quietly behind her.

"Oh, no, no, no! I didn't write it," and the demure little face showed a fleeting smile.

"Then how did you know? For it is signed 'A Friend,' but I don't know whether it was a woman who wrote it or not."

"It was," and Zizi nodded her sleek little black head. She had removed her hat and placed it on a nearby chair, and as she nestled into her furs which formed a dark background, her small white face looked more eerie than ever. "Ninety per cent, of all anonymous letters are written by women, and ninety per cent, of these are signed 'A Friend.' Though usually that is a misstatement."

"May I see the letter?" asked Wise.

"Sure; I'll get it."

It was Zizi who spoke! And rising, she went swiftly across the room, to a desk, and from a pigeonhole took an opened letter, which she carried to Wise, and then dropped back into her seat again. Mrs. Vail gave a surprised gasp, and Olive looked her amazement.

"How did you know where to find that?" she exclaimed, her great brown eyes wide with wonder.

"Dead easy," said Zizi, nonchalantly; "you've scarcely taken your eyes off that spot, Miss Raynor, since the letter was mentioned!"

"But even though I looked at the desk, how could you pick out the very letter, at once?"

"Oh, I looked at the desk, too. And I saw your morning's mail, pretty well sorted out. There's a pile of bills, a pile of what are unmistakably social notes, and, up above in a pigeonhole, all by itself, was this letter. You glanced at it a dozen times or more, so I couldn't help knowing."

Olive laughed. One couldn't help liking the strange girl whose expression was so earnest, even while her black eyes were dancing.

Meanwhile, Penny Wise examined the missive.

"I'll read it aloud?" and he glanced at Olive, who acquiesced by a nod.

"MISS RAYNOR:

"Quit looking for slayer of A. G. or you'll be railroaded in yourself. This is straight goods. Call off all Tecs, or beware consequences. Will not warn twice!

"A FRIEND."

"A woman," Pennington Wise said in a musing voice, after he read it.

"A business woman," added Zizi from her corner.

"A stenographer maybe," Wise went on, and Olive cried:

"Do you mean Jenny?"

"Oh, no; this is written by a woman with more brains than Jenny ever dreamed of. A very clever woman in fact."

"Who?" breathed Olive, her eager face flushing in her interest and anxious to know more.

"I don't know that, Miss Raynor, but—"

"Oh, Mr. Wise," broke in Mrs. Vail; "you are so wonderful! Won't you explain how you do it, as you go along?"

She spoke as if he were a conjurer.

"Anything to oblige," Wise assented. "Well, here's how it looks to me. The writer of this letter is a business woman, not only because she uses this large, single sheet of bond paper, but because she knows how to use it. She is a stenographer,—by that I do not necessarily mean that is her business,—she may have a knowledge of stenography, and be in some much more important line of work. But she is an accomplished typist and a rapid one. This, I know, of course, from the neat and uniform typing. She is clever, because she has used this non committal paper, which is in no way especial or individual. She is a business woman, again, because she uses such expressions as 'quit,' 'railroaded,' 'Tecs,' 'straight goods,'"

"Which she might do by way of being misleading—" murmured Zizi.

"Too many of 'em, and too casually used, Ziz. A society girl trying to pose as a business woman never would have rolled those words in so easily. I should have said a newspaper woman but for a certain peculiarity of style which indicates,—what, Zizi?"

"You've got it; a telegraph operator."

"Exactly. Do you know any telegrapher, Miss Raynor?"

"No, indeed!" and Olive looked astounded at the suggestion that she should number such among her acquaintances. "Are you sure?"

"Looks mighty like it. The short sentences and the elimination of personal pronouns seem to me to denote a telegraph girl's diction. And she is very clever! She has sent the carbon copy of the letter and not the outside typing."

"Why?" I asked.

"To make it less traceable. You know, typewriting is very nearly as individual as pen writing. The differentiations of the machine as well as of the user's technique, are almost invariably so pronounced as to make the writing recognizable. Now these peculiarities, while often clear on the first paper, are blurred more or less on the carbon copy. So 'A Friend,' thinking to be very canny, has sent the carbon. This is a new trick, though I've seen it done several times of late. But it isn't so misleading as it is thought to be. For all the individual peculiarities of the typewriter,—I mean, the machine, are almost as visible on this as on the other. I've noticed them in this case, easily. And moreover, this would be clever writer has overreached herself! For a carbon copy smudges so easily that it is almost impossible to touch it, even to fold the sheet, without leaving a telltale thumb or finger print! And this correspondent has most obligingly done so!"

"Really!" breathed Zizi, with a note of satisfaction in her low voice.

"And the peculiarities,—what are they?" asked Olive.

"The one that jumps out and hits me first is the elevated s. Look,—and you have to look closely, Miss Raynor,—in every instance the letter s is a tiny speck higher than the other letters."

"Why, so it is," and Olive examined the letter with deep interest; "but how can you find a machine with an elevated s?"

"It isn't a sign board, it's a proof. When we think we have the right machine, the s will prove it,—not lead us to it."

"Let me see," begged Mrs. Vail, reaching for the paper. "A friend of mine is a stenographer; maybe she—"

"Excuse me," and Penny Wise folded the letter most carefully. "We can't get any more finger prints on this paper, or we shall render it useless. Now, Miss Raynor, I'm going. I'll take the letter, and I've little doubt it will be a great help to me in my work. I will report to you from time to time, but it may be a few days before I learn anything of importance. Zizi?"

"Yes; I'll stay here," and the girl sat quietly in her chair.

"That means she'll take up her abode with you for the present, Miss Raynor," and Wise smiled at Olive.

"Live here?"

"Yes, please. It is necessary, or she wouldn't do it."

"Oh, let her stay!" cried Mrs. Vail; "she's so interesting—and queer!"

The object of her comment gave her an engaging smile, but said nothing, and beckoning me to go with him, Wise rose to take leave. But I wanted to have a little further talk with Olive on several matters and I told Wise I'd join him a little later.

"Be goody girl, Zizi," he adjured as he went off, and she nodded her head, but with a saucy grimace at the detective.

"My room?" she said, inquiringly, with a pretty, shy glance at Olive. "I'm no trouble,—not a bit. Any little old room, you know."

"You shall have it in a few moments," and Olive went away to see the housemaids about it. Mrs. Vail snatched at a chance to talk uninterruptedly to the strange girl.

"What is your work?" she inquired; "do you help Mr. Wise? Isn't he wonderful! How you must admire him. I knew a detective once,—or, at least, a man who was going to be a detective, but— Oh, do tell me what your part of the work is!"

"I sit by," returned Zizi, with a dear little grin that took off all edge of curtness.

"Sit by! Is that some technical term? I don't quite understand."

"I don't always understand myself," and the girl shook her head slowly; "but I just remain silent until Mr. Wise wants me to speak,—to tell him something, you know. Then I tell him."

"But how do you know it?" I put in, fascinated by this strange child, for she looked little more than a child.

"Ooh!" Zizi shuddered, and drew her small self together, her black eyes round and uncanny looking; "ooh! I donno how I know! I guess the bogie man tells me!"

Mrs. Vail shuddered too, and gave a little shriek.

"You're a witch," she cried; "own up, now, aren't you a witch?"

"Yes, lady, lady! I am a witch,—a poor little witch girl!" and Zizi laughed outright at her own little joke.

If her smile had been charming, her laugh was more so. It was not only of a silvery trill, but it was infectious, and Mrs. Vail and I laughed in sympathy.

"What are you all laughing at?" said Olive, reappearing.

"At me," and Zizi spoke humbly now; "I made 'em laugh. Sorry!"

"Come along with me, you funny child," and Olive led her away, leaving me to be the victim of Mrs. Vail's incessant stream of chatter.

The good lady volubly discussed the detective and his assistant and detailed many accounts of people she had known. Her acquaintance was seemingly a wide one!

At last Olive returned, smiling.

"I never saw anything like her!" she exclaimed; "I gave her a pretty little room, not far from mine. I don't know, I'm sure, why she's staying here, but I like to have her. Well, in about two minutes she had the furniture all changed about. Not the heavy pieces, of course, but she moved a small table and all the chairs, and finally unscrewed an electric light bulb from one place and put it on another, and then, after looking all about, she said, 'Just one thing more!' and if she didn't spring up on to a table with one jump and take down quite a large picture! 'There,' she said, and she set it out in the hall; 'I can't bear that thing! Now this is a lovely room, and I thank you, Miss Raynor. The pink one we passed is yours, isn't it?'

"'Yes; how did you know?' I asked her. And she said, 'I saw a photograph of Mr. Manning on your bureau.' Little rascal! I can't help liking her!"

CHAPTER 11: CASE RIVERS

SO absorbed was I in the new interests that had come into my life, so anxious to be of assistance to Olive Raynor, and so curious to watch the procedure of Pennington Wise, that I confess I forgot all about the poor chap I had seen at Bellevue Hospital,—the man who "fell through the earth"! And I'm not sure I should ever have thought of him again, save as a fleeting memory, if I hadn't received a letter from him.

My dear Brice [he wrote] : I've no right to pilfer your time, but if you have 'a few minutes to squander, I wish you'd give them to me. I'm about to be discharged from the hospital, with a clean bill of health,—but with no hint or clew as to my cherished identity. The doctors—drat 'em!—"say that some day my memory will spring, full armed, back at me, but meanwhile, I must just sit tight and wait. Not being of a patient disposition, I'm going to get busy at acquiring a new identity, then, if the old one ever does spring a come back, I'll have two,—and can lead a double life! No, I'm not flippant, I'm philosophical. Well, if your offer didn't have a string tied to it come in to see me,- please.
Sincerely yours,
CASE RIVERS.

P.S.—The doctors look upon me as a very important and interesting case,—hence my name.

I smiled at the note, and as I had taken a liking to the man from the start, I went at once to see him.

"No," I assured him, after receiving his cordial welcome, "my offer had no string attached. I'm more than ready to help in any way I can, to find a niche for you in this old town and fit you into it. It doesn't matter where you hail from, or how you got here; New York is an all comers' race, and the devil take the hindmost."

"He won't get me, then," and Rivers nodded his head determinedly; "I may not be in the van, just at first, but give me half a chance, and I'll make good!"

This was not bumptiousness or braggadocio, I could see, but an earnest determination. The man was sincere and he had a certain doggedness of purpose, which was evident in his looks and manner as well as in his words.

Rivers was up and dressed now, and I saw he was a good looking chap. His light brown hair was carefully parted and brushed; his smooth shaven face was thin and pale, but showed strong lines of character. He had been fitted with glasses,—a pince nez, held by a tiny gold chain over one ear,—and this corrected the vacant look in his eyes. His clothes were inexpensive and quite unmistakably ready made.

He was apologetic. "I'd rather have better duds," he said, "but as I had to borrow money to clothe myself at all, I didn't want to splurge. One doctor here is a brick! He's going to follow up my 'case,' and so I accepted his loan. It's a fearful predicament to be a live, grown up man, without a cent to your name!"

"Let me be your banker," I offered, in all sincerity; "I—"

"No; I don't want coin so much as I want a way to earn some. Now, if you'll put me in the way of getting work,— anything that pays pretty well,—I'll be obliged, sir, and I'll be on my way."

His smile was of that frank, chummy sort that makes for sympathy and I agreed to help him in any way I could think of.

"What can you do?" I asked, preliminarily.

"Dunno. Have to investigate myself, and learn what are my latent talents. Doubtless their name is legion. But

I've nailed one of them. I can draw! Witness these masterpieces!"

He held up some sheets of scribble paper on which I saw several careful and well done mechanical drawings.

"You were a draughtsman!" I exclaimed, "in that lost life of yours."

"I don't know. I may have been. Anyway, these things are all right."

"What are they?"

"Not much of anything. They're sort of designs for wall paper or oilcloth. See? Merely suggestions, you know, but this one, repeated, would make a ripping study for a two toned paper."

"You're right," I exclaimed, in admiration of the pattern. "You must have been a designer of such things."

"No matter what I was,—the thing is what can I be now, to take my place in the economic world. These are, do you see, adaptations from snow crystals."

"So they are! It takes me back to my school days."

"Perhaps I'm harking back to those, too. I remember the pictures of snow crystals in 'Steele's Fourteen Weeky in Natural Science.' Did you study that?"

"I did!" I replied, grinning; "in high school! But, is your memory returning?"

"Not so's you'd notice it! I have recollection of all I learned in an educational way, but I can't see any individual picture of me, personally,—oh, never mind! How can I get a position as master designer in some great factory?"

"That's a big order," I laughed. "But you can begin in a small way and rise to a proud eminence—"

"No, thanky! I'm not as young as I once was,—my favorite doctor puts me down at thirty,—plus or minus,— but I feel about sixty."

"Really, Rivers, do you feel like an old man?"

"Not physically,—that's the queer part. But I feel as if my life was all behind me—"

"Oh, that's because of your temporary mental—"

"I know it. And I'm going to conquer it, get around it some way. Now, if you'll introduce

me,—and, yes, act as my guarantee, my reference,—I know it's asking a lot, but if you'll do that, I'll make good, I promise you!"

"I believe you will, and I'm only too glad to do it. I'll take you, whenever you say, around to a firm I know of, that I believe will be jolly glad to get you. You see, so many men of your gifts have gone to war—"

"Yes, I know, and I'd like to enlist myself, but Doc says I can't, being a—a defective."

"I wish you were a detective instead," I said, partly to turn the current of his thoughts from his condition and partly because my mind was so full of my own interests that he was a secondary consideration.

"I'd like to be. I've been reading a bunch of detective stories since I've been here in hospital, and I don't see as that deduction business is such a great stunt. Sherlock Holmes is all right, but most of his imitators are stuff and nonsense."

And then, unable to hold it back any longer, I told him all about the Gately case and about Pennington Wise.

He was deeply interested, and his eyes sparkled when I related Wise's deductions from the hatpin.

"Has he proved it yet?" he asked; "have you checked him up?"

"No, but there hasn't been time. He's only just started his work. He has another task; to find Amory Manning."

"Who's he?"

"A man who has disappeared, and there is fear of foul play."

"Is he suspected of killing Gately?"

"Oh, no, not that; but he was suspected of hiding to shield Miss Raynor—"

"Pshaw! a girl wouldn't commit a murder like that."

"I don't think this girl did, anyway. And, in fact, they—the police I mean—have a new suspect. There's a man named Rodman, who is being looked up."

"Oh, it's all a great game! I wish I could get out into the world and take part in such things!"

"You will, old man. Once you're fairly started, the world will be—"

"My cellar door! You bet it will! I'm going to slide right down it."

"What about your falling through it? Do you remember any more details of that somewhat—er—unusual performance?"

"Yes, I do! And you can laugh all you like. That's no hallucination, it's a clear, true memory,—the only memory I have."

"Just what do you remember?"

"That journey through the earth—"

"You been reading Jules Verne lately?".

"Never read it. But that long journey down, down,—miles and miles,—I can never forget it! I've had a globe to look at, and I suppose I must have started thousands of miles from here—"

"Oh, now, come off—"

"Well, it's no use. I can't make anybody believe it, but it's the truth!"

"Write it up for the movies. The Man Who Fell Through the Earth would be a stunning title!"

"Now you're guying me again. Guess I'll shut up on that subject. But I'll stick you for one more helping hand act. Where can I get a room to live in for a short time?"

"Why a short time?"

"Because I must take a dinky little cheap place at first, then soon, I'll be on my feet, financially speaking, and I can move to decenter quarters. You see, I'm going to ask you after all to trust me with a few shekels, right now, and I'll return the loan, with interest, at no far distant date."

His calm assumption of success in a business way impressed me favorably. Undoubtedly, he had been one accustomed to making and spending money in his previous life, and he took it as a matter of course. But his common sense, which had by no means deserted him, made him aware that he could get no satisfactory position without some sort of credentials.

As he talked he was idly, it seemed, unconsciously, drawing on the paper pad that lay on the table at his elbow—delicate penciled marks that resolved themselves into six sided figures, whose radii blossomed out into beautiful tendrils or spikes until they formed a perfect, harmonious whole; each section alike, just as in a snow crystal.

They were so exquisitely done that I marveled at his peculiar gift.

"You ought to design lace," I observed; "those designs are too fine for papers or carpets."

"Perhaps so," he returned, seriously gazing at his drawings. "Anyway, I'll design something,—and it'll be something worthwhile!"

"Maybe you were an engraver," I hazarded, "before you—"

"Before I fell through the earth? Maybe I was. Well, then, suppose tomorrow I so far encroach on your good offices as to go with you to see the firm you mentioned. Or, if you'll give me a letter of introduction—"

"Do you know your way around New York?"

"I'm not sure. I have a feeling I was in New York once,—a long time ago, but I can't say for certain."

"I'll go with you then. I'll call for you tomorrow, and escort you to the office I have in mind, and also, look up a home and fireside that appeals to you."

"The sort that appeals to me is out of the question at present," he said, firmly determined to put himself under no greater obligation to me than need be. "I'll choose a room like the old gentleman in the Bible had with a bed and a table and a stool and a candlestick."

"You remember your literature all right."

"I do, mostly; though I'll confess I read of that ascetic individual since I've been here. The hospital is long on Bibles and detective stories, and short on belles lettres. Well, so long, old man!"

I went away, pondering. It was a strange case, this of Case Rivers. I smiled at the name he had chosen.

He was positively a well educated and well read man. His speech gave me a slight impression of an Englishman, and I wondered if he might be Canadian. Of course, I didn't believe an atom of his yarn about coming from Canada to our fair city via the interior of the globe,—but he may have had a lapse of memory that included his railroad journey, and dreamed that he came in some fantastic way.

And then, as is usual, when leaving one scene for another, my thoughts flew ahead to my next errand, which was a visit to Police Headquarters.

Here Chief Martin gave me a lot of new information. It seemed they had unearthed damaging evidence in the case of George Rodman, and he was, without a doubt, a malefactor,—but in what particular branch of evil the Chief omitted to state. Nor could any rather broad hints produce any result. At last I said:

"Why don't you arrest Rodman, then?"

"Not enough definite evidence. I'm just about sure that he killed Gately, and I think I know why, but I can't prove it,—yet. Your statement that his head shadowed on that glass door was the same head you saw the day of the murder, is our strongest point—"

"Oh, I didn't say that!" I cried, aghast; "I do say it looked like the same head, but I wouldn't swear that it was!"

"Well, I think it was, and though we can't connect up the pistol with Rodman—"

"Did you get the pistol from the Boston man?"

"Yes; Scanlon brought home that bacon. But careful grilling failed to get any more information from Lusk, the man who found the pistol. He tells a straight tale of his visit to the Puritan Building, and his business there, all corroborated by the people he called on. He found that pistol, just as he says he did. And, of course, I knew he told the truth in his letter. If he were involved, or had any guilty knowledge of the crime, he surely wouldn't write to tell us of it! So now we have the pistol, and we know it was picked up in the tenth floor hall near Rodman's door,—but that proves nothing, since we can't claim it is Rodman's weapon. It may be, of course, but there's nothing to show it."

"What does Rodman say for himself?"

"Denies everything. Says he had the merest nodding acquaintance with Gately,—this we know is a lie!—says he knew there was an elevator door in his room, but he had never used it, nor even opened it. Said he hung a big war map over it because it was a good place for a map. We've no living witness to give a shred of evidence against Rodman, except your statement about his shadow,—and that is uncertain at best."

"Yes, it is. I do say it looked like Rodman's head,— that is, I mean, Rodman's head looked like the one I saw that day. But other heads might look as much like it."

"That's the trouble. George Rodman is a slick chap, and what he does that he doesn't want known, doesn't get known! But I'm onto him! And I'll bet I'll get him yet. He's so comfoundedly cool that all I say to him rolls off like water off a duck's back. He knows I've got no proof, and he's banking on that to get through."

"What about Jenny? Can't she tell you anything?"

"She knows nothing about Rodman. And that very point proves that if he visited Gately often, as I think he did, he came and went by that private elevator which connected their two offices, as well as made a street exit for either or both of them."

"Did old man Boyd ever see Rodman leave the Matteawan by way of that elevator?"

"He says he never did, but sometimes I think Rodman has fixed him."

"And Jenny, too, maybe."

"Maybe. And here's another thing. There's somebody called 'The Link,' who figures largely in the whole affair, but figures secretly. I won't say how I found this little joker, but if I can dig up who 'The Link' is, I've made a great stride toward success."

Naturally. I said nothing about Pennington Wise to the Chief of Police, but I made a mental note of "The Link" to report to the detective.

"Reward's offered," we were suddenly informed, as Foxy Jim Hudson burst into the room.

"For what?" asked the Chief, a little absentmindedly.

"For information leading to the whereabouts of Amory Manning."

Martin wheeled round in his chair to look at his subordinate. "Who offered it? How much?"

"That's the queer part, Chief. Not the amount,—that's five thousand dollars, but it's a person or persons unknown who will put up the kale. It's done through the firm of Kellogg and Kellogg,—about the whitest bunch of lawyers in town. I mean whoever offers that reward is somebody worthwhile. No shyster business. I'm for it,— the money, I mean. Do you know, Chief, the disappearance of that Manning chap is in some way connected with the Gately murder? I've got a hunch on that. And here's how I dope it out. Manning saw Rodman,—well, perhaps he didn't see him shoot, but he saw something that incriminated Rodman, and so he,— Rodman, had to get Manning out of the way. And did! You see, Friend Rodman is not only a deep-dyed scoundrel,—but the dye was 'made in Germany '!"

"Well, I'm glad the reward is offered," commented the Chief. "Now some rank outsider'll pipe up and speak his little piece."

"Meaning anybody in particular?" I asked.

With that peculiarly irritating trick of his, Chief Martin not only made no reply but gave no evidence of having heard my question. He went on:

"That makes two rewards. The Puritan Trust Company has offered five thousand for the apprehension of Gately's murderer. This other five thousand adds to the excitement and ought to produce a good result."

"I'm out for both," announced Hudson. "Can't say I expect to get 'em, but I'll make a fierce stab at it. Rodman has an awful big income, and no visible means of support. That fact ought to help."

"How?" I asked.

"Oh, it proves to my mind that he was mixed up in lucrative business that he didn't—well—advertise. 'The Link' was mixed in, too. That is,—I suppose,—'The Link' was a sort of go between, who enabled Rodman to transact his nefarious deals secretly."

"Well, Foxy, you know a lot," and the Chief laughed good humoredly.

I felt that I now knew a lot, too, and as I went away I determined to see Penny Wise at once, and report all I had learned. I dropped in first at my own office, and found Norah in a brown study, her hands behind her head and a half written letter in her typewriter.

She gazed at me absently, and then, noting my air of excitement, she became alert and exclaimed, "What's happened? What do you know new?"

"Heaps," I vouchsafed, and then I told her, briefly, of Rodman's probable guilt and also of the offered rewards.

"Jenny's your trump card," she said after a thoughtful silence. "That girl knows a good deal that she hasn't told. I shouldn't be surprised if she's in Rodman's employ."

"What do you mean?"

"Oh, she's too glib. She admits so many things that she has seen or heard and then when you ask her about others, she is a blank wall. Now, she does know about them, but she won't tell. Why? Because she's paid not to."

"Then how can we get around her?"

"Pay her more." And Norah returned to her typing. But she looked up again to say: "Mrs. Russell called here about an hour ago."

"She did! What for?"

"I don't know. She wanted to see you. She was a bit forlorn, so I talked to her a little."

"I'm glad you did. Poor lady, she feels her brother's absence terribly."

"Yes; we discussed it. She thinks he has been killed."

"Has she any reason to think that?"

"No, except that she dreamed it."

"A most natural dream for a nervous, worried woman."

"Of course. I wonder if she knows there's a reward offered for Mr. Manning?"

"Maybe she offered it,—through the Kellogg people."

"No, she didn't."

"Pray, how do you know, oh, modern Cassandra?"

"I don't know your old friend Cassandra, but I do know Mrs. Russell isn't offering any five thousand dollars. She can't afford it."

"Why, she's a rich woman."

"She passes for one, and, of course, she isn't suffering for food or clothes. But she is economizing. She was wearing her last year's hat and muff, and she maids herself."

"Perhaps she wore her old clothes because she was merely out to call on my unworthy self."

"No. She was on her way to a reception. They're her best clothes now. And a tiny rip in one glove and a missing snap fastener on her bodice proves she keeps no personal lady's maid, as people in her position usually do.

So, I'm sure she isn't offering big reward money, though she loves her brother."

"You're a born detectivess, Norah. You'll beat Penny Wise at his own game, if he doesn't watch out!"

"Maybe," said Norah, and she laid her fingertips gracefully back on her typewriter keys.

Chapter 12: The Link

IT was the next afternoon that Penny Wise came into my office. It was his first visit there, and I gave him a hearty welcome. Norah looked so eagerly expectant that I introduced him to her, for I couldn't bear to disappoint the girl by ignoring her.

Wise was delightfully cordial toward her, and indeed Norah's winsome personality always made people friendly.

I had tried to get in touch with the detective the day before but he was out on various errands, and I missed him here and there, nor could we get together until he found this leisure.

I told him all I had learned from the police, but part of it was already known to him. He was greatly interested in the news which he had not heard before, that there was somebody implicated, who was called "The Link."

"That's the one we want!" he cried; "I suspected some such person."

"Man or woman?" asked Norah, briefly, and Wise glanced at her.

"Which do you think?"

"Woman," she replied, and Penny Wise nodded his head. "Yes, I've no doubt 'The Link' is a woman, and a mighty important factor in the case."

"But I don't understand," I put in. "What does she link?"

"Whom,—not what," said Wise, and he looked very serious. "Of course, you must realize, Brice, there's a great big motive behind this Gately murder, and there's also a big reason for Amory Manning's disappearance. The two are connected,—there's no doubt of that,—but that doesn't argue Manning the murderer, of course. No, this Link is a woman of parts,—a woman who is of highest value to the principals in this crime, and who must be found, and that at once!"

"Did she have to do with Mr. Gately?" asked Norah, her gray eyes burning with interest.

"I—don't—know." Wise's hesitating answer was by no means because of disinclination to admit his ignorance, but because he was thinking deeply himself. "Look here, Brice, can't we go over Gately's rooms now? I don't want to ask permission of the police, but if the Trust Company people would let us in—"

"Of course," I responded, and I went at once to the vice president for the desired permission.

"It's all right," I announced, returning with the keys, "come ahead."

We went into the beautiful rooms of the late bank president.

Pennington Wise was impressed with their rich and harmonious effects, and his quick eyes darted here and there, taking in details. With marvelous swiftness he went through the three rooms of the suite nodding his head as he noted the special points of which he had been told. In the third room,—the Blue Room,—he glanced about, raised the map from the wall, and dropped it back in place, opened the door to the hall, and closed it again, and then turned back to the middle room, the office of Amos Gately, and apparently, to the detective's mind, the principal place of interest.

He sat down in the fine big swivel chair, whose velvet cushioning deprived it of all look of an ordinary desk chair, and mused deeply as his eyes fairly devoured the desk fittings. Nothing had been disturbed, that I noticed, except that the telephone had been set up in its right position, and also the chair which I had found overturned was righted. Wise fingered only a few things. He picked up the penholder, a thick magnificent affair made of gold.

"Probably a gift from his clerks," said I, smiling at the ornate and ostentatious looking thing. "All the other gimcracks are in better taste."

Pennington Wise opened the desk drawers. There was little to see, for all financial papers had been taken away by Mr. Gately's executors.

"Here's a queer bunch," Wise observed, as he picked up a packet of papers held together by a rubber band. He sorted them out on the desk.

They were sheets of paper of various styles, each bearing the address or escutcheon of some big city hotel. Many of the principal hostelries of New York were represented among them. Each sheet bore a date stamped on it with an ordinary rubber dating stamp.

"Important, if true," commented Wise.

"If what's true?" asked Norah, bluntly.

"My deductions," he returned. "These letters, if we can call them letters, doubtless were sent to Mr. Gately at separate times and in separate envelopes."

"They were," I informed him. "One came the morning after his death."

"It did! Which one?"

"It isn't here. All the new mail went to his lawyer."

"We must get hold of it!"

"But,—do tell me what's the import of a blank sheet of paper?"

"These aren't blank," and he pointed to the stamped dates. "They are very far from blank!"

"Only a date,—on a plain sheet of paper,—what does that mean?"

"Perhaps nothing—perhaps everything."

It wasn't like Penny Wise to be cryptic, and I gathered that the papers were really of value as evidence. "Has the writing been erased?" I hazarded.

"Probably not. No. I don't think so." He scrutinized more closely.

"No," he concluded, "nothing like that. The message is all told on the surface, and he who runs may read."

"Read, 'The Waldorf Astoria, December 7,'" I scoffed. "And is the reader greatly enlightened?"

"Not yet, but soon," Wise murmured, as he kept up his investigation. "Ha!" he went on, "as the actor hath it,—what have we here!"

He was now scrutinizing the ends of two burnt cigarettes, left on the ash tray of the smoking set.

"The lady has left her initials! How kind of her!"

"Why, Hudson studied those and couldn't make out any letters," I exclaimed.

"Blind Hudson! These very dainty and expensive cigarettes belonged to a fair one, whose name began with K and S,—or S and K. Be careful how you touch it, but surely you can see that the tops of the letters though scorched, show definitely enough to know they must be K and S."

"They are!" cried Norah; "I can see it now."

"Couldn't that S be an O?" I caviled.

"Nope," and Wise shook his head. "The two, though both nearly burnt away, show for sure that the letters are K and S. Here's a find! Does Miss Raynor smoke?"

"I don't think so," I replied. "I've never seen her do so,—and she doesn't seem that type. And then,—the initials—"

"Oh, well, she might have had some of her friends' cigarettes with her. I was only thinking it must have been a pretty intimate caller who would sit here and smoke with Mr. Gately —here are his own cigar stubs you see and of course, Miss Raynor came into my mind. Eliminating her we have, maybe, the lady of the hatpin."

"And the powder paper!" cried Norah.

"Yes, they all seem to point to a very friendly caller, who smoked, who took off her hat, and who powdered her nose, all in this room, and all on the day Mr. Gately was killed. For, of course, the whole place was cleaned and put in order every day."

"And there was the carriage check," I mused; "perhaps she left that."

"Carriage check?" asked Wise.

"Yes, a card like a piece of Swiss cheese,—you know those perforated carriage call checks?"

"I do. Where is it?"

"Hudson took it. But he won't get anything out of it, and you might."

"Perhaps. I must see it, anyway. Also, I want to see Jenny,—the young stenographer who was—"

"Shall I get her here?" offered Norah.

"Yes," Wise began, but I cut him short.

"I've got to go home," I said. "I promised Rivers I'd see him this afternoon, and take him on some errands. Suppose I go now, and you go with me, Mr. Wise, and suppose Norah gets Jenny and brings her round to my rooms. We can have the interview there; Rivers may not come till later, but I must be there to receive him."

So Penny Wise and I went down to my pleasant vine and figtree, and as we went, I told him about Case Rivers.

He was interested at once, as he always was in anything mysterious, and he said, "I'm glad to see him. What a strange case! Can he be the missing Manning?"

"Not a chance," I replied. "The two men are totally dissimilar in looks and in build. Manning is heavy,— almost stocky. Rivers is gaunt and lean. Also, Manning is dark haired and full blooded, while Rivers is pale and has very light hair. I tried to make out a resemblance, but it can't be done. However, Case Rivers is interesting on his own account;" and I told him the story of his journey through the earth.

He laughed. "Hallucination, of course," he said; "but it might easily lead to the discovery of his identity. That amnesic aphasia business always fascinates me. That is, if I'm convinced it's the real thing. For, you know, it's a fine opportunity to fake loss of memory."

"There's no fake in this case, I'm positive," I hastened to assure him; "I've taken a decided liking to Rivers, and I mean to keep in touch with him, for when he regains his memory I want to know about it."

"Pulled out of the river, you say?"

"Yes, a tugboat picked him up, drowned and frozen, it was supposed. He was taken to the morgue, and bless you, if he didn't show signs of life when he thawed out a little. So they went to work on him and revived him and sent him over to Bellevue where he became a celebrated case."

"I should think so. No clothes or any identification?"

"Not a rag. Or rather only a few rags of underwear,— but nothing that was the slightest clew."

"What became of his clothes?"

"Nobody knows. He was found drifting, unconscious, apparently dead, and entirely nude save the fragments of underclothing."

"Those fragments have been kept?"

"Oh, yes; but they mean nothing. Just ordinary material,—good,—but nothing individual about them."

"Where was he picked up?"

"I don't know exactly, but not far from the morgue, I believe. It was the same day as the Gately murder, that's why I remember the date. It was a dreadfully cold snap, the river was full of ice and it's a wonder he wasn't killed, as well as knocked senseless."

"Was he knocked senseless?"

"I'm not sure, but he was unconscious from cold and exposure and very nearly frozen to death."

"And his memory now?"

"Is perfect in all respects, except he doesn't know who he is."

"A fishy tale!"

"No; you won't say so after you've seen him. When I say his memory is perfect, I mean regarding what he has read or has studied. But it is his personal recollections that have gone from him. He has no remembrance of his home or his friends or his own identity."

"Can't you deduce his previous occupation?"

"I can't. Perhaps you can. He can draw, and he is well read, that's all I know."

We were at my rooms by that time, and going up, we found Case Rivers already there awaiting us. I lamented my lack of promptness, but he gracefully waived my apology.

"It's all right," he smiled in his good humored way, "I've been browsing among your books and having the time of my life."

I introduced the two men, and told Rivers that Wise was the famous detective I had mentioned to him.

"I'm downright glad to know you," Rivers said, earnestly; "if you can do a bit of deduction as to who I am, I'll be under deepest obligation. I give you myself as a clew."

"Got a picture of Amory Manning?" asked Wise, abruptly.

I handed him a folded newspaper, whose front page bore a cut of Manning, and the story of his mysterious disappearance.

Wise studied the picture and compared it with the man before him.

"Totally unlike," he said, disappointedly.

"Not a chance," laughed Rivers; "I wish I could step into that chap's shoes; but you see, I came from far away."

"Tell me about that trip of yours," asked Wise.

"Don't know much to tell," returned Rivers; "but what I do know, I know positively, so I'll warn you beforehand not to chuckle at me, for I won't stand it!"

Rivers showed a determination that I liked. It proved that I was right in ascribing a strong character to him. He would stand chaffing as well as anyone I knew, but not on the subject of his fall through the earth.

"I don't know when or where I started on my memorable journey, but I distinctly remember my long, dark fall straight down through the earth. Now it would seem impossible, but I can aver that I entered in some very cold, arctic sort of country, and I came on down feet first, till I made exit in New York. I was found, but how I got into the river, I don't know."

"You were clothed when you started?"

"I can only say that I assume I was. I'm a normal, decent sort of man, and I can't think I'd consciously set out on a trip of any sort undressed! But I've no doubt my swashing around in the ice filled river did for my clothes. Probably, as related by the Ancient Mariner, 'the ice was here, the ice was there, the ice was all around: it cracked and growled and—something or other—and howled, like noises in a swound.' You see, I still know my 'Familiar Quotations' by heart."

"That's a queer phase," and Wise shook his head. "It may be you are a poet—"

"Well, I haven't poetized any since my recrudescence."

"And that's another queer thing," pursued the detective. "Most victims of aphasia can't remember words. You are exceptionally fluent and seem to have a wide vocabulary."

"I admit it all," and Rivers looked a little weary, as if he were tired of speculating on his own case.

"Now, to change the subject, how are you progressing, Mr. Wise, with your present work? How goes the stalking of the murderer?"

"Haven't got him yet, Mr. Rivers, but we've made a good start. You know the details?"

"Only the newspaper accounts, and such additional information as Mr. Brice has given me. I'm greatly interested,—for,—tell it not to Gath detectives,—I fancy I've a bent toward sleuthing myself."

Pennington Wise smiled. "You're not alone in that," he said, chaffingly, but so good naturedly that Rivers took no offense.

"I suppose it's your reflected light that makes everybody who talks with you feel that way," he came back. "Well, if you get up a stump, lean on me, Grandpa,—I'm 'most seven."

And then we all three discussed the case, in all its phases, and though Rivers said nothing of great importance, he showed such an intellectual grasp of it all, and responded so intelligently to Wise's theories and opinions that the two soon became most friendly.

The announcement of the rewards stirred Rivers to enthusiasm.

"I'm going to get 'em!" he cried; "both of 'em! With all due respect to you, Mr. Wise, I'm going to cut under and win out! Don't say I didn't warn you, and hereafter all you say will be used against you! If there's one thing I need more than another it's ten thousand dollars,—I could even do with twenty! So, here goes for Rivers, the swiftsure detective!"

Not a bit offended, Penny Wise laughed outright.

"Go ahead, my boy," he cried; "here's a bargain; you work with me, and I'll work with you. If we get either Manning or the murderer or both, then either or both rewards shall be yours. I'll be content with what else I can get out of it."

"Done!" and Case Rivers was jubilant. "Perhaps Manning is the murderer," he said, thoughtfully.

"No," I put in. "That won't do. Manning is in love with Miss Raynor, and he wouldn't queer his cause by killing her guardian."

"But Guardy didn't approve of Suitor Manning," Rivers said.

"No; but I know Manning and you don't,—well, that is, I know him only slightly. But I'm sure he's not the man to shoot a financial magnate and a first class citizen just because he frowned on his suit. Try again, Rivers."

"All right: what you say goes. But I'm just starting in, you know. And, by the way, I'm to get a job of some sort today—yes?"

He looked at me inquiringly, but Wise answered.

"Wait a bit, Rivers, as to that. If you'll agree, I'll grubstake you for a fortnight or so, and you can help me. Really, I mean it, for as a stranger you can go to places, and see people, where I can't show my familiar face. Then, when you get the two rewards you can repay me my investment in you. And if you fail to nail the ten thousand, I'll take your note."

"I'll go you!" said Rivers, after a moment's thought. "You're a brick, Penny Wise!"

A tap at the door announced Norah, and with her came Jenny Boyd. Nor was Jenny dragged unwillingly,— she seemed eager to enter,—but her absurd little painted face wore a look of stubbornness and her red lips were shut in a determined pout.

"Jenny knows who 'The Link' is, and she won't tell," Norah declared, as a first bit of information.

"Oh, yes, she will," and Penny Wise winked at the girl. He really gave a very knowing wink, as who should say: "We understand each other."

As they had never met before, I watched to see just how Jenny would take it, and to my surprise she looked decidedly frightened.

Wise saw this too,—doubtless he brought about the effect purposely,—but in a moment Jenny regained her poise and was her saucy self again.

"I don't know for sure," she said, "and so I don't want to get nobody into trouble by suspicioning them."

"You won't get anybody into trouble," Wise assured her, "unless she has made the trouble for herself. Let's play a game, Jenny,—let's talk in riddles."

Jenny eyed him curiously, and then, as he smiled infectiously, she did, too.

"Now," went on Wise, "this is the game. I don't know, of course, whom you have in mind, and you don't know whom I have in mind, so we'll play the game this way: I'll say, 'I know she is a clever woman.' Now you make a truthful statement about her."

Enthralled by his manner, Jenny said, almost involuntarily, "I know she is a wrong one!"

"I know she's pretty," said Wise.

"I know she isn't!" snapped Jenny.

"I know she is black haired and dresses well and owns a scarab hatpin."

"I know that, too," and Jenny was breathless with interest.

"No; that won't do. You must know something different from my know."

"Well, I know she's a friend of Mr. Rodman."

"And of Mr. Gately," added Wise.

"Oh, no, sir, I don't think so!" Jenny's surprise was unfeigned.

"Well, I know she's a telegraph girl."

"Yes: and I know she has more money to spend than she gets for a salary."

"I know she's a good girl."

"Oh, yes, sir,—that way. But she—"

"She smokes cigarettes."

"Yes; she does. Oh, I think that's awful."

"Well, it's your turn. You know she's 'The Link'?"

"I know she's been called that, but it isn't a regular nickname, and I don't know what it means."

"Where is she?"

"Her work, you mean?"

"Yes; she's in the company's office,—" Here Jenny whispered the address to Wise.

"Good girl," he commented. "Keep it dark. No use in telling all these people!"

He turned to my telephone, then said: "No, Brice, you do it. Call Headquarters and tell the Chief to arrest,— what's her name, Jenny?"

"I—I didn't say, sir." The girl's caution was returning.

"Say now, then," commanded Wise. "I know, anyway. It begins with S."

"Her first name,—yes, sir."

"And the last name with K. You see I know! So, out with it!"

"Sadie Kent," whispered Jenny, her nerves beginning to go to pieces at realizaton of what she had done.

"Yes, of course. Sadie Kent. Go ahead, Brice. Fix it all up,—and go to the telegraph office yourself. Meet the officers there. Scoot!"

I scooted. The strong arm of the law works swiftly when it wills to do so. Within half an hour Sadie Kent was arrested at her key in the telegraph office on charge of stealing confidential telegrams sent by officials in Washington to munition plants and steamship companies and delivering them to persons who she knew would transmit them to the German Foreign Office.

When approached, the girl,—the woman rather,—put up a bold bluff, but it was of no avail. She was taken into custody, and all her appeals for mercy denied. All but one. She begged so hard to be allowed to telephone to her mother that Hudson, who was present, softened.

"You can't, my lady," he said, "but I'll have it done for you. Mr. Brice, now, maybe he'll do it."

"Oh, if you would be so kind," and the beautiful brunette, for she was that, gave me a grateful look.

"Just call 83649 Greenwich Square, and ask for Mrs. Kent. Then tell her, please, that—that I won't be home tonight. That's all."

Her voice broke and she sobbed softly in her handkerchief.

They took her away, to be detained pending developments. I made the call and gave the message exactly as she had asked me. A pleasant voice responded, saying the speaker was Mrs. Kent, and she thanked me for sending word.

I hurried back to my rooms. Wise and Rivers were still there but Norah and Jenny had left. I had no sooner got my coat off than Zizi came flying in.

"Oh, everybody," she cried, in a whirl of excitement, "Olive's gone! She's kidnaped or abducted or something. A telephone message came and she flew off, telling nobody but Mrs. Vail, and telling her not to tell!"

"Where's she gone?" I cried, flinging back into my coat.

"Nobody knows. I only got it out of Mrs. Vail this minute, and then only by threatening her with all sorts of horrors if she didn't tell me. She doesn't know where Olive's gone,—nobody knows,—but whoever telephoned said he had Amory Manning with him, just for a few moments and for her to come at once if she wanted to see him. A car would come for her at four o'clock, exactly, and she was to get in and ask no questions. And she did—and she told Mrs. Vail that as soon as she got to Mr. Manning she would telephone back,—in about fifteen minutes. And now it's over an hour! and no word from her! That stupid old woman just walks up and down and wrings her hands!"

"I should think she would! Which way shall we look, Wise?"

"I don't know, I'm sure!" and for once the resourceful detective was absolutely at a loss.

"Oh, Penny Wise," and Zizi burst into tears, "if you don't know what to do, nobody does! Olive will be killed or held for ransom or some dreadful thing! What can we do?"

But the dull silence that fell on us all proved that no one present was able to offer any suggestion.

CHAPTER 13: OLIVE'S ADVENTURE

GIVE me a handkerchief, somebody!" commanded Zizi, and not without reason, for her own tiny wisp of cambric was nothing but a wet ball, which she was futilely dabbing into her big black eyes.

I hurried into my bedroom and hastily grabbed a fresh handkerchief from a drawer, which I brought to the excited girl.

"Thanks," she said, as she grasped it and plied it diligently; "now, men, we must get busy! It's after five o'clock, Olive went away before four,—anything may have happened to her—we must rescue her!"

"We will!" exclaimed Case Rivers, showing more energy than I knew he possessed." What about 'The Link,' Mr. Brice?"

As quickly as I could, I detailed what had happened at the telegraph office, where Sadie Kent had been taken into custody by Hudson's men.

"Did she go quietly?" asked Penny Wise.

"She did not!" I returned; "she put up a fearful fight, tore up a lot of papers from a desk drawer, and lit into the policemen like a tiger cat! She tried to bite Hudson, and yet, he was the one who kind heartedly let her telephone to her mother."

"What!" cried Rivers, "he let her do that!"

"I did it myself, really," I said; and I told how Sadie had begged for the privilege.

"There you are!" Rivers said, positively. "That telephone message was not to her mother!"

"But I called her up," I explained, "and she said she was Mrs. Kent."

"That may be," and Rivers shook his head; "but, don't you see, that was a code call,—a warning. The person who received it, mother or grandmother, caught on to the state of things and set machinery in motion that resulted in the kidnaping of Miss Raynor."

"What for?" I asked, blankly.

"Revenge, probably, but there may be other villainies afoot. Am I right, Mr. Wise?"

"Yes, and mighty quick witted. Then the next step is to go to the 'mother's' house."

"Yes, if we can trace it. It may be a call within a call; I mean, the number Mr. Brice got may be merely a go between—a link—"

"Try it, anyway," implored Zizi; "every minute is precious. I'm so afraid for Miss Olive. You know, she's spunky,—she won't submit easily to restraint, and you don't know what they may do to her!"

"Get Information first," directed Wise, as I started for the telephone. "Find the address of the number you called. You remember it?"

"Yes; of course." And in a few moments I learned that the house was down in Washington Square.

"Get a taxi," said Zizi, already putting on her long black cape, which swirled round the slender figure as she flung one end over her shoulder.

She flew to a mirror, and was dabbing her straight little nose with a powder puff as she talked.

"We'll all go down there, and I don't think we'll have to look any further. Miss Olive is there,—I'm dead sure! Held by the enemy! But she's game, and I don't believe we'll be too late, if we hustle like a house afire!"

And so, with the greatest speed consistent with safety, we taxied down to the house in Washington Square.

The Kent apartment was on the third floor, and as Zizi dashed up the stairs, not waiting for the elevator, we three men followed her.

Zizi's ring at the bell brought a middle aged woman to the door, who looked at us rather blankly.

I was about to speak, when Zizi, insinuating her small self through the partly opened door, said softly:

"We've a message from 'The Link.'"

It acted like magic, and the woman's face changed to an expression of welcome and serious anxiety, as we all went in.

It was rather a pretentious apartment, with fine furnishings in ornate taste. We saw no one save the woman who admitted us, and heard no sound from other rooms.

"You expected it?" and Zizi's air of secret understanding was perfect.

"Expected what?" said Mrs. Kent, sharply, for she was apparently on her guard.

"Sadie's arrest," and Zizi's black eyes narrowed as she looked keenly at the other.

But the woman was not to be trapped. She glanced at us each in turn, and seemed to conclude we were not friendly visitors for all Zizi's pretense.

"I know nothing of any arrest," she said, evenly; "I think you have mistaken the house."

"I think not," and Penny Wise looked at her sternly. "Your bluff won't go, madam,—Sadie, 'The Link,' is arrested, and the game is up. Will you answer questions or will you wait until you, too, are arrested?"

"I have nothing to say," she mumbled, but her voice trembled, and her nerve was deserting her. Inadvertently she glanced toward the closed door of the next room, and Zizi's quick eyes followed the glance.

"Is Miss Raynor in there?" she flung out so quickly that Mrs. Kent gasped. But she recovered her poise at once and said, "I don't know what you mean,—I don't know any Miss Raynor."

"Oh, tut, tut!" and Zizi grinned at her; "don't tell naughty stories! Why, I hear Miss Raynor's voice!"

She didn't at all, but as she listened, with her head cocked on one side, like a saucy bird, Mrs. Kent's face showed fear, and she listened also.

A muffled scream was heard,—not loud, but clearly a cry for help.

Without further parley, Rivers made a dash for the door and though it was locked, he smashed into the rather flimsy panel and the old hinges gave way.

There, in the adjoining room was Olive Raynor, a handkerchief tied across her mouth and her angry eyes flashing with rage.

Holding her arm was George Rodman, who was evidently trying to intimidate her, but without complete success.

Zizi flew to Olive's side, and snatched off the handkerchief.

Rodman was perfectly cool. "Let that lady alone," he said; "she is my affianced wife."

"Affianced grandmother!" retorted Zizi. "You can't put that over, Mr. Rodman!"

"Save me!" Olive said, looking from me to Penny Wise and back again. Her glance fell on Rivers, but returned to me, as her face assumed a look of agony.

I couldn't quite understand, as she must know that with us all there her danger was past.

"Are you his betrothed?" Case Rivers said, bluntly.

"No!" Olive replied, in an indignant tone; "never!"

"Then—" and Rivers seemed about to remove Rodman's hand from Olive's arm by force, but Rodman himself spoke up:

"One moment, please," he said, quietly, and bending over, he whispered in Olive's ear.

She turned deathly white, her lips quivered, and she seemed about to fall. Whatever the brief words were, they wrought a marvelous change in the girl's attitude. She lost her air of defiant wrath, and seemed a helpless, hopeless victim of the man who held her.

"Are you engaged to me?" Rodman said, looking at Olive, with a threatening scowl.

"Yes," she managed to whisper, but so agonized was her face that it was palpable she spoke under coercion.

I was uncertain what to do; Wise, too, looked nonplussed, but Rivers, though a stranger to Olive, seemed imbued with an irresistible chivalry, and drawing nearer to her, he said:

"Is that man forcing you to say that against your will?"

Rodman's grip tightened on Olive's arm, and his glowering face looked sternly into hers. She made no reply in words, but her piteous glance told all too clearly that Rivers' assumption was correct.

And yet, what could we do? Olive had assented to Rodman's assertion, and we could scarcely demand a girl from her fiancé.

Zizi mastered the situation by saying, triumphantly: "We've got 'The Link!' She's under arrest!"

"What!" cried Olive, and then, dropping her arm, Rodman whirled toward her:

"There!" he cried, "your secret is out! Unless—" He made a gesture as if to put his arm round her.

With a cry of revulsion, Olive shrank from him, and her face showed that she preferred his threatening attitude to his endearing one.

"You let that lady alone, unless she desires your attentions," said Rivers, his innate desire to protect a woman in distress showing in his repressed eagerness to get at Rodman.

"You mind your own business!" shouted Rodman, angrily, as he put out his arm and drew Olive to him. "You're mine, now, aren't you, dearie?"

The disgust on the girl's face, and the shrinking of her form as she tried to draw away from the leering face so near hers was too much for Rivers. He assumed a threatening attitude, and said, "You take your hands off that lady! She doesn't want—"

In defiance, Rodman drew Olive nearer, and raising her bowed head was about to kiss her angry, beautiful face, when she uttered a despairing scream.

That was the match in the powder keg!

Unable to hold back longer, Rivers sprang forward and wrenched Olive from Rodman's grasp.

With a snarl, Rodman lunged at Rivers, who deftly stopped him with an uppercut. Rodman came back with a smashing facer, and Rivers replied in kind.

Zizi, who had flown to Olive's side, and was tenderly soothing her, watched the two men, breathlessly. Something savage in her nature responded to the combat, and she flushed and paled alternately as one or the other of the angry men seemed to have the upper hand.

Olive hid her face in her hands, not wanting to look, but Zizi was with the fight, heart and soul.

It was give and take, with such rapidity that I trembled for Rivers' safety. Rodman was a formidable antagonist, and far heavier than the gaunt man who met and returned his blows.

But Rivers was skilled, and made up in technique what he lacked in strength.

So desperate was the struggle, so blindly furious the two men, that Pennington Wise and I were fearful of results. With a simultaneous impulse we made a dash to separate the combatants, but were obliged to get back quickly to save ourselves from the rain of blows.

Never had I seen such a wild, unbridled fight compressed into such a short time, and I wondered what Rivers had been in a fighting way before he lost his identity.

Fighting and boxing had never been favorite forms of entertainment with me, but this contest absorbed me. It was primitive, instinctive,—the rage of Rodman pitted against the angry indignation of Rivers.

I had not thought of the latter as a weakling, but neither had I looked upon him as a strong man, and I should have judged that in a bout with Rodman he would have gone under.

But not so; his lean, gaunt frame was full of latent strength, his bony fists full of dexterity.

He rushed in, fell back, sidestepped, with the dazzling quickness of a trained fighter. He showed knowledge and skill that amazed me.

Rodman, too, fought for all he was worth, but he impressed me as being not an experienced fighter,—and not a fair one.

Wise, too, was watching Rivers with wonder and admiration, and he also kept his alert gaze on Rodman.

Fascinated, we watched as Rodman clinched, and Rivers with a smile, almost of contempt, threw him off. Then Rodman, bellowing like an angry bull, made a head on rush for Rivers, who neatly sidestepped, letting his furious antagonist have it on the side of his head.

Even this didn't knock any sense into Rodman, and he was about to plunge again, when Wise, seeing a chance, said:

"Now, Brice!"

Springing in, I hooked my arm around Rivers' neck, and yanked him away from Rodman, now struggling, half spent, in Wise's grasp.

"Let up, Rivers!" I cried, sternly; "what do you mean?"

He glared at me, not sensing what I said, and then, Rodman, breaking loose, came at him madly, Rivers slithered out of my clutch and caught the other a smashing blow on the ear. This, landing just as Rodman was off his balance from his break away from Wise, spun him around and sent him down with a crash which knocked all the fight out of him, and he made but a half hearted attempt to rise.

Satisfied, Rivers turned to me, and then, with a half apologetic glance at Olive, murmured:

"Sorry! Couldn't help it, Miss Raynor. Brute!"

The last was addressed to his fallen foe, and was met by a vindictive glance, but no other retort.

Rodman, however, was pulling himself together and we were of one mind as to our next procedure, which was to get Olive Raynor away from that house.

"Beat it," Wise decreed; "you're a good one, Mr. Rivers! My hat's off to you. Now, if you're fit, and you look it, will you and Mr. Brice take Miss Raynor home, and I'll stay here and clear up this little disturbance. Hop along with them, Ziz; I'll join you all at the house as soon as I can."

The faithful taxi was waiting, and Rivers and I put the two girls in, and followed them. Rivers was very quiet and seemed preoccupied. He looked not at all like a conqueror, and I guessed that the fight had stirred some chord of remembrance, and he was now struggling with his lost memory. In silence we went most of the way home.

Before we reached the house, however, he shook off his reverie with an impatient gesture that said, as clearly as words could have done, that he had failed to catch the elusive thread that bound him to the past and that he had returned to the present.

Olive saw it, too, and putting out her hand, said, frankly:

"I owe you deep gratitude, Mr. Rivers. I suppose I was in no real danger, with you men there, but I must confess I was glad to have that wretch punished."

Her lovely face glowed with righteous indignation, and Zizi's pert little countenance showed deep satisfaction.

"You gave it to him, good and plenty, Mr. Rivers," she fairly crowed; "it was a treat to see you put it all over him! Now, you've knocked him out physically, Penny Wise will mop up the floor with him mentally and morally! What did he do to you, Miss Olive? Why did he make you say you were his girl?"

The look of agony returned to Olive's face, as if she had just recollected what the man had said to her.

"He threatened me," she said, slowly; "with an awful threat! I can't think about it! Oh, I don't know what to do! I can't tell it—I can't tell it to anybody—"

"Wait till you get home," I counseled her, and Rivers added, "And wait till Mr. Wise comes. He's the man you must tell, and he will advise you. But, I say, we're getting at things, eh, Brice? 'The Link' under arrest, Wise onto Rodman, and he won't let go of him, either, and Miss Raynor safe, —whew! I feel as if we should just forge ahead now!"

"Sure we will!" declared Zizi, her little face glowing with anticipation. "Never you mind. Miss Olive, dear; whatever that man threatened, Penny Wise will look after him."

"But—" began Olive, and then stopped, for we had reached her home.

"Oh, my darling child," exclaimed Mrs. Vail, as we went in, "where have you been? I've been nearly crazy!"

I think we all felt a sudden twinge of shame, for none of us had thought to relieve the poor lady's suspense as to Olive's fate! We ought to have telephoned, at least. But she was now smiling and happy at the safe return of her charge and eager to know all the details of the adventure.

Both Olive and Zizi went off with Mrs. Vail, who was chattering volubly, and I was left alone with Rivers.

"The fight,—on which let me congratulate you,—"stirred some old memory?" I said, inquiringly.

"For a few moments, yes;" he returned, looking deeply thoughtful. "But it was both vague and evanescent, I couldn't nail it. Oh!" and he made an impatient gesture, "it is maddening! I seem just on the edge of complete recollection,—and, then,—it's gone again, and my mind is a positive blank regarding it. But, it's no use worrying, Brice," and he spoke cheerfully, "I'm sure it will come, some day. Until then I shall be Case Rivers, and if I die under the name, I'll try, at least, not to disgrace it."

"You didn't disgrace it today," I said, heartily. "You put up a first class fight, and in a righteous cause."

"I couldn't stand it to see Miss Raynor bullied by that brute," he returned, simply, "and then, too, I felt a natural antagonism toward him on my own account. No," as I started to speak, "I know what you're going to say, and I don't think I knew him before I lost my memory. Maybe I did, but it wasn't that that startled me to thinking back. It was something else,—some other impression, that made me have a fraction of a reminiscence of something,—oh, I don't know what, but I'm going to take it as an omen of future good fortune."

CHAPTER 14: WHERE IS MANNING?

"YOU'RE to stay for dinner," a voice said, | speaking from the shadows at the other end of the long room.

As I looked toward it, Zizi's little white face gleamed between the portieres, and in another moment she slid through and was at my side.

"Miss Raynor says so, and Mrs. Vail adds her invitation. They're going to keep Penny Wise when he returns, and Miss Raynor—"

"Miss Raynor wants to thank Mr. Rivers for his good work," and Olive herself followed in Zizi's footsteps. She was smiling now, but her lips were tremulous and her eyes showed unshed tears.

"Nothing to thank me for," returned Case Rivers, quickly, "on the contrary, I want to apologize for such an exhibition of wrath before a lady. But I confess I lost all self control when I saw that brute intimidating you. If you absolve me of offense, I am thoroughly glad I did him up! And you do?"

"Indeed, yes!" and Olive's frank gaze was sincere but sad, too. "I was terribly frightened, —and,—I am still."

"Why?" cried Rivers, abruptly, and then added, "but I've no right to ask."

"Yes, you have," Olive assured him, "but—I've no right to tell you. Mr. Rodman holds a threat over my head, and—and—"

Just then Wise arrived, and Mrs. Vail came into the room with him.

Olive welcomed him gladly, and then, as dinner was announced, we all went to the dining room.

"No discussion of our momentous affairs while we eat," Wise commanded, and so we enjoyed the occasion as if it were a social affair.

The conversation was interesting, for Pennington Wise was a well informed man and a good raconteur; Rivers proved to be most entertaining and clever at repartee; and though Olive was very quiet, Mrs. Vail kept up an amusing chatter, and Zizi was her own elfin self and flung out bits of her odd talk at intervals.

We returned to the big library for coffee, and then, almost abruptly, Wise began to question Olive as to her adventure that afternoon.

"Mr. Rivers was quite right," he said, "in assuming the telephone call sent by Sadie Kent to her 'mother' was a trick. Mighty clever of you," he turned to Rivers, "and it led to the arrest of Rodman. The woman called Mrs. Kent is not Sadie's mother, but a companion in crime. For Sadie, 'The Link,' is a criminal and a deep one! But first, Miss Raynor, let us have your story."

"When I answered the telephone call," Olive began, "a man's voice said, rather brusquely, 'We have Amory Manning here. If you want to see him, come here at once.' I said,—of course, I was terribly excited,—'Where are you? who are you?'

The voice replied, 'Never mind all that. You have to make quick decision. If you want to see Manning, a taxi will call for you in five minutes. Tell nobody, or you will queer the whole game. Do you consent?' I may not give his exact words, but that was his general meaning. I had to think quickly; I did want to see Mr. Manning, and I feared no harm. So I said I agreed to all the stipulations, I would tell no one, and I would go in the taxicab that would come for me."

"But you told me," put in Mrs. Vail, who liked to feel her importance.

"Yes," went on Olive, "I felt I must leave some word, for I had an uneasy feeling that all was not right. If Amory Manning was there, why didn't he telephone himself? But, I reasoned, he might be, well—in fact, I thought he was,—held for ransom, and in that case I was ready and willing to pay it. So, I said nothing to Zizi, for I knew she would tell—"

"Wow! Yes!" came from Zizi's corner, where she sat on a low ottoman.

"And so, I went alone. The taxi was at the curb when I left this house. I got in, and was taken to the house in Washington Square. I felt no fear until, after Mrs. Kent admitted me, she showed me into a room where I found myself confronted by Mr. Rodman. Mrs. Kent remained with me, but I saw at once she was not friendly.

" ' Where is Mr. Manning?' I asked. Mr. Rodman only laughed rudely and said he hadn't the slightest idea. And then I knew it was all a trap,—but I didn't know why I was tricked there. And then," Olive paused, and a deep blush came over her face, but she shook her head and went bravely on, "then he tried to make love to me. I appealed to Mrs. Kent, but she only laughed scornfully at my distress. He said if I would marry him he would protect me from all suspicion of being implicated in—in the death of my guardian! Of course, that didn't scare me, and I told him I wasn't suspected now, by anybody. Then he dropped that line of argument and told me if I didn't marry him,—he would—oh, that part I can't tell!"

"Blackmail!" said Wise, looking at her intently.

"Yes," she replied, "and it was an awful threat! Then, he saw I was indignant and not to be intimidated—oh, I pretended to be much more courageous than I really was,—and he began to talk more politely and very seriously. He said, if I would call off Mr. Wise and make no further effort to run down my uncle's murderer, he would send me home safely, and molest me no further. I wouldn't agree to this; and then he grew ugly again, and lost his temper, and—oh, he talked dreadfully!" Olive shuddered at the recollection, and her lips quivered.

With quick sympathy, Zizi moved noiselessly from her place, and, kneeling at Olive's side, took her hand. With a grateful glance at the comforting little fingers caressing her own, Olive went on:

"He stormed and he threatened me, and that Kent woman joined in and said terrible things! And I was so frightened I couldn't pretend I wasn't any longer,—and I didn't know what to do! And then the bell rang, and Mrs. Kent went to the door, and as I looked hopeful,—I suppose, for I welcomed the thought of anybody's coming,—Mr. Rodman threw a handkerchief around my mouth and tied it behind my head. 'There, my lady,' he said, 'you won't scream for help quite as quickly as you planned to!' And I couldn't make a sound! Then, when I heard familiar voices,—Zizi's and Mr. Wise's, I knew I must make myself heard, and with a desperate effort, I got out a groan or wail for help, though that awful man stood over me with his hand raised to strike me!"

"You poor darling!" exclaimed Mrs. Vail, putting her arm round Olive, "it was fearful! Why, once I heard of a case like that—no, I read it in a book,—and the girl fainted!"

"Well, I didn't faint, but I almost collapsed from sheer fright lest I couldn't make a loud enough sound to be heard by you people."

"Oh, we were coming!" said Zizi, "I saw by the old hen's face she had you boxed up in there, and I was going to do some ground and lofty yelling myself, if Mr. Rivers hadn't smashed in the door just as he did."

"I couldn't hold back," said Rivers, "I gave way to a blind impulse,—and I'm glad I did!"

"I'm glad, too," and Olive gave him a grateful smile.

"But then," cried Zizi, "he made you say you were engaged to him "

"Yes," and Olive paled as with fear. "I can't tell about that—"

"You said you weren't, and then he whispered to you, and then you said you were," went on Zizi, remorselessly reviewing the scene.

"I know it,—but—oh, don't ask me! Perhaps, I'll tell— later,—if I have to,—but—I can't—I can't."

Olive's head drooped on Zizi's shoulder, and the eerie little voice said, "There, there,—don't talk any more now, Miss Olive, dear. Penny Wise, you carry on the conversation from this point."

"All right," said Wise, "I'll tell my story. George Rodman is in the hands of the police, but I doubt very much if they can prove anything on him. He's a sly proposition, and covers his tracks mighty well. Moreover, as to the murder of Mr. Gately, Rodman has a perfect alibi."

"Your First Lessons in Sleuthing always say, 'distrust the perfect alibi,'" murmured Zizi, without looking up from her occupation of smoothing Olive's softly banded hair.

"Yes,—manufactured ones. But in this case there seems to be no question. A Federal detective, who has had his eye on Rodman for some time, was in Rodman's office at the very time Mr. Gately was killed."

"But Mr. Rodman went down on the same elevator I did, soon after the shooting," I exclaimed.

"How soon after?"

"Less than half an hour. And Rodman got on at the seventh floor."

"That's all right, the Federal Office man knows that. They went down together from the tenth,—Rodman's floor,—to the seventh, and then after they looked after something there, Rodman went on down alone."

"All right," I said, for I knew that Wise and the Federal Detective were not being hoodwinked by any George Rodman!

"And here's the situation," Wise went on; "Sadie Kent is a German telegraph spy. She is called 'The Link,' because she has been an important link in the German spy system. A trusted employee and an expert operator of long experience, she has stolen information from hundreds of telegrams and turned it over to a man who transmitted it to Berlin by a secret avenue of communication. A telegram has been sent to Washington asking for a presidential warrant to hold her until the case can be investigated. She is also one large and emphatic wildcat! She bites and scratches with feline ferocity, and is under strong and careful restrictions."

"And she is the one," I said, "whose identity we learned from Jenny—and,—oh, yes, whose identity you guessed, Mr. Wise, from some cigarette stubs, and "

"Oh, I say," Wise interrupted me, shortly, "we must get the truth from her by quizzing, not by clews. We've arrested her, now, and—"

Olive stirred uneasily, and Zizi, after a quick, intelligent glance at Wise, which he answered by a nod, rose to her feet, and urged Olive to rise and go with her.

"You're all in, Miss Olive," she said, gently, "and I'm going to take you off to sleepy by. Tell the nice gentlemen good night, and come along with your Zizi zoo. Upsy diddy, now," and smilingly, Zizi persuaded Olive to go with her. "You come, too, Mrs. Vail," Zizi added, because, I noticed, of an almost imperceptible nod from Wise in the elder lady's direction. "We just simpully can't get along without you."

Pleased at the flattering necessity for her presence, Mrs. Vail went from the room with the two girls. "I'll be back," she called out to us, as she left the room.

"She won't," said Wise, decidedly, after the sound of footsteps died away, "Zizi'll look out for that. Now, Brice, I've important new information. I didn't want to divulge it before Miss Raynor, tonight, for she has had about all she can bear today. But it begins to look as if Sadie Kent sold her stolen telegrams to Rodman, and he—can't you guess?"

"No," I said, blankly, and Rivers said, "Tell us."

"Why, I believe he turned them over to Gately."

"Gately! Amos Gately mixed up in spy business! Man, you're crazy!"

"Crazy does it, then! Haven't we positive proof that Sadie Kent was in Gately's office the day he was killed?"

"How? I said, wonderingly. "Did she kill him?"

"Lord, no! But didn't I size her up from the hatpin? and didn't your girl trace the powder paper? and didn't we see cigarette stubs with the S.K. monogram,—in Mr. Gately's private office,—and his own cigar stubs there, too, as if she had been there in intimate chat!"

"Are you sure about the powder paper?" I cried, impressed by the realization of Norah's hand in the discovery.

"Yes; we know, at least, that she has bought them from that shop. You see, she has lots of money beside her salary from the telegraph company."

"Rather!" said Rivers, "if she's selling Government secrets!"

"Well," I said, after the whole disclosure began to sink into my brain, "if Sadie Kent sat around in Mr. Gately's office, smoking and chatting, with her hat off, and her powder papers in evidence, she was pretty friendly with him!"

"Of course she was," and Wise looked grave. "That's what I dread to tell Miss Raynor. For it implicates Amos Gately in some way; either he is mixed up in the spy racket,—or—Miss Kent was his friend—socially!"

"Oh, come now," I said, "don't let's say that sort of thing."

"But, my dear man, unpleasant though it be to assume an intimacy between the bank president and the handsome telegraph girl,—yet, isn't that preferable—to—"

"To brand him with the shameful suspicion of receiving spy secrets!" Rivers completed the sentence. "Yes, it is! The most disgraceful revelations of a liaison would be as nothing compared with the ignominy of spy work!"

"I know that," I hastened to explain myself, "but I can't connect either disgrace with Amos Gately! You didn't know him, Wise, and you, Rivers, didn't either. Nor did I know him personally,—but I did know,—and do know, that no breath of suspicion can be attached to Amos Gately's whole career! Why, he was a synonym for all that is best in finance, in politics, in society! I'm glad you didn't hint this before Olive Raynor! It would have crushed the poor child."

"She'll have to learn it sooner or later," and Wise shook his head. "There's no doubt about it in my mind. You see, 'The Link' usually took her news to Rodman and he secretly, and by means of the secret elevator, carried it to Gately who gave it over to the agents of the German Government."

"Do you know this?" asked Rivers.

"I couldn't get Rodman to admit it, but when I taxed him with something of the sort, he flew into such a rage that I'm sure I struck the truth."

"Where's Rodman now?"

"The Department of Justice has his case in hand. They'll look after him. But I don't see how we can connect him with the murder of Gately. I don't for a minute doubt he'd be quite capable of it, but he wasn't there at the time."

"Was Sadie Kent?" and Rivers frowned thoughtfully.

"Not at the time of the shooting. Brice, here, can testify to that."

"Not unless she was in hiding," I said, "and she wasn't, for I looked in the cupboards and all that. We seem to have proved Sadie there before the murderer was, but I don't suspect her of shooting Gately."

"Nor I," agreed Wise, "but it was unusual for her to go to Mr. Gately's office. It must be that she had grown more daring of late, and had some hold over Gately, so that she felt safe in going there."

"Can't they get all that out of Sadie?"

"She's a slippery sort. She pretends to speak frankly, but what she tells means little and is misleading."

"Where is she?"

"For the moment, down at Kenihvorth House. Detained there till they're sure of the persons working with her."

"She'll get away," said Rivers, "she ought to be in jail."

Now it was a strange thing, but this casual prophecy of Rivers' was fulfilled the very next day!

I was in my office, absorbedly conversing with Norah on the all engrossing subject of the Gately case, when Zizi dashed in.

"Alone I did it!" she exclaimed, and tossing the folds of her voluminous black cape over her shoulder, she folded her arms and assumed the attitude of Napoleon; scowling from under her heavy black brows, though her eyes were dancing.

"What have you done?" I asked, while Norah gazed enchanted at the dramatic little figure.

"Returned the missing 'Link' to her rightful owners!"

"What! Sadie?"

"The same. You know, Mr. Rivers said she'd break loose from that Whatchacallit House, and make trouble— also, which she done!"

"Tell us about it," I urged.

"That's what I'm here for. Mr. Wise sent me to tell you that,—and a lot of other messages. Well," and Zizi's black eyes snapped with satisfaction, "somebody called this morning to see Miss Raynor. And that somebody was none other than Sadie, 'The Link!' She sent up a different name, —I forget what, now,—and Miss Olive went down to see her. And she blackmailed Miss Olive good and plenty! You see, little Ziz was listening from behind a convenient portiere, and I heard it all. The whole idea was that if Miss Olive would quit all investigations, there would be no tales told. But if she kept up her detective work,—that is, if she kept Mr. Wise on the job, then revelations would be made about her guardian, Mr. Gately, that Sadie said would blast his name forever. Olive seemed to understand just what these revelations were, for she didn't ask, but she was scared to pieces, and was about ready to give in when I slid into the game. But,—before I joined the confab I called up Penny Wise on an upstairs telephone and invited him to come along hastily and bring a squad of policemen or something that could hold that 'Link'!

"Then I sauntered into the library, where the blackmailing session was being held, and I stood by. We had a war of words,—'The Link' and I,—but it didn't amount to much, for I was really only sparring for time till Penny Wise blew in. But I kept Miss Olive quiet, and I gave 'The Link' a song and dance that made her think some! I told her we knew she wrote the blackmailing letter to Miss Olive, signed 'A Friend,' and that she could be jailed for that! She wilted some, but carried it off with a high hand and soon Penny came and he had his little helpers along. They were in uniform, and they seemed mighty glad to get back their longlost friend and comrade, 'The Link'!"

"You clever little piece!" cried Norah, "to think of your getting that girl again, after she had broken loose! Didn't they appreciate it?"

"Yes," and Zizi smiled, modestly; "but it's all in the day's work. I don't care much about appreciation, except from Mr. Wise."

She had thrown off her long cloak, and her slender, lithe little figure leaned over the back of a chair. "But," she cried, twirling round suddenly to me, "I did do one more little trick! When they were taking Sadie away, I sidled up to her, and—oh, well, I s'pose I am a direct descendant of some light fingered gentry,—I picked her pocket!"

"What did you get?"

"Her pocket,—by which I mean her little leather hand bag, was never out of her hand for a minute! The way she hung on to it,—fairly clutched it,—made me think it contained something of interest to our side. So I just picked it on general principles. And I got the goods!"

"What?" cried Norah and I together.

"Some stuff in code, or in cipher,—I dunno just what it was. But Penny took it, and he's tickled to death to get it. Gibberish, of course, but he'll make it out. He's clever at ciphers, and it will likely be the final proof of 'The Link's' perfidy,—and,—" here Zizi's head drooped, and her eyes saddened,—" maybe it will show up Mr. Gately or—"

"Or whom?"

"You know! But," she brightened again, "here's something else yet! I'm on the job day and night, you know, and, if you inquire of me, I'd just as like spill it to you, that Miss Olive is a whole lot interested in that fascinating Mr. Rivers!"

"Oh, now," and Norah looked reproof at the saucy, smiling girl, "Miss Raynor is the fiancée of Amory Manning."

"Nixy! she told me she never was engaged to Mr. Manning. And when I tease her about Mr. Rivers, she blushes the loveliest pink you ever saw, and says, 'Oh, Zizi, don't be a silly!' but then she sits and waits for me to be a silly again!"

"But she hasn't seen Rivers half a dozen times," I said, smiling at Zizi's flight of imagination.

"That's nothing," she scoffed; "if ever there was a case of love at first sight, those two have got it! They don't really know it themselves yet, but if Amory Manning wants Miss Olive, he'd better come out of hiding and win her while the winning's good! And it's my belief he'd be too late now! And here's a straw to show which way that wind blows. The picture of Mr. Manning that was on Miss Olive's dresser has disappeared!"

"That may not mean anything," I said, for I didn't think it right to encourage Zizi's romancing.

"But I asked Miss Olive about it, and she hesitated and stammered, and never did say why she had put it away. And, too, you ought to see her eyes smile when she expects Mr. Rivers to call! He's making a lace pattern for her, and they have to discuss it a lot! Oho, oho!"

The mischievous little face took on a gentle, tender look and Norah smiled with the sympathy of one who, like all the rest of the world, loves a lover.

"But," I said, musingly, "none of this brings us any nearer to the discovery of Amos Gately's murderer, or to the discovery of Amory Manning,—which are the two ends and aims of our present existence."

"Did it ever occur to you, Mr. Brice,"—Zizi's face grew very serious,—" that those two quests will lead you to the same man?"

I looked at her,—stunned to silence. Then, as suddenly shocked into speech, "No!" I fairly shouted, "it never did!"

CHAPTER 15: WISE'S PIPE DREAM

THE mystery was a baffling one. I learned from Pennington Wise that he had a pipe dream that Amory Manning had killed Amos Gately.

But, save for the faithful Zizi, he could find no one to share his suspicion. It was too absurd. In the first place, had Manning done the deed, he never would have hung around the scene of the crime as he did, for nearly an hour. I remembered perfectly his demeanor and expression, as I saw him, with Olive Raynor that afternoon. He was deeply concerned, greatly shocked, and most considerate and thoughtful of Olive, but there was no shadow of guilt on his fine, strong face.

I had looked at him closely both during the excitement of the tragedy itself, and later, as we were in the street car, and I noted his grave, serious countenance, but though he seemed puzzled and anxious, there was no mark of Cain on his brow.

I told Wise this, and he listened, duly impressed, but, as he finally owned up, he saw no other way to look.

"It wasn't Rodman," he asserted; "that chap is a traitor and a spy, but he's no murderer. And, too, he was in cahoots with Gately, and the last thing he wanted was to lose his patron. It wasn't Sadie, of course; she too, wanted Gately alive, not dead. I know the unwillingness of Olive's guardian to listen to Manning's suit, seems a slight motive,—yet where can we find a suspect with a stronger one?"

"We haven't as yet," I returned, "but there must be people implicated in that spy business,—if that's a true bill against Gately—"

"Oh, it's a true bill, all right. Amos Gately was a wolf in sheep's clothing! Miss Raynor will have to know it sooner or later. She really knows it now, but she won't let herself believe it."

"What about that paper Zizi took from Sadie Kent?"

"That's what I'm working on. Meet me this afternoon at the Raynor house, and I may be able to tell you."

The big, cheerful library at Olive's house had come to be our general meeting place of an afternoon. I usually dropped in there about four o'clock, and was pretty sure to find Wise or Rivers or both there. Zizi was a whole vaudeville show herself, and Olive was always cordial and hospitable. Mrs. Vail, too, was a gentle old lady, and I had grown to like her.

So I went, as Wise suggested, and found him poring over the mysterious paper.

Looking at it for the first time, I saw merely a lot of letters, pen written, and arranged in long rows that ran clear across the sheet.

There were perhaps twenty rows or so, and each row held about thirty letters. They were carefully aligned and evenly spaced, and, without doubt, contained a hidden message.

"I've unraveled a lot of cryptograms in my time," said Wise, "but this isn't a cryptogram. I mean it isn't in cipher code,—there's some other way of getting at it."

We all studied it. Olive, Zizi, Wise, and I bent our heads over the table where it lay, while Mrs. Vail looked on from a little distance, and babbled about some man she knew once, who could solve secret writings.

Suddenly Zizi jumped up, and running around the table, viewed the paper from the other side.

She cocked her funny little head sidewise, and then wagged it knowingly as she took a few steps further and looked at the paper from another angle. All round the table she went, and finally, with a murmur of apology, took up the paper and held it laterally in front of her eager eyes.

"Whee!" she crowed in an ecstasy of satisfaction; "I've got it! You have to have a pattern to read it by."

"A pattern!" I repeated, blankly.

"Yep! A paper with holes in it,—a key paper."

"Oh!" and Wise looked as if a light had burst upon him. "That's it, Ziz! You're the wonderchild, after all! Stoo-pid! Stoo-pid!" and he beat his forehead in self abasement. "And, oh! I say, Brice, what did you tell me once about Swiss cheese?"

"Swiss cheese?"

"Yes; don't you remember? A carriage call check— with holes in it."

"Oh, that thing. Yes; it was on Mr. Gately's desk,— Hudson, the foxy detective, took it."

"Can we get it?"

"Of course, by sending for it."

"I'll go!" cried Zizi; "where? Headquarters?" and she was already flinging on her coat.

"Let her go," said Wise, giving the girl a quick, appreciative glance. "She'll beat any other messenger, and she'll find it."

We heard Zizi's imperative little voice demanding a cab from the telephone, and a bit later heard the street door close behind her.

"You see," and Wise explained it to us, "Zizi noticed,— and then I did,—these letters. At first glance they seem to be perfectly regular, but noted closely there are some, here and there, that are a microscopic fraction of space nearer or farther away from others. And that shows what kind of a cipher it is. We may be mistaken about the carriage check, but I truly believe when we get it we can read the message this paper carries. We certainly can't without it."

This was so true that we laid the paper aside until the return of our winged Mercury.

She came soon, and waved triumphantly the perforated card she had gone in quest of.

"Here you are!" she cried; "let me try it as a reward for getting it."

"All right, go to it," said Wise, and flinging off her cape, Zizi bent over the puzzle.

"It's it! It's it!" she cried, exultantly. "See, oh, Wise One!"

The detective took the paper and the card.

"You see," he said, generously sharing the first sight of the solution with us, "this card has seven holes, at irregular distances. By placing it in the right position on this solid bank of letters, certain ones show through the holes, and these,—I hope,— will spell the message."

And it did. After re-adjusting the key card several times, Wise finally got it right, and the letters that could be seen through the holes in this card, as he moved it along, spelled coherent words and sentences. Of course, the other letters were not to be used.

He read the message aloud, and as we suspected, it was information concerning the shipment of munitions, and told of certain sailing dates.

"Spy work of the cleverest type," Wise exclaimed; "you see, 'The Link' got her information from stolen telegrams, and recorded it in this way, so it would be unintelligible to anyone not having this card,—or a duplicate of it."

I scrutinized with interest the letters as they showed clearly through the little round holes.

"The information is of no particular value now," Wise said; "it refers to yesterday as the sailing date. The point is, that this card,—this key card, was found on—"

He paused: a glance at Olive's agonized face stopped the words he would have uttered. But we all knew. That card, found on Amos Gately's desk, or in his desk drawer, proved that he was implicated in the interception of these messages, that he was guilty of treason to his country!

Wise tried to help matters by saying, hastily, "Perhaps it was a plant! Perhaps this card was put where it was found by some sly scoundrel for the purpose of misleading—"

"Don't!" said Olive, faintly; "you are kind, Mr. Wise, but you are saying that merely to give me a ray of comfort and hope. You know better. You believe,—and I fear I must believe,—my guardian was involved in some wrong, some grave wrong—and—"

She broke down utterly and sobbed in Zizi's arms which were opened to receive her.

Feeling that our further stay was an intrusion, Rivers and I took leave, and Wise came along with us. We three went down to my rooms, and continued our confab without the embarrassment of Olive's presence.

"It's clearing itself up pretty quickly in some respects," Wise said as he settled himself with a cigar, and passed the box to Rivers. "I'm not so surprised as some at Gately's perfidy. It seems the Government has been onto him for some time,—at least, they suspected him, and were secretly investigating his private affairs. That Sadie person—"

"By the way, Wise," I interrupted him, "you sized her up perfectly! Did you ever hear about that, Rivers? Mr. Wise saw only the girl's hatpin, and from it he drew an exact portrait of 'The Link' herself. How did you do it, Wise? Tell us the details."

"Like all those deductions it was simpler than it sounded," the detective said, smiling. "You see, Mr. Rivers, the head of the pin was a big good-looking scarab. I don't know yet whether it was a real one, but if not it was a first class imitation. This argued a person of education and taste. The average young woman doesn't lean toward scarabs. Then, there was a short bit of a human hair caught in the setting. This was black, rather coarse, and strong, denoting a healthy, buxom brunette. Hair is a clear indication of physical appearance, as a rule. That's how I know you aren't Amory Manning," he broke off suddenly and looked at Case Rivers. "I've had his description from Miss Raynor and from Brice, here, and they agree that Manning had dark, heavy hair, rather—footballish type. Yours is light, fine, and a little scant. And you have all the characteristics that belong to it. Oh, yes, I admit I've been trying to fasten Manning's identity on you, but without success."

"Don't apologize," laughed Rivers, "I've been trying to connect up with the missing Manning myself, but I can't work it. So, I'm out for the reward for finding that elusive individual. But I fear he's gone beyond recall."

"By the way," Wise put in, "I've found out who offers the reward. And, if you please, it's none other than the United States Government!"

"Why?" Rivers asked, interestedly.

"Well, it seems Manning is,—or was,—a Secret Service man and he was set on the trail of Amos Gately. He worked secretly, of course, and—"

"And he was kidnaped by Gately's friends!" I cried; "by some of Rodman's underlings, and put out of the way! I don't believe Manning is alive!"

"Go on about the hatpin, Mr. Wise, won't you?" urged Rivers. "I think I'm going to grow up to be a detective and I'm taking notes."

"Well," said Wise, good humoredly, "as I remember it, I mentioned the lady's good teeth. This, because the prints on the rather soft gold of the pin were straight and even."

"You said she was proud of them," I put in.

"A glittering generality," and Wise laughed. "Aren't all girls proud of good teeth? Also, I assumed she had rather flashy tastes, for the scarab, large, and of a bright greenish blue color, was not a quiet affair. A strong perfume clung to it, which also indicated a certain lack of refinement."

"And you said untidy habits," I reminded him.

"Because the pin was bent to a real crookedness. Also, it had been broken and mended. The break proving probable carelessness, and the mending seemed to me to show that she was sentimentally fond of it, for it was skilfully mended and the cost of that would have bought a new one, I should judge. I assumed her to be somewhat intellectual to care so much for a scarab, and I deduced her fairly well off to own and to care for the rather valuable trinket. None of these deductions amounted to much by itself, but the combination helped us to find a way to look for the owner. Of course, the cigarette stubs and the powder paper helped, too. In fact, Miss Kent left pretty strong evidences of her call on Mr. Gately. But,— she didn't kill him. Now, who did? We are learning lots of things, but not one shred of evidence have we yet found against any individual as the actual murderer."

"No," I agreed. "You see, the shadow of the head that I saw on the glass door couldn't have been Rodman's."

"And so it may have been anybody's. I mean, it shows that heads look pretty much alike, when merely shadowed on a thick, waved glass."

"Yes," I mused, "it may have been anybody's. But whose? It seems as if we ought to have a suspect by this time."

"I'll get you a suspect," spoke up Case Rivers. "I'm going into this thing for all I'm worth. The way lies through the Rodman crowd. 'The Link' sold her information to Rodman and he took it to Gately, but of late, 'The Link' became more bold and went straight to Gately herself. Now, there must be others concerned, and an interview with Miss Kent would give us an inkling of who they are. She's lost some of her bravado, by this time, I've no doubt, and I'm going to chase her up. Then, too, I want to go to Mr. Gately's office. I've never been there yet! Don't think, Wise, that I'm butting in on your game, but sometimes two heads are better than one, if one is a nameless wanderer on the face of the earth."

"All right, Rivers," and Wise nodded genially, "go in and win. We're together on this matter. And when it's over, I'm going to take up your case, and see just how, when, and where you fell through the earth."

"I wish you would," and Rivers looked earnestly at the detective, "for I see that trip every night in my dreams. I see myself falling through—oh, I won't bore you with that same old story!"

"It doesn't bore me, but just now we'll put all our energies on the present puzzle. We must get Gately's murderer, and then we must get Amory Manning."

"Zizi says—"I began.

"I know she does," returned Wise, looking thoughtful. "Zizi says Manning is the murderer. But the kid has no reason to say it but a hunch. She's a witch though for hunches, and I keep her idea in mind."

"No," and Rivers spoke positively, "it doesn't seem to me that Manning is the murderer. If he was in the Secret Service, he may be purposely in hiding now, for some reason entirely unconnected with Amos Gately's murder."

"Very likely," assented Wise. "Only, as I say, I often remember Zizi's notions because they so often pan out correct."

"She's a marvel, that child," said Rivers; "where'd you get her?"

"She's my model. In civilian life, I'm by way of being an artist, you know. I sketch her over and over, but never have I successfully caught her smile. She's a witch child, a sprite."

"Yes; she seems gypsy born. But clever! And of a charm."

"All that," agreed Wise. "And a good little thing. Devoted to me, like a faithful dog, and yet, absolutely impersonal. Oh, I couldn't get along at all without Ziz."

And almost as he spoke the door opened and Zizi came gliding in. Her mode of entering a room was one of her individual characteristics. She slid in softly and unobtrusively, yet one was at once aware of her. It seemed to electrify the atmosphere, and the place was brighter and more vital in feeling. She moved across the room as quietly as a shadow, she said no word, yet her whole presence spoke.

"Hello, Ziz," and Wise smiled at her. "Watcha want?"

"Mr. Rivers," she replied, flashing her black eyes at him. "Miss Olive sent me. And she wants the other crystal."

"A new mystery?" and Wise laughed. "I can't see through the other crystal! Has it to do with a pair of glasses?"

"No," and Rivers took out a pocket book, from which he extracted some flimsy paper. These proved to be tracings of snow crystals similar to those I had seen him drawing while he was still in the hospital.

"How lovely!" Zizi exclaimed, as she took the traced patterns. "You see," and she showed them to Wise, "Miss Olive is making lace work,—and Mr. Rivers makes her these patterns. Aren't they exquisite?"

They were. They were forms of snow crystals, than which there is nothing more beautiful, and Rivers had adapted and combined them into a delicate lace like pattern, which Olive was to copy with linen threads, or whatever women use to make lace out of.

"I was going to take them round," Rivers said; "I hope the delay hasn't bothered Miss Raynor."

"Oh, no," Zizi assured him, "but she is impatient to see this new design and couldn't wait. So I offered to run down for it. I knew you were here."

"But I'm just going up to Miss Raynor's," Rivers spoke as if disappointed, "and the patterns are my only excuse for a call! So, if you please, Miss Zizi, I'll take them to the impatient lady, and I'll go at once."

"I think she's gone out, Mr. Rivers, she was about to go as I left. If you telephone you'll likely catch her."

Quite unembarrassed at our knowing smiles, Rivers took up my desk telephone and called Olive's number. While waiting for the response he picked up a pencil from my pen tray, and idly drew a snow crystal on the big desk blotter.

I watched him, for his skill fascinated me. He drew the dainty six sided figure with the accuracy of a designer. The tiny fronds, all six alike, made a lovely hexagonal form as it grew beneath his fingers.

He was apparently unconscious of what he was doing, and drew without thinking, for he spoke to us several times while waiting for the desired connection.

At last Olive answered him, and he dropped the pencil and talked to her. In a wheedlesome mood, he persuaded her to defer her proposed errand until he could join her and he would accompany her. The kindly familiarity with which he carried on the conversation and the jaunty assurance he showed that she would accede to his request proved to us, listeners perforce, that there was good comradeship between them.

Rivers hung up the receiver, and turned to me with a boyish smile. "I'm going now," he said, "Miss Raynor is waiting for me. I'll see you again, tonight, Brice." And with a general nod of farewell he went off.

Zizi sat staring at my desk.

The strange child was thinking of something,—more, she had made a discovery, or had sensed some new information.

She leaned over the desk, her outstretched hands resting on the big blotter and her black eyes wide with an expression of surprised fear.

"Look!" she cried; "look!"

But her slender finger pointed only to the snow crystal that Rivers had drawn. It was a graceful figure, not quite finished, but a delicate tracery of one of the myriad forms that snow crystals show. How often I had looked at the lovely things as they rested for a moment on my dark coat sleeve when I was out in a snowstorm. And after seeing Rivers draw them so skilfully, several times, they had taken on a new interest to me. But what had so moved Zizi I could not imagine. It was as if the little drawing were fraught with some dreadful significance of which I knew nothing.

Nor was Pennington Wise any more aware than I of the girl's meaning.

He smiled quizzically, and said, "Well, Zizi, girl, what's hypnotizing you? That drawing of Rivers'?"

"Yes," and Zizi turned her big black eyes from my face to Wise's, and gave a queer little sigh.

"Out with it, girlie," urged Wise. "Tell your old Penny Wise what's the matter."

"Will you do what I want?" she asked, her voice tense and thrilled with strong feeling.

"Yes; to the limit."

"Then look at that thing! That snow crystal!"

"Yes, I've looked," and after a moment's close scrutiny Wise turned his eyes again to the eerie face, so vividly emotional, so white with that unnamed fear.

"You look, too, Mr. Brice," and I did.

"Note the design," Zizi went on, "see just how the fronds are marked. Isn't it funny how people always draw or scribble while they're waiting to get a telephone call?"

"Oh, come now, Ziz," and Penny Wise patted her arm, "you're putting up a game on us. We know Rivers draws these things beautifully. Why act as if you never knew it before?"

"Come with me," and Zizi rose and began to put her long black cloak round her, shivering with excitement as she did so. "You come, too, Mr. Brice."

We obeyed the strange child, for I remembered how Pennington Wise respected what he called her "hunches," and before going downstairs she directed that I call a taxicab.

In the cab she said nothing, having already bade us go to Amos Gately's office, and arrange to get into the rooms.

And then, when we were there, when I had obtained the keys from the bank people and had entered the dim, quiet rooms, Zizi went straight to the middle room, straight to Amos Gately's desk, and lifting the telephone from where it stood on the big desk blotter, she disclosed the exact counterpart of the snow crystal we had seen drawn at my desk by Case Rivers!

CHAPTER 16: THE SNOWFLAKE

I LOOKED at the design with interest, but without at first grasping its true significance.

Pennington Wise looked at it aghast. "Where did it come from?" he exclaimed.

"It's always been there," said Zizi. "I mean, I saw it there one day when I was in this room with Mr. Hudson, I—I—"

"Didn't know you'd ever been here, Ziz," and Wise smiled at the earnest little face.

"Yep, I was; and I happened to move the telephone, and under it was that drawing. I didn't think anything about it, as evidence, but I looked at it 'cause it was so pretty. And I put the telephone back over it again."

"But I searched this room," and Wise looked mystified.

"You probably didn't lift the telephone, then," Zizi returned, shaking her elfin head, while a deep sorrow showed in her black eyes.

"I don't believe I did," Wise mused, thinking back. "I did pick up most of the desk fittings to examine them but I suppose I didn't take hold of the telephone at all."

"'Course not!" Zizi was always ready to defend Wise's actions. "How could you know there was a picture under it? But, oh, Penny, what does it mean?"

"Wait,—let's get at it carefully. On the face of it, it would seem as if Case Rivers must have drawn this figure of a snow crystal. Everybody has some peculiar habit, and especially, lots of people have a habit of drawing some particular thing when waiting at a telephone.

"I've asked half a dozen men of late, and every one says he scribbles words or draws some crude combination of lines. But each one says he always does the same thing, whatever it may be. Now, I imagine, very few men draw snow crystals,—and fewer still, draw them with this degree of perfection. Again, granting they did, would any other individual draw this identical design, with this accuracy of drawing, that Case Rivers drew on the desk blotter at your house, Brice?"

"I should say it would be impossible that anyone else could have done it," I replied, honestly, though I began to see where our investigation was leading us.

"It is impossible," declared Wise. "Two men might draw snow crystals, but they would not both choose this particular one."

"It's exactly the same," Zizi murmured, "for I brought Mr. Brice's with me: here it is."

Calmly the girl took from her little hand bag a piece torn from my desk blotter. It held the drawing done by Rivers while he was waiting for his telephone call and it was the precise duplicate of the figure drawn on the blotter of Amos Gately's mahogany desk.

"The same pencil—or, rather, the same hand drew those two," Wise said, positively, and I could not contradict this.

Snow crystals are said by scientists to show hundreds of different shapes, and almost any illustrated dictionary or text book of natural science shows several specimens. This one we were looking at was of simple but beautiful design and I felt sure Rivers had copied it from some picture as one can rarely keep a real snowflake long enough to copy its form.

Anyway it was stretching the law of coincidence a little too far to believe that two men would idly draw the same form on a desk blotter while telephoning.

Of course, this sketch on Amos Gately's desk need not have been made while the artist's other hand held the telephone receiver, but its juxtaposition to the instrument indicated that it was.

"Of course, Mr. Rivers drew this," Zizi declared, her little head bobbing as she turned her black eyes from one of us to the other.

She wore a small turban made entirely of red feathers,—soft breast feathers of some tropical bird, I suppose. The hat set jauntily on her sleek black hair, and the motions of her head were so quick and birdlike, that she gave me a fleeting remembrance of the human birds I saw in the play of Chantecler.

"Of course he did," assented Wise, very gravely; "and now we must go on. Granting, for the moment, that Case Rivers,—as we call him,—drew this little sketch, he must have been in this office the day of Amos Gately's murder. For I've been told that the blotter on this desk was changed every day, and any marks or blots now on it were therefore made on that day. If he did it, then,—or, rather, when he did it, he was telephoning to somebody—"

"Well," put in Zizi, "perhaps he was just sitting here, talking to Mr. Gately. Maybe, he might draw those things when he just sits idly as well as when he telephones."

"Yes; you're right. Well, at any rate, he must have been sitting here, opposite Mr. Gately, on that very day. And I opine he was telephoning, but that makes no difference. Now, if he was here, in this office, on that day,—what was he here for, and who is he?"

"He is the murderer," said Zizi, but she spoke as if she were a machine. The words seemed to come from her lips without her own volition; her voice was wooden, mechanical, and her eyes had a faraway, vacant gaze. "I don't know who he is, but he is the man who shot Mr. Gately."

"Oh, come, now, Ziz," Wise shook her gently, "wake up! Don't jump at conclusions. He may be the most innocent man in New York He may have been in here calling on Gately early in the day, and his errand may have been of the most casual sort. He may have had cause to telephone, and as he sat waiting for his call, he sketched the snowflake pattern, which is his habit when waiting. But that he was here that day is a positive fact,—to my mind. Now, it's for us to find out what he was here for, and who he is. I don't favor going to him and asking him pointblank. That peculiar phase of amnesia from which he is suffering is a precarious matter to deal with. A sudden shock might bring back his memory,—or, it might—"

"Addle his brain!" completed Zizi. "All right, oh, Most Wise Guy! But when you do find out the truth, it will be that Case Rivers in his right mind and in his own proper person killed Mr. Gately."

"Hush up, Ziz! If you have such a fearful hunch keep it to yourself. I'm not going to believe that, unless I have to! It has always been my conviction that Rivers is,—or was, a worthwhile man. I feel sure he was of importance in some line,—some big line. Moreover, I believe his yarn about falling through the earth."

"You do!" I cried, in amazement. "You stand for that! You believe he fell into the globe at Canada,—or some Northern country, and fell out again in New York City?"

"Not quite that," and Wise smiled. "But I believe he had some mighty strange experience, of which his tale is a pretty fair description, if not entirely the literal truth."

"Such as?"

"Why, suppose he fell down a mine shaft in Canada. Suppose that knocked out his memory. Then suppose he was rescued and sent to New York for treatment, say, at some private hospital or sanitarium. Then suppose he escaped, and, still loony, threw himself into the East River—oh, I don't know—only, there are lots of ways that he could have that notion about his fall through the earth, and have something real to base it on."

"Gammon and spinach!" I remarked, my patience exhausted; "the man had a blow or a fall or something that jarred his memory, but his 'falling through the earth' idea is a hallucination, pure and simple. However, that doesn't matter. Now we must follow this new trail, and see if we can get a line on his personality. He can't tell us what he was here for,—if he doesn't remember that he was here."

"Perhaps he does remember," Wise spoke musingly.

"Nixy!" and Zizi's saucy head nodded positively; "Mr. Rivers is sincere now, whatever he was before. He doesn't remember shooting Mr. Gately—"

"Stop that, Zizi!" Wise spoke more sharply than I had ever heard him. "I forbid you to assume that Rivers is the murderer,—you are absurd!"

"But I've got a hunch—" Zizi's black eyes stared fixedly at Wise, and—"

"Keep your hunch to yourself! I told you that before! Now, hush up."

Not at all abashed, Zizi made a most wicked little moue at him, but she said no more just then.

"We have a new direction in which to look, though," Wise went on, "and we must get about it. You remember, we found a hatpin here that led us to Sadie, 'The Link,' as straight as a signboard could have done."

"Yes," scoffed Zizi, "with the help of Norah and her powder paper, and Jenny and her tattle tongue!"

"All right," Wise was unperturbed; "we got her all the same. Now, perhaps the Man Who Fell Through the Earth also left some indicative clews. Let's look round."

"He couldn't leave anything more indicative than the drawing on the blotter," persisted Zizi." He drew on Mr. Brice's blotter today and he drew on this blotter of Mr. Gaiety's the day Mr. Gately was killed. That much is certain."

"So it is, Zizi," agreed Wise; "but nothing further is certain as yet. But we may find something more."

As he talked the detective rummaged in the desk drawers. He pulled out the packet of papers that had interested him before.

"I'd like to read these," he said; "you see, they're dated in chronological order, and they must mean something."

"It's where they come from," said Zizi, with an air of wisdom; "you see, Waldorf means a certain message in their code book, and St. Regis means another; Biltmore paper means another, and so on."

"Right you are, as usual," Wise said, so approvingly that Zizi smiled all over her queer little countenance.

"Part of 'The Link's' spy business," she went on, and I cried out in denial.

"Oh, come off, Mr. Brice," she said, "you may as well admit, first as last, that you know Mr. Gately was mixed up in this spy racket. I don't know yet just how deeply or how knowingly—"

"You mean," I caught at the straw, "that he was a go between, but didn't know it?"

"I thought that at first," said Wise, "I hoped it was so. That, of course, would argue that he was infatuated with Sadie and she wound him round her finger and used him to further her schemes, while he himself was innocent. But the theory, though a pretty one, won't work. Gately wasn't quite gullible enough for that, and, too, he is more deeply concerned in it all than we know."

"Yes," I agreed; "these letters,—I mean, these blank sheets,—were sent to him by mail. One came the day after he died."

"I know it. And, as Zizi says, they mean something definite in accordance with a prepared code.   For instance, a sheet of Hotel Gotham paper, dated December tenth, might mean that a certain transport, indicated in the code book by that hotel, was to sail on that date."

"That's a simple, child's play explanation," said Zizi,— "but it may be the right one."

"Certainly," Wise assented, "there may be other explanations and more complicated ones. But it doesn't matter now. The receipt of these letters,—blank letters,— was of secret value to Gately, and proves him to have been pretty deeply mixed up in it all."

"But what about Mr. Rivers?" spoke up Zizi; "where does he come in?"

"It looks black," Wise declared. "He was here that day secretly. That is, he didn't come in at Jenny's door. She doesn't recognize him, I asked her. Therefore, he came in by one of these other doors, or up in the secret elevator. In either case, he didn't want his visit known. So he is a wrong doer, with Gately, and—probably, with Rodman. They're all tarred with the same brush. The trail of the spy serpent is over them all."

"No!" cried Zizi, and her face was stormy, "my nice Mr. Rivers isn't any spy! He hasn't anything to do with that spy matter!"

"Why!" I exclaimed; "you said he was the murderer!"

"Well, I'd rather be a murderer than a spy!" Her eyes snapped and her whole thin little body quivered with indignation. "A murder is a decent crime compared to spy work! Oh, my nice Mr. Rivers!"

She broke down and cried convulsively.

"Let her alone," said Wise, not unkindly, after a brief glance at the shaking little figure. "She's always better for a crying spell. It clears her atmosphere. Now, Brice, let's get busy. As Zizi says, you must admit that there's no doubt that Amos Gately was pretty deeply into the game. Even if he was unduly friendly with Sadie Kent, it was indubitably through and because of their dealings together in the stolen telegram business. The way I see it is that Sadie sold her intercepted messages to the highest bidder. This was George Rodman, but above him was Amos Gately. Oh, don't look so incredulous. It isn't the first time a bank president has gone wrong on the side. Gately never was unfaithful to his office, he never misappropriated funds or anything of that sort, but for some reason or other, whether money gain, or hope of other reward, he did betray his country."

I couldn't deny it,—or, rather, I could deny it, but only because of my still unshattered faith in Amos Gately. I could bring no proof of my denial.

"But," I said, musingly, "we haven't yet proved Gately mixed up in—"

"What!" cried Wise; "isn't this enough proof? These blank letters, for that's what they are,—the proved visit here of Sadie, 'The Link,' and the fact that Gately was shot,—by someone,—with no known reason,—all that goes to show that the murderer had some secret motive, some unknown cause for getting Gately out of the way."

"I see it, as you put it," I said, "but I will not believe Amos Gately a spy,—or conniving at spy business until I have to. I shall continue to believe he was a tool—an innocent tool—of the Rodman and Sadie Kent combination."

"All right, Brice, keep your faith as long as you can, but, I tell you, you'll soon have to admit that I'm right. Gately, as we all know, was a peculiar man. He had few friends, he had little or no social life, and he did have secret callers and a secret mode of entrance and exit from his offices. All this shows something to hide,—it is unexplainable for a man who has nothing to conceal."

"All right, Wise," I said, finally, "I suppose you are right. But still we must continue our search for the murderer. We don't seem to progress much in that matter."

"Not yet, but soon," Wise said, optimistically; "the ax is laid at the root of the tree—we are on the right track—"

"Meaning Case Rivers?" I cried, in alarm.

"Meaning Case Rivers,—perhaps," he returned. "I'm not as sure as Zizi is that the evidence points to him as the murderer, but we must conclude that he was in this room the day of the murder,—and what else could he have been here for?"

"What else?" I stormed. "Dozens of things! Hundreds of things! Why, man alive, every person who set foot in this room on that day didn't necessarily kill Amos Gately!"

"Every person who set foot in this room on that day is his potential murderer," Wise returned, calmly. "Every person must be suspected,—or, at least, investigated."

"Well," I said, after realizing that he spoke truly, "you investigate the question of Rivers' visit here that day. I don't want to do that. But I'm going down to Headquarters now, and perhaps I'll dig up something of importance."

And I did. A visit to the Chief told me the interesting tale of the further discoveries of Sadie Kent's industries. It seems the Federal agents had found a complete and powerful wireless station in a cottage at Southeast Beach, a fairly popular summer resort. The cottage was seemingly untenanted, but some unexplained wires which ran along the rafters of an adjoining house led to the discovery of the auxiliary wireless station.

Experts had broken into the locked house and had found a cleverly concealed keyboard of a wireless apparatus. Further search had disclosed the whole thing, and, moreover, had brought out the fact, that the adjoining cottage was occupied by two apparently innocent old people, who were really in the employ of Sadie Kent.

"The Link" was a person of importance, and though she passed for a mere telegraph operator, she was one of the most important links in the German spy system in the United States.

In the room where the wireless apparatus was found there were also quantites of letter paper from the various hotels of New York City.

These sheets, abstracted from the writing rooms of the hotels, were the code system used in forwarding the stolen intelligence.

It all hung together, and the bunch of those hotel papers found in Gately's desk, and especially the fact that one reached his address the day after his demise proved, beyond all doubt, his implication in the despicable business.

Now, I thought, to what extent or in what way was Case Rivers concerned? Surely the man had been in

Gately's office on that fatal day. I had no idea that he had killed the banker,—that was only Zizi's foolishness,—but he had certainly been there.

It came to me suddenly that if Rivers could be taken again to the Gately offices, the rooms, the associations, might possibly bring back his lost memory, and let him reinstate himself in his real personality. To be sure, this might prove him the murderer, but if so, it would be only the course of justice; and, on the other hand, if it explained his innocent or casual call on Gately that, too, was what the man deserved.

And so I went at once to see Rivers. I found him in his rooms, the ones he had taken while he was to assist Wise in his work, and he greeted me cordially.

"The plot thickens," he said as I told him of Sadie's wireless station. "I knew that girl was a sly one. She's one of the most important people in the big spy web. She's one of their spyders, who spin a pretty web and attract gullible flies. Amos Gately fell for her charms,—you know, Brice, she is a siren,—and somehow she lured him into the web she so deftly spun. To my mind, Gately was a good, upright citizen, who fell for a woman's wiles. I'm not sure about this, it may be he was mixed up in spy work before Sadie came on the scene,—but I'm certain she was accessory before, during, or after the fact."

"Accessory to his murder?" I asked.

"Not necessarily; but strongly accessory to his wrongdoing in the matter of treason. I think she, for a time, worked Gately through Rodman, but, latterly, she grew bolder or found she could do more by personal visits and she came and went by the secret elevator, pretty much as she chose."

"I hate to have Miss Raynor know this," I said with a covert glance at Rivers, to see how he took the remark.

"So do I," he said, as frankly as a boy; "I may as well tell you, Brice, that I love that girl. She is, to me, the very crown of womanhood. I have worshiped her from the first moment I saw her. But, understand, I have no hopes,—no aspirations. I shall never offer my hand and heart to any woman while I have no name to offer. And I shall never have a name. If I haven't yet discovered my own identity I never can. No, I'm no pessimist, and I know that some time some sudden shock might restore my memory all in a minute, yet I can't bank on such a possibility. I've talked this over with Rankin,—he's the doctor who's following up my case,—time and again. He says that a sudden and very forcible shock is needed to restore my memory, and that it may come and—it may not. He says it can't be forced or brought about knowingly,—it will have to be a coincidence,—a happening that will jar the inert cells of my brain—or, something like that,—I don't remember the scientific terms."

Rivers passed his hand wearily across his forehead.

I was in a quandary. I had gone to see the man with full purpose of luring him to Gately's office and confronting him with the sketched snowflake on the blotting pad. Now, since he had confided to me his love for Olive Raynor, I shrank from doing anything that might prove him to be Amos Gately's murderer. For I was fond of Miss Raynor, in a deeply respectful and unpresumptuous fashion. And I had noticed several things of late that made me feel pretty sure that her friendship for Rivers was true and deep, if indeed it were not something more than friendship. This, to be sure, would argue but a fickle loyalty to the memory of Amory Manning, but as Norah and I agreed, when talking it over, Miss Raynor had never shown any desperate grief at Manning's disappearance,—at least, not more than the loss of a casual friend might arouse.

But I knew where my duty lay. And so I said, "Rivers, I wish you'd go round to Mr. Gately's office with me. Don't you think that if you were there,—and you never have been,—you might chance upon some clew that has escaped the notice of Wise or Hudson or myself?"

"Righto!" he said; "I've thought myself I'd like to go there. Not, as you politely suggest, to find overlooked clews, but just as a matter of general interest. I'm out, you know, to find the murderer, and also to trace the vanished Amory Manning."

CHAPTER 17: ZIZI'S HUNCH

"HE'S afraid," and Norah wagged her head sagaciously, while her gray eyes had an apprehensive expression.

"Afraid of what?"

"Afraid of the truth. You see, Mr. Brice, our friend Rivers is nobody's fool. He's onto most points regarding this case, and now, he's getting onto himself. That astute little scrap of humanity, Zizi, knows he is. Of course, living with Miss Raynor, as she does, she has opportunities every day to see Mr. Rivers, for he's eternally hanging around the Raynor house. Oh. I don't mean he's an idler; not by a long shot. On the contrary, his middle name is efficiency! He puts over a lot of work in a day."

"What sort of work and how do you know so much about him?"

We were in my office, waiting for Rivers, who had promised to come to see me, and to look into the Gately rooms. It was now nearly half an hour after the time he had set for his call, and as it was not his habit to be tardy, I was surprised. I had begun to look upon Rivers as a man of importance, not only in the matters with which we were associated, but he showed so much general ability and force of character that I wondered who or what he would turn out to be. For I felt sure he would find himself, and even if he never discovered who he had been he would make a new name and a well worthwhile individuality for himself yet.

Norah, too, admired him, and seemed to know as much of his capabilities, or more, than I did myself.

"I don't know just what sort of work, but I think it's connected with the mysteries we're up against ourselves.

And I know about him, because Zizi told me. She sees everything he does,—when she's with him, I mean. Not a gesture or motion escapes her notice. And she's watching his attitude toward Miss Raynor. She says,—Zizi does,— that Mr. Rivers is over head and ears in love with Olive, but he won't tell her so because he is, as he puts it, a self named man! Zizi heard him call himself that when talking to Miss Raynor, and then he just looked away, and resolutely changed the subject. But she thinks,—Zizi does,—that he's working night and day to find out who he is, and she's sure he'll find out. And also, he's working to find Mr. Gately's murderer, and he's hunting for Amory Manning. No wonder the man's busy!"

"Well, why is he afraid to come here?"

"I'm not sure that he is; but you know Zizi has a hunch that he's the murderer, and I think maybe he is. That snowflake sketch proves he was there that day and as his presence isn't accounted for, why may he not have been the slayer? And, why may he not have an inkling or a suspicion of it, and dread to verify his fears?"

"But, good gracious, Norah, even granting he was in Gately's office that day, he needn't have done the shooting. There are about one million other errands he could have been there on. Perhaps he was a commercial traveler, selling laces, and drew the design for a sample."

"Sometimes, Mr. Brice, you talk like a Tom-noddy! Drummer, indeed! I can tell you whatever calling Case Rivers followed, it was far different from that of a selling agent! I'll bet he was a lawyer, at least!"

"At least!" I mocked her; "understand, pray, I consider my profession somewhat above the least of the professions!"

"Yes, for you dignify it to a high standing," and the gray eyes flashed me the smile of appreciation that I was looking for. I may as well admit that I was growing very fond of those two gray eyes and their owner, and I had a pretty strong conviction that after the present case was all settled I should turn my attention to the winning of the exclusive right to the tender glances those eyes could give.

But just now, I had to exclude all distracting thoughts, and forcing my mind back to the present situation, I again marveled at the non appearance of Case Rivers.

"Perhaps he's fallen through the earth again," Norah suggested; "by the way, Mr. Brice, what do you think about that fall? Mr. Rivers is no doubt under some strange hallucination, but all the same, may there not be some foundation on which he based his dream?"

"Maybe! There must be! That mind of his is too sure fire to hang on so desperately to a mere dream. He had some experience of a strange nature, and it included something that he looks upon as falling through the earth—"

"Such as?"

"I don't know. But I've a vague idea of a motor accident. Say, a motor car ran into a stone wall, and he was hurled high in the air, and landed in the East River—"

"But I don't see how that implies falling through the earth."

"Well, say he slid down a high bank to reach the river—"

"There's no high bank near the morgue, and he was fished out in that locality."

"But he needn't have fallen in there! In fact, he couldn't have,—he must have floated or drifted a considerable distance to have had his clothing torn from him—and to have reached the state of exhaustion and freezing that so nearly culminated in death."

"Yes, but even yet, you haven't suggested anything like falling through the earth."

"All right, Miss Smarty, what's your idea? I see you're dying to spring something."

"Only what I've thought from the beginning. I believe he was in some cold country, Canada, or somewhere, and fell down through a mine shaft, or into a deep old well, or perhaps merely an excavation for a new, large building. But, anyway, whatever it was, his last impression was of falling down into the ground. Then when he struck he was knocked unconscious. Then, he was taken to a hospital, or somewhere, and as the fall had utterly blotted out his memory, he was kept in confinement. Then, somehow he broke loose and came to New York,— or, maybe, he was brought to New York for treatment by the doctors and he got away and either threw himself into the river or fell in accidentally, and when he was rescued he still remembered the fall but nothing else concerning his disaster."

"Good enough, Norah, as a theory. But seems to me, in that case, he would have been sought and found by the people who had him in charge."

"Ah, that's the point of it all! They don't want to find him! They know just where he is, and all about him, but they won't tell, for it suits their base purposes to have him lost!"

"Well, you have cooked up a scheme! And he killed Amos Gately?"

"Maybe, but if so, he did it unknowingly. Perhaps these people who are looking after him, secretly hypnotized him to do it—"

"Oh, Norah! come off! desist! let up! Next thing you know you'll be having him in the movies! For you never thought up all that stuff without getting hints for it from some slapstick melodrama!"

"Oh, well, people who are absolutely without imagination can't expect to see into a mystery! But, you won't see any Mr. Rivers this morning,—I can assure you of that!"

She turned to her typewriter, and I took up my telephone.

I could not get Rivers at his home address, and I next called up Miss Raynor.

She replied, in agitated tones, that Rivers had been to see her for a few minutes, and that he had left half an hour before. She begged me to come around at once.

Of course, I went.

I found her in a strange state of mind. She seemed like one who had made a discovery, and was fearful of inadvertently disclosing it.

But when I urged her to be frank, she insisted she had nothing to conceal.

"I don't know anything, Mr. Brice, truly I don't," she repeated. "I mean, anything new or anything that I haven't told you. Mr. Rivers was here this morning for a very short call. He said that while his memory had not returned, he had a queer mental impression of being on a search for a paper when he fell through the earth."

"Did he go down into the earth to seek the paper?" I asked, thinking it best to treat the matter lightly.

"No," she returned, in all seriousness, "but the believes he was commissioned to hunt out a valuable paper, of some sort, and while on the quest he fell through the earth, by accident. It was the shock of that that impaired his memory."

"Sufficient cause!" I couldn't help saying.

Olive bristled: "Oh, I know you don't believe his story,—almost nobody does,—but I do."

"So do I!" and Zizi was in the room. One could never say of that girl that she entered or came in,—she just— was there,—in that silent, mysterious way of hers. And then with equally invisible motions she was sitting opposite me, at Olive's side, on a low ottoman.

"I know Mr. Rivers very well," Zizi announced, as if she were his official sponsor, "and what he says is true, no matter how unbelievable it may sound. He says he fell through the earth, and so he did fall through the earth, and that's all there is about that!"

"Good for you, Zizi!" I cried. "You're a loyal little champion! And just how did he accomplish the feat?"

"It will be explained in due season," and Zizi's big black eyes took on a sibylline expression as she gazed straight at me. "If you were told, on good authority, that a man had crossed the ocean in an aeroplane, you'd believe it, wouldn't you?"

"Yes; but that doesn't seem to me a parallel case," I demurred.

"Neither is Case Rivers a parallel case," Zizi giggled, "but he's the real thing in the way of Earth Fallers. And when you know all, you'll know everything!"

The child was exasperating in her foolish retorts and yet so convincing was the determined shake of her little black head that I was almost tempted to believe in her statements.

"You're a baby sphinx, Zizi," and Olive looked at her affectionately, "but honestly, Mr. Brice, she keeps my spirits up, and she is so positive herself of what she says that she almost convinces me. As for Mrs. Vail, she swallows everything Zizi says for law and gospel!"

"And just what is it you say, now, Zizi?" I asked.

"Nothin' much, kind sir. Only that Case Rivers is a gentleman and a scholar, that, his memory is on the home stretch and humming along, and that if he's after a paper,—he'll get it!"

"And, incidentally he's Amos Gately's—"

A scream of agony from Zizi interrupted my speech, and jumping to her feet she danced round the room, her forefinger thrust between her red lips, and her little, eerie face contorted as with pain.

"Oh, what is it, Zizi?" cried Olive, running to the frantic girl.

Mrs. Vail, hearing the turmoil, came running in, and she and Olive held Zizi between them, begging to know how she was hurt.

Catching an opportunity, Zizi looked at me, over Mrs. Vail's shoulder, and the message shot from her eyes was fully as understandable as if she had spoken. It said, "Do not mention any hint of Case Rivers' possible connection with the Gately murder, and do not mention the snowflake drawn on the blotter in Mr. Gately's office."

Yes, quite a lengthy and comprehensive speech to be made without words, but the speaking black eyes said it as clearly as lips could have done.

I nodded my obedience, and then Zizi giggled and with her inimitable impudence, she turned to Olive, and said: "I'm like the White Queen, in 'Alice,' I haven't pricked my finger yet, but I probably shall, some day."

"What were you screaming about, then?" asked Mrs. Vail, inclined to be angry, while Olive looked amused and mystified.

"Emergency," and Zizi grinned at her. "First aid to the injured,—or, rather, prevention, which is worth a pound of first aid!"

"You're crazy!" said Mrs. Vail, a little annoyed at being fooled so. "I thought you were nearly killed!"

"When you knew a lady once who was nearly killed did she yell like that?" asked Zizi, with an innocent smile.

"Yes!" exclaimed Mrs. Vail; "but how did you know I once saw a lady nearly killed?"

"Mind reading!" replied Zizi, and then Pennington Wise arrived, and we all shamelessly ignored Mrs. Vail and her yarns to listen to his report.

"There's a lot doing," he said," and," he added, gently, "I'm sorry to bring you unpleasant news, Miss Raynor, but you'll have to know sooner or later—"

"I do know," said Olive, bravely; "you're going to tell me my guardian was—was not a good man."

"That is so; it is useless to try to soften the truth. Amos Gately was the receiver of important Government secrets, learned by Sadie Kent, the telegrapher. She carried them to Rodman, who in turn transmitted them to Gately, who, it seems, had a way of getting the information to the enemy. Of course, the secret wireless station, recently discovered, was used, as well as other means of communication. I won't go into details, Miss Raynor, but Amos Gately was the 'man higher up,' who thought himself safe from discovery because of his unimpeachable reputation for integrity, and also because of the infinite precautions he had taken. Indeed, if he had not fallen a victim to the personal charms of 'The Link,' his share in the wrong might never have been learned."

Olive listened to all this, white faced and still,—her lips a tense, drawn line of scarlet,—her expression a stony calm.

Zizi, watching her closely, and with loving care, slipped her little brown paw into Olive's hand, and noted with satisfaction the faint answering smile.

"Perhaps," Olive said, after a thoughtful pause, "it is as well, then, that Uncle Amos did not—did not live to be—disgraced."

"It is," said Wise, gravely; "he would have faced a Federal prison had it all been discovered while he lived. That will be Rodman's fate,—if he is not held for the crime of murder. But I think he will not be. For his alibi clears him and it was to escape the graver charge that he has told so much of the spy business."

"And so," I said, "we are as far as ever from the discovery of the murderer?"

"You never can tell," Wise returned; "it may be we are on the very eve of solving the mystery. Rivers is on the warpath—"

"I think I ought to tell you, Mr. Wise," Olive broke in, "that Mr. Rivers was here this morning, and he seems to have a slight glimmer of returning memory."

"He has? Good! Then it will all come back to him. I've been looking up this aphasia amnesia business, and quite often when the patient begins to recover his memory, it all comes back to him with a bang! Where is Rivers?"

"He went away—I don't know where" Olive's lips quivered, and so plainly did she show her feelings that we all saw at once she feared that Rivers had fled, because of his returning memory.

"It's all right," declared Zizi, stanchly; "Mr. Rivers is white clear through! He'll come back, soon, and he'll bring the paper he's after."

"What paper?" demanded Wise.

"The poipers! the poipers!" scoffed Zizi; "did you ever know a case, oh, Wise Guy, that didn't revolve round and hinge on a poiper? Well, the dockyments in the case is what he's a soichin' for! See?"

When Zizi acted the gamine she was irresistibly funny and we all laughed, which was what she wanted to lighten the strain of the situation. Rivers was a mystery, indeed. Every one of us, I think, felt that he might be connected with the Gately affair. All of us, that is, but Olive,—and who could tell what she thought?

But Pennington Wise had a question to ask, and he put it straightforwardly.

"That day you were lured to Sadie 'The Link's' house, Miss Raynor," he began, "you said, or rather, you agreed when Rodman said you were his fiancée. Will you tell us why?"

Olive flushed, but more with anger than embarrassment.

"The man threatened me," she said, "he first tried to make love to me, and when I repulsed him, he told me that unless I would promise to marry him he would tell something that would be a living reproach to the memory of my dead guardian. I declared he could say nothing against Amos Gately. Then he whispered that Mr. Gately was a spy! I couldn't believe it, and—yet, I had seen just a few things,—had heard just a few words, that filled my heart with a fear that Mr. Rodman was speaking the truth. So I thought I'd better say what he asked me to, though I knew I'd kill myself rather than ever marry him. But I wasn't greatly afraid, except that I knew I was in his power. Oh, I don't like to think about that day!"

Olive broke down and hid her face in her hands, while Zizi's thin little arms crept round her and held her close.

"Only one more query, Miss Raynor," and Wise spoke very gently; "are you,—were you engaged to Amory Manning?"

Olive lifted her face, and spoke composedly: "No, Mr. Wise, I was never engaged to him. We were good friends, and I think he had a high regard for me, but no words of affection ever passed between us. I admire and respect Mr. Manning as a friend, but that is all." And then a lovely blush suffused Olive's face, followed quickly by a look of pain,—and we knew she was thinking of Rivers, and his possible defection. Never have I seen a woman's face so easy to read as Olive Raynor's. Perhaps because of her pure, transparent character, for in my enforced intimacy with her, as I managed her estate, I had learned that she was an exceptional nature, high minded, fine, and conscientious in all things.

"I cannot think," Olive went on, "that Mr. Manning will ever be found. I think he has been killed."

"Why?" asked Wise, briefly.

"You know, he was a Secret Service man. Many times he has had the narrowest escape with his life, and—I'm not sure of this,—but I think now, he was on the track of the nest of spies with which my—with which Mr. Gately was mixed up. A few slight incidents, otherwise unexplainable, make this clear to me now, though I never suspected it before. My uncle disliked Mr. Manning, and it may have been because he knew he was in the Government's employ. And though I know Mr. Gately would never have moved a finger to put Amory Manning out of the way, yet George Rodman may have done so. Oh, it's all so mysterious, so complicated,—but of this I'm sure, Case Rivers is in no way connected with the whole matter. He is a man from some distant city, he is unacquainted in New York, and he" here Olive broke down utterly and fell into a hysterical burst of weeping.

Zizi rose and gently urged Olive to go with her from the room.

A silence fell as the two girls disappeared. It was broken by Mrs. Vail, who remarked, dolefully, "I do hope that nice Mr. Rivers will come back, for dear Olive is so in love with him."

"What!" cried Pennington Wise, "Miss Raynor in love with Rivers! That will never do! Why, we've no idea who he is. He may be a fortune hunter of the lowest type!"

"Oh, no, no!" denied Mrs. Vail, "he is a most courteous gentleman."

"That doesn't count," stormed Wise; "although, perhaps, I spoke too strongly just now when I called him names!"

"Especially as he has no name!" I put in; "in fact, he calls himself a self named man!"

Wise smiled: "He is a witty chap," he conceded, "and I like him immensely. But it's up to us, Brice, to safeguard Miss Raynor's interests, and a possible suitor for the hand of an heiress ought, at least, to know his own ancestors! And then, again, unless he recovers his memory and can deny it, there's a fair chance that he had some hand in the Gately murder. We can't get away from that snowflake pattern drawn on the blotter. Rivers was there, in that room, he sat at Gately's desk, opposite Gately himself,—I mean, of course, this is the way I reconstruct the matter,—and if he didn't shoot Gately then and there, at least, we have no proof that he didn't."

"I think he did," I admitted, for Wise's statement of the matter was convincing,—and beside, Norah thought so, too.

"Well, you think again!" came in a wild little voice, and there was Zizi at my elbow fairly shaking her little clenched fist in my face. "Mr. Badman Brice, you've got a lot of follow up thinks a coming to you, and you'd better begin 'em right now!"

She looked like a little fury as she danced around my chair and exploded the vials of her wrath. "That Mr. Rivers is a perfectly good man,—I know! He and Miss Olive are in love,—but they don't hardly know it themselves,—bless 'em! And Mr. Rivers he won't tell her, anyway, 'cause he's a nobleman,—one of Nature's maybe,—and again, maybe he's a real one from Canada, or wherever he hails from. But, anyway, he no more killed anybody than I did!"

"All right, Ziz,—bully for you! As a loyal friend you're there with the goods!"Wise smiled at her. "But after all, you've got only your loyalty to bank on. You don't know all this."

"I've got a hunch," said Zizi, pounding one little fist into the other palm, "and when it comes to certainty,— Death and Taxes have nothing on my hunches!"

CHAPTER 18: CLEAR AS CRYSTAL

"HELLO, people! What's the matter, Zizi? I'll be on your side! Bank on me, little one, to the last ditch. And, by jumping Jupiter, Brice, I believe the last ditch is coming my way! No, I haven't got a strangle hold on that eloping memory of mine yet, but I 'ave 'opes. I've had a glimmer of a gleam of a ray of light on my dark, mysterious past, and I beflew myself straight to good little old Doctor Rankin, who's my Trouble Man every time. And he says that it's the beginning of the end. That any day, almost any hour now, I may burst forth a full memoried and properly christened citizen."

"Good for you, old chap," and thrilled at the elation in his tones, I held out my hand. "Go in and win!"

"Oh, won't it be fine when you remember?" cried Mrs. Vail, wringing her hands in excitement; "why, I knew a man once—"

"Yes," Rivers encouraged her, in his kindly way, "what happened to the lucky chap?"

"Why, he was affected something as you are,—or, as you were—" but Wise couldn't stand for what seemed likely to be a long story.

"Excuse me, Mrs. Vail," he interrupted her, "but, really, I must run away now, and I want a word or two with Mr. Rivers first."

The good lady subsided, but it was plain to be seen she was disappointed.

"May I come in?" and a smiling Olive appeared in the doorway. "Am I wanted?"

"Are you wanted?" the eager, hungry smile Rivers gave her was pathetic. For it was so spontaneous, so gladly welcoming that it was as if a light was suddenly

extinguished when the man, on second thought, hid his
real feelings and advanced with a courteous but rather
formal air.

"You're always wanted," he resumed, lightly, but the
joy was gone from his tones, and a mere friendly greeting
resulted. Surely, he was a gentleman, but he would make
no advances while uncertain of his claim in full to that
title.

And then, he looked at her curiously, as if wondering
whether she would hold any place in his restored
memory,—should the restoration really occur.

It was Zizi who broke the silence that fell on us all.

"I want my way, Penny," she said, in such a wistful,
pleading tone, that I felt sure no breathing human heart
could refuse her.

"What is your way, Zizi?" Wise said, gently.

"I want us all to go—all of us,—over to Mr. Gately's
office—"

"Come ahead!" cried Rivers; "I promised old Brice,
here, that I'd go this very day, and I broke my
appointment. Sorry, old man, but I had to see Friend
Doctor, on the jump. Let's go now, in accordance with the
Witch's whim, and we'll take the big wagon, and all go."

He often called Zizi the Witch, or the Elf child, and
she liked it from him, though she usually resented any
familiarity.

She smiled at him, but I noted an undercurrent of
sadness in her gaze, and I knew she was thinking of the
evidence of the snow crystal.

For though Zizi liked Rivers a lot, and though she
really had faith in his innocence of wrongdoing, yet her
whole fealty was to Pennington Wise, and her hunch
about the snowflake drawing might lead to disastrous
results in more ways than one.

Olive shrank from going to her guardian's office,—she
had never been there since the tragedy,—but a few
whispered words from Zizi persuaded her to agree to
accompany us.

And to help matters, I told her that if she preferred not to go into Mr. Gately's rooms, she could remain in my office with Norah, while we went.

Mrs. Vail insisted on being of the party, and ran briskly off to get her bonnet.

The atmosphere seemed peculiarly charged with a feeling of impending disaster, and yet, not one of us would have held back. Pennington Wise was very grave and quiet; Zizi, on the other hand, was as one electrified. She sprang about with quick, darting motions, she giggled almost hysterically and then suddenly became most gentle and tender. She ran for Olive's wraps herself, and bringing them, put them on with the careful air of a mother dressing her child.

Olive, herself, was as one dazed. She, now and then, looked toward Rivers with a shy, yet wistful glance, and he looked back with a big, hearty smile that seemed to warm her very soul.

We piled into the big touring car and made a quick run to the Puritan Building.

Then we all went to my office first. Norah did the honors as prettily as any hostess in her own home, and her ready tact helped Olive to overcome her dread of the place.

"Well," said Rivers, at last, "what are we waiting for? I thought we were to go over to Mr. Gately's rooms. Perhaps Miss Raynor and Mrs. Vail would prefer to stay here with Miss MacCormack."

"No." said Olive, firmly, "I want to go, too."

Norah looked at her uncertainly. Then, probably realizing that for Olive to remain behind would be harder than to face whatever might happen, she said, quite casually, "Very well, Miss Raynor, let us all go."

I think we were all imbued with a sense of fear, a sort of premonition that the visit across the hall would be productive of grave results.

Rivers was the most light hearted of the party, and yet I somehow felt that his cheerfulness was forced.

"The keys, Brice?" he said; "oh, you have them. All right, my boy, go ahead."

And then the same stillness that was on the rest of us fell on him, too, and we entered the rooms in silence.

I went first, through Jenny's room, on to the middle room, and paused just beyond the desk.

Rivers was next, but Zizi pushed her lithe little body through the group, and came through the door just ahead of him.

Rivers entered with the strangest look I have ever seen on any human face. It was a transition,—not sudden but gradual,—from the dark of forgetfulness to the dawn of memory.

And then, just as he neared Amos Gately's desk, Zizi, without seeming insistence,—indeed, without seeming intent,—guided him to the chair opposite Mr. Gately's desk chair.

Mechanically, almost unconsciously, Rivers dropped into the seat and sat at the great table desk,—just where, presumably, the slayer of Amos Gately had sat.

With one of her sudden, swift motions, Zizi put the telephone receiver into his left hand, which involuntarily opened to take it, and thus exposed to view the snow crystal drawn on the blotter.

A dead silence fell on us all as Rivers sat there staring at the little sketch. He fairly devoured it with his eyes, 'his face, meanwhile, becoming set,—like a face of stone.

Then, raising his blank, staring eyes, his gaze sought out Olive and, looking straight at her, he gave a low, piercing cry,—wrung from him as from a soul in mortal agony,—and said:

"I killed Amos Gately!"

I think the scene that followed this announcement was the strangest I have ever experienced. For myself, I felt a sudden sinking, as if the bottom had fallen out of the universe. In fact, a whimsical idea flashed through my stunned brain that I was "falling through the earth,"—or into a bottomless pit.

The white faces that I looked at meant nothing to me,—I saw them as in a dream, so dazed was my intelligence.

And then, they assumed their individuality and I saw that Olive's lovely countenance was a complete blank; like me, she failed to grasp the full meaning of Rivers' confession.

Mrs. Vail, her eyes closed, lay back limply in a chair, and groaned audibly, while Norah buried her face in a nearby silken curtain and sobbed.

Pennington Wise looked like a man who has just heard the worst,—but who expected it. However, the shock had unnerved him, I could see by his tightly clenched hands and set lips, as he strove to control himself.

Rivers sat like a stone statue, only his eyes, desperate in their concentration, showed the fearful mental strain he was suffering.

Zizi,—bless her!—stood behind him,—hovering, watchful,—more like a guardian angel than a Nemesis, and with her eerie, elfin face full of anxious suspense.

Rivers drew a long sigh; he looked round the room, appraisingly, his quick, darting glance taking in every detail, he scanned the desk and all the things on it, he looked through into the farther room,—the Blue Room,— and saw the great war map hanging on the wall, and then he rose, straightened his broad shoulders, and shook himself as one who arouses from sleep.

Breathlessly, we who watched, saw a great light come into his eyes,—a new self respect, a new sense of importance showed in his whole bearing and, with a smile of infinite tenderness he looked at Olive and said:

"I am Amory Manning!"

Zizi yelled. There is no other word for it. Her shrieks of joy filled the room, and she danced about waving her thin little arms like a veritable pixy.

"It's all right!" she cried, in ecstacy, "Oh, Penny, it's all right!"and with a spring across the room, she landed in Wise's arms, who patted her shoulder, and said:

"There, there, Ziz, don't flatten out now!"

Meantime, Rivers was finding himself. He stood still, with his hands tightly grasping the chair back, and his face working as he received and classified the memories crowding thickly back upon his burdened brain.

"Wait a minute," he said, struggling with his thoughts, "I know all about it, but—"

"Amory!" cried Olive, "that's your voice! I know you now!"

We could all note the change in his speech. Until this moment Rivers had spoken in the peculiar tones I had noticed the first time I met him. Monotonous tones, almost devoid of inflection. Now, his voice was normal, and even more melodious than the average.

Surely, the man had found himself, but if he was really Amory Manning,—well, my mind refused to go further.

And he had also said that he killed Amos Gately!

But I felt no need of asking questions, or even of wondering, for the man before us looked so responsible, so capable of self explanation, that like the rest of the assembly, I merely waited his further speech.

"There's so much to be told," he said, and his smile changed to a look of pain. He gave another glance at Olive, and even took a step toward her,—then he seemed to collapse, and sinking back into the chair he had vacated, he hid his face in his hands and groaned.

"Go on!" whispered an imperious little voice; and Zizi was behind him again, her hand on his shoulder, her tones urgent and encouraging.

"I will!" and Manning, for we felt no doubt of his identity now,—spoke firmly and bravely. He did not look at Olive, and it was clear that this was intentional.

Instead, he turned to Zizi, and seemed to address himself to her.

He couldn't have done better if he wanted helpful sympathy, for the black eyes that gazed at him were soft and tender with something like a maternal sweetness.

This mood of Zizi's, rarely shown, was one of her chiefest charms, and Manning gratefully accepted it, and let it help him.

"Shall I tell all,—now and here?" he asked, glancing at Pennington Wise.

"Yes," said the detective, after a moment's thought. "Yes, if you will."

"Very well, then." Manning was entirely composed now, but it was evident he was holding himself together by a strong effort. Also, he carefully refrained from looking in Olive's direction.

This alarmed me a little, for to my mind, it argued him a guilty man, and, that, in fact, he had declared himself to be.

Norah and I exchanged glances of understanding,— "or, rather, of not understanding,—and Manning began his story.

"I think I will begin right here," he said, in a slow, methodical way, and with the air of one who has a disagreeable duty to perform, but who has no intention of shirking any part of it.

"I remember everything—everything,—and it is not all pleasant remembrance! But it must be told, and then I must go at once and report to my superiors.

"I am Amory Manning, a special agent in the Secret Service. I was detailed by the Government to hunt down a certain branch of the enemy spy system in New York

City, and in pursuance of my duty, I learned that Amos Gately was the man I sought."

Manning still kept his glance averted from Olive, indeed, he looked almost constantly at Zizi, whose dark little face, lovely in its sympathy, seemed to drink in his every word.

"I knew all about Rodman, I was on the trail of Sadie, 'The Link,' and I came here, that afternoon, primarily to get an incriminating paper, which would have been positive evidence against Gately, and I had orders to arrest him if he was unable to clear himself.

"We had a stormy interview, and I found the man was guilty of the blackest treason. He had been a receiver of the stolen information sold by 'The Link,' and had transmitted it, by secret channels of his own, to the enemy government. I charged him with this, and he put up a fight. I tried to overcome him, and take him peaceably, but he was desperate and evaded my grasp. He ran toward that map in the other room, and I stood just here, where I am now sitting. I had overturned the chair in our struggle and as I suddenly saw him push aside the map and enter what was beyond all doubt a secret mode of exit, I fired at him. Of course, I meant merely to wing him,—merely to prevent his escape,—but as I fired he turned and received the bullet in his heart. Of course, I didn't know this at the time, nor did I know where he had gone. But I heard the car descend, and knew that it must be a private elevator.

"I ran into that room, and finding the elevator entrance, behind the map, fastened, I flew out to the hall and downstairs. In my haste, there being no car waiting, I thought I could get down faster by the stairs. But after running down two flights, I saw a waiting elevator and got in. I had dropped my pistol somewhere when trying to stuff it into my overcoat pocket as I ran downstairs. But I gave no thought to anything save preventing the escape of my prisoner. Of course, I didn't then know how seriously he was hurt.

"I failed to find the exit from the private elevator, and never dreaming it was in the building next door, I hunted this building for quite a time. I investigated the ground floor, the basement and sub basement, but couldn't find it. Greatly puzzled, I began the search all over again, and then, Olive,—Miss Raynor, came, and—later, I found that others had discovered the dead body of the man I had shot.

"I waited only to be sure of this, and then started at once to report to the Federal Bureau."

"I know it," I interrupted, unable to keep quiet, as the recollection surged over me, "and you went down Third Avenue on the street car—"

"I did," Manning's face showed only an intense effort at reconstructing the scene, "I was going to stop at my rooms on the way, for something I needed, and—"

"Wait a minute," Wise said, "I'm interested in the Case Rivers phase of your existence. Don't forget you're the Man Who Fell Through the Earth."

A strange smile passed over Manning's face.

"I'm just coming to that," he said; "I am that man, and I can tell you right now, how, where, and why I made the trip!"

All eyes were upon him. This strange talk,—and he had been so sensible up to now. Was the hallucination of falling through the earth destined to mar his newly returned sanity?

"Go on," repeated Zizi, and the calmness of her voice restored Manning's poise, and also raised my hopes of a plausible explanation.

"You were with me, Brice," Manning looked at me, as if for corroboration.

"Yes: I was in the car with you, but we were not near enough to speak. There was a big crowd,—and I was standing at the rear end, while you were well forward. But I say, Rivers, it's hard to believe that man in the car was you! Why, you're not the same type—"

"Wait a minute," the speaker waved his hand as if to check interruption, "I am Manning,—I'll explain later,— but now I want to get that occasion well in hand. I got off the front end of the car,—I don't know what you did,— and as I stepped off, a sudden fierce blast of wind nearly took me off my feet. I was right in the middle of the street but it seemed the middle of a howling blizzard, and as I took a step,—I went down an open manhole into the sewer.

"This I distinctly remember,—the street cleaners were working there, shoveling the snow into the sewer. They had no business to leave the manhole open and unguarded, but that black squall was so sudden and terrific, no one could see or know anything for the time being.

"However, I knew perfectly well, as I fell in, what had happened, but then,—and I remember this, too,—I fell and fell,—down, down,—it seemed for miles; I was whirled dizzily about,—but still I fell—on and on,— interminably. I felt my consciousness going,—at first, abnormally acute, my senses became dulled, and I had only a sensation of falling—ever falling—through the earth!

"There my memory ceases. And as I next remember finding myself in a bed in Bellevue Hospital, and as I have had detailed to me the full account of my being found floating, nearly dead, in the East River, I can only accept the inevitable conclusion that I was carried by the rush of the sewer, straight out to the river, and picked up for dead.

"That a sign of life was found, after I was taken to the morgue, was of the nature of a miracle, and only the most desperate efforts fanned that little spark into resuscitation. The rest you know. The shock, the exposure, the cold, and perhaps a blow or two on my head, all combined, resulted in a total loss of memory as to my identity or to the events of my former life.

"I had only remaining the positive recollection of that fall—" Manning shuddered,—"that interminable, that never ending fall through the earth."

"But you fell through water," said Wise, his eyes staring at the narrator of all this.

"Not to my knowledge. My realization of falling only lasted until I struck the water in the sewer. That, doubtless, knocked me out for good and all,—mentally, I mean. I have to thank my wonderful vitality and strong constitution for the fact that I really lived through the catastrophe. Think what it means! Hurtled through that rushing torrent of a sewer half filled with melted snow and water,—flung out into the river, dashed about among the floating cakes of ice, and all with sufficient force to tear off my clothing,—and yet to live through it!"

"Going some!" cried Zizi, and the sparkle of her dancing eyes and the delight on her small, smiling face, made the rude phrase seem quite fit for the occasion.

"And so," Manning went on, quietly, "I have accomplished my quests. I have been working hard to discover three things,—my own identity, the whereabouts of Amory Manning, and—the slayer of Amos Gately. I, myself, am the answer to all three questions."

A silence fell; and then Olive spoke.

"You are no slayer,—you are no murderer. You shot Mr. Gately by accident, in the pursuance of your duty. You are not only exonerated, but you did a deed, in freeing the world of a traitor, that entitles you to a Distinguished Service Cross! I respected my guardian,—I was fond of him,—but now I know what he was. I have only contempt and hatred of him! You, Amory, are a hero!—-my hero."

Olive held out her hands with a beautiful gesture of affection, and Manning strode across the room to her side.

"Now I have the only forgiveness I care for," he said, and his face was radiant. "Now, I must go at once, and report. My duty lies to my country,—to my government!

Oh, there are so many things yet to think of! They,—the Government,—offered a reward for me!"

"Which you have won yourself!" exclaimed Penny Wise."

"Yes," chuckled Zizi, "and you've won the reward offered for Mr. Gately's—" she hesitated,—"for the man who freed the world of one more traitorous viper!"

"And, incidentally," I added, "you've cleared up the puzzle of the man who fell through the earth!"

"It is well that. Gately is no more," Manning said, musingly; "he was especially dangerous because he was in such a high position and so trusted by everybody. Rodman was an equal scoundrel, but he worked inconspicuously. Gately banked on his reputation for honor and probity,—used his own well earned fame to further the meanest cause on earth!

"Whatever happens, I'm glad he is unable to do further harm. I didn't mean to kill him—it was an accident,—but the world is well rid of him."

"Amen," said Olive, softly.

"Well, the end justifies the means," said Mrs. Vail, a little hysterically. "Why, once I heard of—"

Ruthlessly, I shut her off.

"Accept my greetings, Mr. Manning," I said, offering my hand to our new found friend. "I'm proud to know you!"

And then there was a scene of handshaking and smiling welcome such as any hero might be proud to receive.

"Wait a minute," Manning said, at last, "that day, I was hunting a paper, you know. If it was sent off, there will yet be trouble from it. Has it been found, do you know, Mr. Wise?"

"No; what sort of a paper?"

"One of the stolen telegrams. It was concealed, I had reason to think, somewhere in Gately's desk—"

"Do you know that?"

"I think so—wait,—I had just thought I knew where to look for it, when Gately said something that made me telephone for assistance in his arrest. I was waiting for an answer to my call—"

"When you drew the snow crystal!" Zizi cried.

"Yes," he smiled. "And then, I saw something that hinted a possible hiding place—ah, here it is!"

He stepped to the desk and picked up the heavy, ornate gold penholder. He fussed with it a moment, and then, unscrewing it in the middle, showed that it was a cleverly constructed place to hide a tiny roll of thin paper.

There was such a roll in it, and pulling it out, Manning grinned with glee. "All right," he cried, joyfully; "this is the paper, a Government secret! See, you read it by that carriage call check, and it's safe now!"

It was a paper filled with rows of letters, such a paper as had been found in Sadie's possession and also in Rodman's.

"Now, I am satisfied," Manning declared; "and now I must go straight down to the Federal Bureau. But first-"

"Sure!" said Zizi, reading his thoughts; "we're excused!"

And with a saucy smile, she flew over and kissed Olive heartily. Then, with an imperious air, she took command, and almost before we knew it she had herded every last one of us, except Olive and Manning, across the hall to my office.

I was the last to go, and Manning smiled broadly as he called after me, "I want Miss Raynor to say once more that she exonerates me, and then I'll report to my other Superior!"

Laughing happily, I entered my office, and found it a scene of hilarious gayety. Mrs. Vail was positively cavorting about, as Norah waltzed her up and down the room; Pennington Wise was sitting on the corner of my desk whistling dance music for them, and Zizi, her arms waving, executed a sort of glory dance of her own making up.

After a time, the door of the Gately room opened, and Olive's blushing face appeared, followed by that of the Man Who Fell Through the Earth.

"I want to correct a misstatement of mine," she said; "I told you I wasn't engaged to Amory Manning—but,—I am!"

The two came over to my office, and the ovation we gave them was second only to our reception of Manning himself a few moments before.

"Are you sure it is Manning?" Wise teased her.

"Yes," said Olive, most seriously. "You see he was in disguise when he was himself, and so—"

Her voice was lost in the shout that went up at her remark, and she looked around in bewilderment.

"She's right," said Manning, smiling; "I was. You see, when I became a Secret Service man, I had certain peculiar duties assigned me and it was important that I shouldn't be known. So I adopted a permanent disguise,— oh, nothing much,—merely a mild dye for my hair and beard, which washed off easily, and a pair of big, horn rimmed specs, which were really rather becoming than otherwise. But Olive, and many of my acquaintances knew me only in this way. I wore a Vandyke beard, and a small mustache of the Charles I type.

"Then you see, when I was taken in at the hospital, and shaved, I continued to adopt a clean-shaven face. Also, the dye was thoroughly washed out in the sewer, and as my memory was washed out with it, I experienced no surprise at finding a light haired man in my mirror.

"Olive tells me, too, that my voice was of a totally different caliber, due, no doubt, to a certain vacuity made in my brain by the loss of my memory. Oh, well, that's the story. And but for my peculiarity of drawing snow crystals,—a thing I've done just about all my life,—and but for Zizi's quick-witted realization of this habit of mine, I might never have regained consciousness of my true personality!"

"Probably something else would have brought it about," said Wise, "but your drawing of the snow crystals began with Brice's first interview with you. I ought to have found that drawing on Gately's desk long ago! Stoopid!" and he beat his head in mock self abasement.

"Yes," said Zizi, giving Wise a smile that was both impudent and affectionate, "you should have, oh, Wise Guy ! You ought to have found that snowflake drawing for yourself."

"Oh, that's what I have you for, Ziz, to look up clews for me."

"Of course you do, Penny Wise. I'm only your Pound Foolish, but at least, I can see through a clew that is as dear as crystal!"

THE END

Resurrected Press Mysteries From Louis Tracy

The Albert Gate Mystery
Four men murdered and a fortune in diamonds belonging to the Turkish Sultan stolen, while the Foreign Office official in charge has gone missing. Was it a common jewelry theft or was it a case of international intrigue? This is the question that barrister detective Reginald Brett must solve.

The Bartlett Mystery
When Ronald Tower is murdered on his way to a bridge game on the yacht Sans Souci it at first appears a common crime. But as Rex Carshaw finds, a tragic case of mistaken identity leads to political scandal among the rich and powerful of New York.

The Strange Case of Mortimer Fenley
When the wealthy Mortimer Fenley is struck down by a shot from an express rifle on the steps of his mansion, detectives Winter and Furneaux of Scotland Yard must find the culprit. Was it the artist who claimed he was painting a picture at the time of the shot? The disaffected younger son? Or is there another suspect?

The Stowmarket Mystery
For five generations the Fergus-Hume family has been cursed. Each of the baronets has met a violent end. When the fifth baronet is found slain by a ceremonial Japanese dagger, suspicion falls on his cousin David. It falls to barrister detective Reginald Brett to prove his innocence and find the real murder in a case that spans two continents and as many centuries.

Resurrected Press Mysteries by J. S. Fletcher

The Orange-Yellow Diamond
When an elderly pawnbroker is murdered in the London parish of Paddington, a young, down on his luck writer is accused of the crime. But then it's found the pawnbroker had had in his possession an extraordinary South African diamond worth over eighty-thousand pounds — a diamond that's now missing. It falls to Melky Rubenstein to unravel the mystery and prove the young man's innocence.

The Middle Temple Murder
When an elderly man's body is found on the steps of chambers in the Midde Temple, one of the Inns of Court, it falls to newspaperman Frank Spargo and Detective-Sergeant Rathbury to solve the crime. The murdered man, for indeed it was murder, was found with no money or identification on his person except for a piece of paper with the name and address of a young barrister. Who is the victim? Why was he killed? Who is the murderer?

Scarhaven Keep
Bassett Oliver, the famed actor, has gone missing. When Oliver fails to show for a rehearsal, aspiring playwright Richard Copplestone finds himself sent to the small village of Scarhaven on the northern coast of England to track down the actors movements. What he finds is mystery. Find the answers as Copplestone unravels the mystery of Scarhaven Keep.

Visit www.resurrectedpress.com

Resurrected Press Mysteries from the Dr. John Thorndyke Series

Dr. John Thorndyke - Lecturer on Medical Jurisprudence and Forensic Medicine. Before Bones, before CSI, before Quincy, M.E– there was Dr. John Thorndyke solving the most baffling cases of Edwardian London using the latest tools of medical science. Read about his cases in:

The Eye of Osiris
John Bellingham, noted Egyptologist has vanished not once but twice in the same day. Now Dr, Thorndyke must unravel the tangled claims on his estate, solve the riddle of the missing man and find the "Eye of Osiris".

The Mystery of 31 New Inn
When Dr. Jervis is whisked away in a coach with no windows to an unknown location to treat a man in a coma from undivulged causes it is Dr. Thorndyke who must come up with the solution.

The Red Thumb Mark
The first of Dr. Thorndyke's cases finds him trying to prove the innocence of a young man accused of being a diamond thief despite the fact that his finger print was found at the scene of the crime.

John Thorndyke's Cases
More cases of medical mysteries as told by his trusted assistant Jervis, M.D. Eight stories of crime and deduction in Edwardian London.

Visit www.resurrectedpress.com

Resurrected Press Mysteries by John R. Watson & Arthur J. Rees

The Hampstead Mystery

High Court Justice Sir Horace Fewbanks found shot dead in his Hampstead home, a butler with a criminal past, a scorned lover and a hint of scandal. These are the elements of the Hampstead Mystery that Detective Inspector Chippenfield of Scotland Yard must unravel with the assistance of the ambitious Detective Rolfe. But will he be able to sort out the tangled threads of this case and arrest the culprit before he is upstaged by the celebrated gentleman detective Crewe. Follow the details of this amazing case at it plays out across Hampstead, London and Scotland until it reaches a stunning conclusion in the courts of the Old Bailey.

The Mystery of the Downs

When Harry Marsland was caught in a sudden down pour he sought shelter at Cliff Farm. Met at the door by a young woman clearly expecting someone else he is only too glad to get inside to wait out the storm. When they hear a noise upstairs in the deserted house they investigate only to discover the body of the farm's owner, Frank Lumsden, dead of a gunshot wound. Who then, killed Lumsden, and why? Who was the woman expecting and did she have any roll in the murder? These are the questions that private detective Crewe must answer in The Mystery of the Downs.

Visit www.resurrectedpress.com

Other Resurrected Press Mysteries

Mysteries on a Train

Before the Orient Express there was:

The Rome Express by Arthur Griffiths
A man is found dead in his first class sleeping compartment on the express from Rome to Paris. Who was his murderer? The Countess? The English General? His brother the clergy man? The maid who has disappeared? Is the French justice system up to solving the crime? Read about it in The Rome Express.

The Passenger from Calais by Arthur Griffiths
Colonel Basil Annesley finds he is the only passenger on the train from Calais to Lucerne. That is until a mysterious woman shows up at the last minute to book a compartment. Who is after her? What is her secret? Is she a criminal or a victim? Read about it in The Passenger from Calais

Visit us at www.resurrectedpress.com

About Resurrected Press

A division of Intrepid Ink, LLC, Resurrected Press is dedicated to bringing high quality, vintage books back into publication. See our entire catalogue and find out more at www.ResurrectedPress.com.

About Intrepid Ink, LLC

Intrepid Ink, LLC provides full publishing services to authors of fiction and non-fiction books, eBooks and websites. From editing to formatting, from publishing to marketing, Intrepid Ink gets your creative works into the hands of the people who want to read them. Find out more at www.IntrepidInk.com.

www.ingramcontent.com/pod-product-compliance
Lightning Source LLC
Chambersburg PA
CBHW071310250626
47159CB00004B/1374